JADED JEWELS

A COZY CORGI MYSTERY

MILDRED ABBOTT

JADED JEWELS

Mildred Abbott

for
Alastair Tyler
&
Winifred Hera

Copyright © 2021 by Mildred Abbott

All rights reserved.

No part of this book may be reproduced in any form or by any electronic or mechanical means, including information storage and retrieval systems, without written permission from the author, except for the use of brief quotations in a book review.

Cover, Logo, Chapter Heading Designer: A.J. Corza - SeeingStatic.com

Main Editor: Desi Chapman

2nd Editors: Ann Attwood & Anita Ford

3rd Editor: Corrine Harris

Recipe provided by: Cloudy Kitchen - CloudyKitchen.com

Visit Mildred's Webpage: MildredAbbott.com

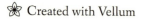 Created with Vellum

The puzzle pieces spread out in front of me, crystal clear as I mentally sorted each one. In the back of my mind, the image covering the metaphorical puzzle box glowed like a beacon, but each time it illuminated, I flipped the switch, plunging the overtly obvious back into shadows, then scattered the pieces once more in an attempt to rearrange them into something else. If I was at home curled up with a book in front of the fireplace with my beloved corgi, Watson, napping by my side, perhaps I could've forced them into some other incarnation. Perhaps if I could pace beside the shelves covering the walls of the mystery room in the Cozy Corgi Bookshop, I'd find some misplaced pieces with weirdly shaped angles that would transform the inevitable.

Neither happened, and in the small, elegant bathroom of Prime Slice, there wasn't even room to pace, so no chance of stumbling upon new puzzle pieces, metaphorical or otherwise. Instead, I paused, gripped the edge of the marble around the sink, and stared in the gilded mirror. Being a redhead, my complexion never boasted a golden tan, but my face was beyond pallid, ghostly white, and as I leaned forward, I was horrified to notice beads of sweat. My forehead was glistening nearly as much as the pounded-silver corgi earrings dangling on either side of my face. I grabbed a couple of the cloth-thick paper towels from beside the sink and ran cold water over them before wringing them out and covering my face, without the least worry about the small amount of lip gloss I'd applied at the start of the evening.

The cool sensation helped, at least a little bit, making my heart rate slow while forcing my brain to jump tracks. There was no need to continue rearranging the puzzle pieces. They wouldn't form any other image, no matter how I tried to stuff them together. I needed to accept what was happening and deal with it.

Deal with it?

That thought caused me to lower the paper towels and stare back into the mirror. Even in the moment, I knew it was a horribly cliché thing to do—to look into a mirror during a second of introspection.

Actually, I skipped the introspection and jumped right to self-reprimands.

There was nothing to *deal with*. Despite the beads of sweat, attempted pacing, and mental gymnastics, I wanted what the puzzle pieces promised. I did. I'd even been aware they were coming. I'd felt them falling into place for months. It was just... well... I thought the final few would fall gradually, maybe with the last one finishing the entirety of the puzzle with the soft easy click in front of the Christmas tree in a little more than three months.

Whether I should have been or not, I wasn't prepared for it to happen so fast. I'd grown suspicious over dinner, then as we'd ordered dessert, I quickly made my escape to the bathroom. If I'd thought, if I'd known, I would've... What? Worn something different, put on some other hue than mustard, chosen something besides a broomstick skirt? Swept my hair up? Plastered on more makeup?

Why? Like any of that mattered.

With a deep breath, I closed my eyes once more, cutting off my reflection and letting the image of the completed puzzle pieces illuminate in the back of my mind once more without being dimmed.

After a couple more deep breaths, though admittedly shaky ones, my nerves shifted from the kind strictly causing nausea and allowed a few types to bring in the pleasant racing, butterflies... happiness.

As I looked at my reflection once more, I smiled and gave a nod to myself. Sure, Prime Slice wasn't where I pictured, and the timing wasn't what I'd predicted, but... none of that mattered either.

After drying my face, I left the bathroom and started to walk back through the restaurant. Some of the pleasant anticipation dampened once more as I glanced around the upscale steakhouse and remembered another night I'd been here—another date, with another man. One who'd ended up being a murderer, who'd killed for me on more than one occasion, the last time being only a couple of weeks ago.

No... I didn't want this... not there. Not with that memory so close by.

"Fred!"

With a yelp, I turned at the sound of my name, then relaxed at the sight of three friends gathered around the table.

Paulie, who'd been the one to call out to me, winced at my reaction. "Sorry. I wasn't trying to startle you. Didn't know you were here—we barely got our drinks." He lifted his glass of white wine as if offering proof. "You can join us, if you'd like."

Good Lord, how long had I been in the bathroom if they'd arrived, gotten seated, and already been served drinks?

"Yeah!" Officer Campbell Clifton Cabot gestured toward the empty chair. "Please do."

"What is wrong with you two? I hardly doubt Winifred is here by herself." Athena scoffed at the two men, then turned her narrowed gaze on me as I approached, her dark eyes barely visible through her thick false eyelashes. "You look distraught. Has there been a murder?"

"Goodness no, not that I'd—" Barely catching myself, I stopped short of admitting a murder would've been much less nerve-racking. "No. Just here for dinner. Thank you for the invitation, though. And we've only barely ordered dessert." Dessert... Clearly, I'd been in the restroom longer than I'd realized. Who knew how long the dessert had been sitting there, waiting.

Eyes still narrowed, the corner of Athena's perfectly painted lips curved slightly, suggesting the sharp older woman had instantly leaped to the correct conclusion. "Well, it's good to see you, but we won't hold you up from... anything."

Paulie and Campbell exchanged quizzical glances at Athena's quick dismissal and knowing tone.

Latching on to the distraction, I glanced toward the purse sitting by Athena's feet, which wore lemon-yellow high heels. "No Pearl this evening?"

Athena didn't seem fooled, but she played along. "As if I go anywhere without Pearl."

At her name, a tiny white head popped out of the purse's opening.

"Ah, there you are." I bent, reaching out to scratch the toy poodle's head. The little dog gave my fingers a cursory look, but instantly angled, attempting to look around me. "Sorry, sweetheart. I had to leave your boyfriend at home. He can't fit into a purse as easily as you. Not that I'm strong enough to carry him if he did."

Whether she understood me or simply didn't catch Watson's scent any stronger than the corgi hairs that were an ever-present fashion accessory, Pearl offered a little sigh before sinking back to the privacy of Athena's purse.

"Are you sure you're okay, dear?" Athena's whisper drew my attention back up. As I was kneeling, the two of us were eye to eye.

Athena's closer inspection shot an arrow of guilt

through me. She was always perfectly put together, ready to grace the cover of any international fashion magazine. Why hadn't I realized what tonight was going to be? Why hadn't I dressed up a little, put in more effort. Not that I'd look as glamorous as Athena Rose, regardless of the level of effort.

And again, since when did I worry about clothes or makeup or any such nonsense? I swallowed, forced a nod, and stood. "Yes, thank you."

A moment later, with no recollection of my parting words to Paulie or Campbell, I continued toward the front room. Once more I was stilled by the sight of the man sitting alone at the table for two in front of the large window looking out over starlit mountains. Sure enough, two plates of dessert sat, untouched, in front of Leo. As his honey-brown gaze found me, as if he felt me enter the room, it was perfectly clear his nerves mirrored my own.

Another shot of guilt ran through me. Leo was nervous enough, and I was adding to it. Forcing a smile, I finished the remaining steps and sat down. "I ran into Athena, Paulie, and Campbell." I felt myself relax a little. "And Pearl."

The tenseness of Leo's shoulders eased somewhat at the explanation of my extended absence. "Oh. That's nice. I didn't even see them come in."

"Sorry, though." I gestured toward our plates of white-chocolate bread pudding. "I didn't mean to keep you waiting."

One of his broad shoulders shrugged and seemed to tense back up. "It's okay." He smiled, one clearly as forced as my own, but it still managed to light up his handsome face. "Fred, I..." He sucked in a shaky breath. "Winifred, I—"

A loud burst of laughter rang from the room at Leo's back, and he flinched, much like I had done when Paulie called my name.

He chuckled self-consciously and quickly snagged a fork. "Let's dig in. I bet it's still warm." With that, he scooped up a large portion and suffocated any words he might be tempted to say.

Both relief and a fresh wave of nerves rushed through me, but I followed suit, not tasting the dessert in the slightest. Even so, I was glad for the distraction, giving me a few more moments to pull myself together. At another laugh, I glanced over Leo's shoulder into the adjoining room, which housed the large grills. While Prime Slice charged a premium for their cuts of steak, they were also known for their gimmick of having their guests cook their steaks themselves. The woman laughing— someone I didn't recognize, a tourist maybe—was pouring on too much of whatever sauce she'd chosen, causing flames to lick up nearly a foot over her steak.

Unfortunately, the distraction didn't help. As my gaze was inevitably drawn to another table, the accordion of time seemed to fold in upon itself, revealing the shadowed figures of Sergeant Branson Wexler and me.

And like that, the shadows shifted into full-on Technicolor, everything rushing back. Branson had chosen elk steak; I'd had buffalo. We'd discussed the death of Eustace Beaker at his daughter-in-law's coffee shop—he'd choked on a scone. I thought it was murder. Branson hadn't been so sure. Then he'd turned the conversation to flirting, romance, to a date.

There was a chance I was wrong about Leo's intentions for the evening, but I didn't think so. And... no. Just no. This couldn't happen here, it couldn't happen right then, not with memories of that vile man playing in my mind. "Branson brought me here once."

Leo jerked to attention so suddenly his elbow hit the table, causing the glasses to shake. "What?"

"Branson." I gestured behind him, toward the table where the two of us had sat. From the corner of my eye, I saw Athena, Paulie, and Campbell carrying their raw steaks toward the grill room. "He brought me here once." I searched for something else to say, but finished with a muttered, "He had elk."

Leo sat with that, a muscle twitching in his jaw, a hardness entering his eyes. "The thought of how many times you were alone with that monster. The fact that he's still out there, that he could be—"

"Don't." I shot out my hand, taking his, giving it a squeeze and holding on. "We're okay. And we're safe. I wasn't trying to ruin the mood." Okay, that wasn't true, but still. "I was just having a flashback. I'd forgotten we'd been here."

Though that specific anger only Branson Wexler could induce remained in Leo's eyes, he seemed to fully relax the rest of the way, the building anticipation vanishing. "Well, how about we finish up the bread pudding and get home to Watson, leaving all memories of Branson right here."

Relief washed over me as well, though not surprisingly, so did disappointment. As nervous as I was, as unprepared as I'd been for what was about to happen, I *did* want it. We were ready. But... I'd put a stop to it, for better or worse. "Yeah. Let's do, and we'll see if the steak we bring him will be good enough to earn Watson's forgiveness for leaving him by himself."

"Considering what it cost, it better." Leo laughed, nearly sounding like himself. "Although, knowing him, it'll take two."

"He is as much of a diva as my uncle." Chuckling along, I released my grip and started to pull my hand back.

Leo snagged it, linked our fingers, and held my gaze, his expression warm and earnest. "I love you."

At that, my nerves finally washed entirely away. "I know... and I love you too." I wished I hadn't mentioned Branson. We could've made a new memory for Prime Slice, superseding anything that happened before. "Leo, I'm sorry if I—"

"Don't be sorry. Not for anything." Rising slightly, Leo reached across with his free hand cupping my face, and kissed me, then held my gaze once more. "Thank you for going on this adventure with me."

"Congrats, you two!"

At the loud interruption, Leo and I both flinched again, and he dropped his hand from my cheek.

Once more, time contracted and went *so* much farther back than just a couple of years as I stared at my ex-husband standing by the table.

"Gar—" The name was only halfway out of my lips before I realized my mistake. This man, whoever he was, could've nearly passed for Garrett Griffin's twin, although more the way Garrett had looked a decade before. There were other differences as well—Garrett hadn't been quite as good-looking, his jaw not so chiseled, nor his dark hair as thick.

"Leo, you sure didn't waste any time, did you?" The stranger reached across the table, taking my left hand as if he knew me. "Let's see how that diamond..." His words faded, and puzzlement filled his eyes as he stared at my bare finger, his expression quickly replaced by one of horror as a deep blush rose over his handsome cheeks. He cleared his throat and dropped my hand, taking a step back. He looked between Leo and me. "Sorry, I... I mistook you for, um..."

"Hi!" Another voice spoke as a figure came to stand beside the man, though neither voice nor form solidified in my mind for several seconds. "Fancy running into you two here."

Blinking, I forced my focus on the woman and took much longer than normal to recognize Alessandra Costa, but even then it required glancing at her shiny Pink Panther jacket to offer the final clue. "Hi." I smiled, maybe? "It's a busy night." I glanced over to Leo, ready to make a passible joke, but was pulled up short by the look of devastation and anger over his features as he glared at the man.

Alessandra noticed as well and glanced back and forth between the two of them.

As much as I liked puzzle pieces, none of them clicked into place to help me figure out who this man was or how he was somehow aware of Leo's intentions. I held out my hand toward him, the one he'd grabbed only moments before. "I'm Winifred Page. I'm sorry, I don't think we've met."

"No. We haven't." The man was still looking at Leo before glancing at my hand, though he didn't take it. "I'm sorry. Like I said, I mistook you... both of you... for people I knew. Sorry."

"Fred, this is Julian LaRue." Still looking like his world had crumbled, Leo sighed in defeat and spoke through slightly gritted teeth. "His parents own Aspen Gold."

Aspen Gold, of course, the jewelry shop downtown. *Those* puzzle pieces easily clicked together, and I instantly hurt for Leo.

Julian bypassed introduction protocol. "Leo, listen, I'm sorry. I—"

Alessandra flipped her long black hair over her shoulder in an obvious steal of attention. "I have to say, every time I come here, I can't help but feel more and more proud of Pasta Thyme, especially with the remodel I did when I took it over from my folks." She leaned forward, lowering her voice to a gossipy tone. "I know that people say we overcharge for pasta... our *house-made* pasta, but at least *we* don't require people to cook it themselves." She was clearly doing her best to remedy the awkward situation, whether she understood the details around it or not, and while things were little more than politely cordial between us, I warmed toward her for the effort. "Speaking of..." She straightened once more and grabbed Julian's hand. "Let's get this thing going. You promised to cook mine for me, and I plan on working up quite the appetite over dirty martinis while you sweat over the grill."

Julian grimaced over his shoulder as Alessandra pulled him away.

Leo and I watched them head toward the host stand—clearly, Julian had spotted us the second they'd entered and hurried our way—then we looked toward each other.

For several awkward moments, the debate behind Leo's eyes was perfectly clear, and when he reached a snap decision, I didn't try to stop him.

"Well..." He stood, dug into his pocket, and pulled out a ring-sized box. "This is definitely not how I pictured, but why pretend you don't already know what's going to happen after that display..." Leo managed a good-natured smirk before a nervous smile curved his lips as he knelt on one knee beside the table, setting off a murmur of excitement from surrounding tables. "Winfried Page, I love you with my entire soul. I think I have since I laid eyes on you and Watson when you showed up with that owl feather."

The restaurant disappeared, as did any nerves or misgivings. It didn't matter that I wasn't dressed in something special. The history at the restaurant didn't register—we might as well have been alone on the moon, for all I could tell. This was Leo. This was me. This was us. And there was no question about what *we* were. If there had been, the thrilled leaping my heart was doing would've shoved it fully away.

His voice grew stronger, steadier, as he paused to open the box, then looked back up. "It would be the greatest honor of my life—"

It wasn't laughter from the grill room that interrupted us that time, but a scream. One that was quickly followed by a second, and then someone yelling, "Fire!"

Sure enough, a quick glance away from the massive diamond ring sparkling from black velvet revealed roiling flames quickly covering the far wall as people rushed out of the grill room.

Athena emerged, a supportive arm wrapped over Paulie's shoulder, and Campbell stepped into view, fire extinguisher in his hands.

He aimed toward the flames, looked confused, then paused long enough to pull the pin free for a second attempt. At the first jet of foam, the extinguisher slipped from Campbell's hands. He picked it up quickly enough, but it didn't matter. It was too late, much too late.

Despite the fire, the early September night held a chill, and I pulled my scarf a bit tighter around my neck.

"Here." Leo had been standing beside me and shifted behind to pull me close, doing a better job of wrapping an arm around my neck than any scarf. "It's cold."

"Very chivalrous, Mr. Lopez." While I infused teasing into my tone, I let myself sink against him.

"What do you mean?" He chuckled softly beside my ear. "I was talking about me. I'm trying to keep from freezing out here."

Unbidden, a laugh burst from me, louder than was appropriate given the firefighters were still finishing up the last bit of the blaze. I ignored a couple of reprimanding glances. "Well, glad I can help."

His only response was to pull me in a little

nearer yet.

I wasn't sure how much time passed—not a lot. The fire department had come quickly, but a third of Prime Slice was little more than charred matchsticks surrounding the blackened grills that almost seemed to be taunting from the rubble.

As with all things dramatic, the crowd gathered to watch the fire grow, but now with it dying to its final embers, people began to disperse. We'd stayed, both to make sure everyone was safe and to offer support to Campbell, who was a bit of an emotional mess. He and Paulie sat on the ground close to us, Athena standing over them. Though her purse was slung over her shoulder, she held little Pearl to her chest.

For the thousandth time in the last little while, Campbell let out a groan. "I'm going to lose my job, my life savings."

"No, you're not." Paulie wrapped a thin supportive arm over Campbell's shoulders. "It's all going to be okay."

"You're not going to lose your job, Campbell," Athena chimed in. "You're Chief Dunmore's nephew after all. This is America—nepotism is alive and well." When she caught me gaping at her, Athena winked and bent down to pat Campbell's free shoulder. "As far as your life savings, you're barely more than a baby; how much could you have really?"

"Athena!" Leo barked out her name, then had to stifle a laugh.

Chuckling as well, Athena bent farther, with an easy grace—impressive considering her age, the coolness of the evening, and the fact she held the dog to her chest—and pressed a kiss to the top of Campbell's head. "You didn't mean any harm. If anything, Tom Colter owes you a debt. He'll be able to use that insurance money and buy grills twice as large."

"That's probably true." Leo spoke up again, his tone taking a serious turn. "And we were fortunate none of the flames traveled to any of the other buildings or jumped to the trees. The national park is safe." Spoken like the park ranger he was born to be.

Words vanished as a new set of flashing lights washed over the scene. When the late-arriving police cruiser came to a stop, the lights continued.

"Oh." Campbell issued his most forlorn groan yet. "I've been worried about the wrong things. Detective Green is going to flay me alive."

And though Paulie gave Campbell's shoulders another squeeze, none of us were able to offer any comfort in *that* arena.

Like she could feel his presence, Detective Susan Green didn't have to scan the crowd when she emerged from the cruiser and glared with laser precision right at her partner of nearly a year. She pointed at Campbell—hard enough that if she weren't across the street, her finger probably would've stabbed him right through the heart—then she turned and headed toward the edge of what remained of the fire, where she spoke to the fire chief, Shelly Patel.

"If you want to run, child, now's your chance." Athena didn't sound like she was teasing. "Pearl and I can put on a distraction while you make your getaway." She glanced toward Leo and me. "You'll help too, right?"

"No." Campbell's voice quavered, but after a second, he slipped out from the weight of Paulie's arm and stood. "Whatever Detective Green decides to do, I have it coming. She's always right. I'll deserve whatever she does."

The years had taught me to respect Susan Green, and though I'd judged him flighty at first, I'd grown to respect Officer Cabot as well. With his unflinching willingness to face Susan's wrath, that respect grew. I started to verbalize the sentiment, but someone else laughing on the edge of the crowd caught my attention.

Alessandra Costa shoved the jeweler's son playfully away before covering her mouth. Laughing as well—I searched for his name and stumbled upon it quickly enough. LaRue, Julian LaRue—Julian leaned closer and whispered something else, eliciting another burst of laughter, audible over Alessandra's grip over her mouth.

Her attention flicked in our direction, and the hand fell away, as did the revealed smile. With a shame-faced expression, her gaze shifted to her feet. Beside her, Julian seemed puzzled, then turned to where Alessandra had looked. He flinched but gave a little wave before refocusing on Alessandra with another whisper. As one, they turned and joined a few others heading toward the parking lot on the untouched side of Prime Slice.

Hadn't I just been laughing as well? I shouldn't be judging them for doing the same as firefighters brought the blaze to its end. Perhaps it was the sour feelings I had toward Julian for spoiling Leo's proposal, for embarrassing him. Although... there was a tone to Alessandra's laughter. Something almost mocking... maybe gleeful. Strange, considering the drama and scandal the restaurant she'd inherited from her parents had endured.

"On the first night I've had off in weeks, *weeks*,

Campbell"—Susan's rage-filled voice yanked me back from Alessandra and Julian—"I find out my partner, Officer Cookie Dough for Brains, decides to become an arsonist."

"Hey." Paulie leaped to his feet. "He feels bad enough. Don't take that tone with—"

The stabbing finger that had been pointed from across the street finally found a target and jabbed Paulie in the chest with enough force that he stumbled back a couple of steps. "I will end you, little man."

"Susan."

Leo's whispered reprimand earned him a glare from Detective Green, but she lowered her hand. Though she didn't apologize, she refocused on her original target. "Why, for the love of all that is holy, can you not seem to have a lick of common sense in that head of yours? Who else, above the age of twelve, uses a meat skewer to engage in a pretend sword fight?" Though her voice had been deadly low, as she finished, it ended in a screech. "Especially with a hunk of flaming meat on the end of it?" The finger shot back up and finally found its target in the center of Campbell's chest.

He didn't stumble backward or even wince, though it had to hurt. Instead, Campbell looked straight into his superior's eyes without flinching. "I'm sorry."

"Sorry!" Susan's voice shot up again as she gestured wildly behind her, encompassing the ruined steakhouse. "What good does sorry do?"

"I'll..." Campbell's voice broke as he reached into the rear pocket of his jeans. "I'll turn in my badge."

"Campbell." I whispered his name as Athena and I both reached out and touched his arm at the same time.

"Oh for..." Susan stared at the star glistening in the flashing lights, and then her gaze met mine. A miracle must've occurred as a smirk quirked the corner of her lips, and she gave her trademark eye roll. "Care to trade sidekicks, Fred? Yours might shed and eat you out of house and home, but at least you can put him in a cage when you want to." She turned back to her partner. "Keep your badge, Campbell. When you're not being a complete moron, you're a *slightly* above-adequate police officer."

Campbell looked close to tears, but who could say whether it was more from relief or embarrassment? He slipped his badge back into his pocket and then, clearly needing comfort, reached up to stroke Pearl, who was still clutched in Athena's embrace.

Susan scowled at the little dog before glancing at

her feet then looking up at me in confusion. "Where is Officer Fleabag anyway?"

"Home." I shrugged. "Prime Slice doesn't allow dogs."

Susan glanced back toward Pearl, considering. "Well, I guess that little thing probably doesn't qualify."

Athena merely lifted her chin haughtily but refrained from comment.

"Technically"—Campbell found his voice once more—"The meat on the end of the sword wasn't flaming. Just—" He wisely took a couple steps back at Susan's glare.

"Apparently, it was flaming enough to burn down part of the restaurant." Susan encompassed Paulie in her reprimand. "And it wasn't a *sword*, no matter what your adolescent minds pretended!"

"I'm struggling with that very thing." A new voice joined us, and it was a testament to Susan's presence that none of us had noticed the fire chief heading our way. Unlike Susan's, Shelly Patel's tone was kind when she addressed Campbell. "Officer Cabot, you're *sure* it was your kabob that set the blaze?"

Once more, though shame filled his eyes again,

Campbell didn't look away as he met responsibility in the face. "Yes. It was mine."

"But *I* started it," Paulie jumped in, moving closer to Campbell, though maintaining a large arc to keep well out of Susan's reach. "I held up my skewer and yelled 'En garde.'" He shrugged and finished with a mutter, "We were watching the *Three Musketeers* last night, so..."

"Paulie's didn't have meat on it, though." Campbell countered, as if the two of them were fighting for responsibility. "I just moved too quickly, swiped mine off the grill not thinking about it and..." He shrugged as well. "When our swords hit, the meat flew off and landed against the lady's purse beside the wall. By the time we'd stopped laughing, it was only then we realized the fire started."

"They weren't *swords!*" Susan rubbed her temples.

Bypassing that, Shelly narrowed her eyes. "But your steak was on fire?"

Another shrugged. "I guess so. Another lady close by kept pouring a bunch of sauce all over hers, making the fire flare."

Shelly made a humming sound and glanced back toward the rubble.

"Are you thinking this is somehow arson?"

Before Shelly could answer me, Susan lowered her hand and gave me another eye roll—"Disappointed you didn't stumble across a dead body this time, huh?"—though there was a touch of humor in her tone. "Gotta find a crime somewhere."

"No." Shelly turned to me. "It would seem like a rather large coincidence that a flaming piece of meat would fly across the restaurant at the exact same moment someone tried to burn the restaurant down." She shot Susan a commiserative expression. "And thank goodness there's no dead body this time around."

"Oh"—Susan made another sweeping gesture toward Prime Slice—"don't speak too soon. If you let Fred wander through the ashes, I'm certain she'll find someone."

"I think you can sit this one out, Fred." Chuckling, Shelly smiled at me, then glanced down at Leo's and my interlocking fingers, and her smile grew. "That reminds me, I hear congratulations are in order. Prime Slice is the place to do it! Or at least was. Ajay and I celebrated our anniversary here last month."

Paulie, Athena, Campbell, and Susan all looked at us at the same time, each with various expressions of confusion and dawning understanding.

"How in the world?" I gaped at Shelly. "You were in the middle of fighting a fire and..." I finished with a shake of my head. I knew the gossip power of small-town life in Estes Park was a powerful force, but still...

"I *knew* it!" Athena reached out and grabbed my hand, as Julian had done at the table. "I could *feel* it. And it's about time. The two of you..." She halted when she saw my bare ring finger, her perfectly sculpted brows knitting before she glanced back up at Leo and me. "Oh, I thought..."

"Um..."

There was so much misery in that one syllable from Leo that I jumped in. "Leo was about to put the ring on my finger when the fire started." I moved my hand toward him. "Do you still have it? Or did it get left behind in the rush out?"

His brows lifted questioningly, hopefully. "No. I have it."

I smiled at him, trying to recapture that moment from the restaurant when everything else had disappeared. I wasn't able to, but I poured all the love I could into my gaze. "Good."

Leo slid the box from his pocket and opened it up. His lips moved wordlessly, like he was getting ready to finish his question, and then he glanced at our friends around us, the partially burnt restaurant, and cringed.

"Leo Lopez!" Athena's gasp cut through the tension. Clearly she'd not noticed his reaction as she stared at the ring in his fingers. "That diamond! It's..." She swallowed. "Well... park rangers must make a lot more than I realized, or you've been saving for a very, very long time. It's stunning!"

I followed her gaze. Though I'd seen the ring in the restaurant, it had barely been a glance, and I'd been much more focused on Leo in the proposal than the diamond. But now I really saw it, I blinked, shocked. It was huge and reflected the beams of the flashing lights from the police cruiser and fire truck.

Leo returned from staring at the restaurant to look at Athena, the ring, then at me. "I... ah..."

Taking the ring from him, I slid it onto my finger. I didn't bother to look down at it, just held his gaze, trying to communicate so much in the middle of such chaos.

Athena, Paulie, Campbell, and Shelly all cheered. After a few heartbeats, Susan clapped, before punching Leo in the shoulder. "Congratulations, you two."

. . .

There was no greeting pitter-patter of heavy, tiny feet as we opened the door and stepped into my little cabin in the woods. The lamp I'd left on in the living room illuminated my chubby corgi sitting on the hearth of the unlit fireplace. It was a rare occasion when Watson entered Leo's presence without slipping into a state of euphoria, but the glare from his narrowed chocolate eyes confirmed that even one of his favorite humans in the world was just as much in the doghouse as his mama.

"Hey, buddy." Leo cooed and went down to one knee before I'd even shut the door behind us. "I'm sorry we left you for so long. We missed you."

Watson didn't so much as blink, though one of his foxlike ears twitched. After a second, the other did as well.

Knowing him like I did, I was certain what he was listening for—the crinkle of a paper bag, maybe the crunch of tinfoil.

I laid a hand on Leo's shoulder, a sinking feeling settling in my gut. "I'm sorry, Watson. We didn't bring you home any steak."

Leo looked up at me with a groan. "Oh no! In the midst of everything... I wasn't even thinking."

"I can make you some chicken." I was aware the pleading in my tone indicated an unhealthy imbalance of power in the relationship between me and my corgi, but... it was what it was. "I might have some sausage in the freezer, I could—"

Watson stood, foregoing the languid stretch he normally gave when getting up from a nap. Not that he'd been napping. It appeared he'd been sitting there glaring at the door, waiting. When he trotted toward us, Leo made a relieved sound, but it was for naught. With a chuff, Watson strolled past, barely out of arm's length, and disappeared into the dark kitchen. A couple heartbeats later the plastic flap of the dog door sounded, making it clear we were in for a few days of the cold shoulder.

After a sigh, Leo stood. "I can go to the grocery store. Maybe if I got a couple of steaks—"

"They're closed." I sighed and then forced a laugh at the panicky, guilty feeling coursing through me. "Surely this shows we're insane. We're talking about a dog. Is he the master or us?"

"He's Watson." Leo stated the name as if that was self-explanatory.

And it was. "I know, you're right. He's Watson." I gazed into the dark of the kitchen, hoping to hear the flap of the dog door as he returned to give us a second chance. Yes, I was more than aware he was spoiled to a ridiculous degree, and that his little tantrum was just that, a show of power. But underneath it all, I really did think it hurt his feelings to be left behind. To be forgotten only added insult to the injury. "Maybe we'll think of some special treat tomorrow."

"A bribe, you mean?" Leo grinned.

"Yes. That's exactly what I mean." I laughed, then sighed again, feeling exhausted. Only then did I notice that Leo's gaze dipped toward my left hand.

"Fred..." Leo's voice was barely a whisper as he reached to grasp it. "I'm sorry. Tonight was just... I'd hoped..."

"Hey." I lifted my free hand and cupped his face, as he so often did with me, then waited until his eyes met mine. "We're engaged. No matter how it happened." Though I meant the words in a form of comfort, as they rang out between us, a flicker of excitement rose in me again, and the smile that grew was thoroughly genuine as my heart fluttered in happiness. "We're getting married." Then, in a very-un-Fred-like manner, I giggled.

He studied me for a few seconds longer, seemed to find the assurance he was looking for, then beamed. "We're getting *married*."

As he pulled me into a kiss, poor Watson, for the second time that evening, was completely forgotten.

The following morning, no force on the face of the earth—be it fire, engagement, or the ignition of nuclear codes—would've allowed my finicky corgi to have been forgotten, overlooked, or misunderstood. He made certain of that.

Watson woke us before the alarm went off by pacing around the bed, his claws clacking on the hardwood floor. Once we were both up, he resituated in his own bed and took a nap while Leo and I got ready. Then, as we made our breakfast, we offered him a wide assortment of choices, and just as he'd done the night before when he'd finally returned from the dog run and we'd offered him a bevy of options, he turned up his nose. That had been startling enough the first time, but to still do so after breakfast? That had to have been the longest time he'd ever gone without eating. When Leo left to report to the national park and attempted to give a good-bye pat, Watson ducked his head out of the way with a grunt.

Despite knowing it was useless, I attempted to affix Watson's leash so we could take our morning stroll through the woods. As soon as he saw it, he hid under the bed. Giving up, I decided to simply head to the Cozy Corgi. He had such a stubborn streak, I thought I was going to have to carry him to the car, but that particular personality flaw was one we shared, and I finally set my foot down. "Fine. Stay here and pout if you must. But you'll be by yourself. And it's a very busy day." My hair pooled on the floor as I leaned over to peer under the bed, only to meet Watson's scowl. "I won't be able to come back in the middle to check on you. You'll be alone until this evening." That wasn't true; no doubt my guilt would get the better of me within an hour. Watson probably knew that.

Still, it wasn't until I stood at the open door jangling the keys to my volcanic-orange Mini Cooper that he finally trotted out from his hiding space. That is, if *slugs* are able to trot, as that was the pace he chose from the bedroom to the front door and then miraculously moved even slower—possibly at a snail's pace; I'm assuming their shell impedes their speed—to the car. With a solitary burst of energy, he jumped from the passenger side to the back seat and faced the opposite direction. He didn't curl up with his back to me, he quite literally sat down on his haunches, as if at attention, and faced the back seat of the car, not even looking out the window.

Irritation flitted, but the sight of him looking so ridiculously stubborn melted my heart, and I chuckled. It was the wrong thing to do of course, and I earned myself the briefest of glares, which only made me chuckle again.

Watson was silent as we drove into town toward the bookshop and bakery. I barely noticed—actually, barely noticed the road as I drove when my hand gripped the steering wheel and the light caught on the diamond, captivating me. It'd been so long since I'd worn an engagement ring. My first wedding band hadn't had a diamond at all. I knew nothing about diamonds, less than nothing. I didn't have a clue how many carats it was, hadn't the foggiest about quality, cut, or any other diamondy attributes. But it was large and sparkly and... it slid sideways as I angled the steering wheel when I pulled onto Elkhorn Avenue... too large. The ring itself, that was. I'd noticed it as I'd gotten ready that morning, feared it would slide off my finger as I washed my face. I made a mental note to go to Aspen Gold at some point that day to see if they could resize it. I might not have a clue how big of a diamond it was, but it didn't look cheap. The last thing I wanted was for it to fall off without me noticing.

A horn blaring pulled my attention back from the ring and onto the road. At some point I'd come to a red light, while I couldn't remember stopping, it seemed we were several seconds into green and I was holding up traffic.

Watson chuffed from the back seat.

We made it to the Cozy Corgi without car wrecks or lost diamonds, but not without trademark corgi disapproval all the way from the car to inside. Proving the adage that old dogs can't learn new tricks to be true, Watson turned on the charm as Ben Pacheco, my assistant bookseller and one of Watson's three human superheroes, came into view. As he had before during times of frustration with his mama, Watson spared a side-eye glance my way as he licked ferociously over Ben's face, a cloud of corgi hair billowing around them at their embrace.

Ben had plopped all the way to the floor to keep from losing his balance at Watson's greeting, and though he didn't quit lavishing love on my little grump, he grinned up at me. "I take it our mascot here is annoyed with you and using me to rub it in?"

"See, Watson?" He didn't look my way as I addressed him. "You're not nearly as clever as you think." I winked at Ben and pointed upstairs. "Got it in one. I'm going to let you hang out with His Majesty on your own and head to the bakery to get my first dirty chai of the day." I was halfway up the steps when I glanced over my shoulder. "In fact, maybe I'll even get a *treat!*"

Ben and I both flinched, and our gazes went from Watson to each other as my corgi's favorite word didn't prompt so much as a whisker twitch. "Whoa." Ben actually paled. "You're in for real trouble this time."

"So it seems." Pathetic as it might be, I had to admit my feelings were hurt, which was probably exactly Watson's point as it had been the night before. By the time I reached the top of the steps, I decided the two of us should probably enter couples counseling.

"Couples counseling?" Katie turned from where she was rearranging Cozy Corgi merchandise above the little dog-sized apartment in the built-in shelving. "Why?" Worry filled her tone. "Are things bad with you and Leo? I thought—"

"No, I meant Watson and me. I didn't realize I said that out loud." I started to explain Watson's mood, then realized where Katie had been going before I'd interrupted. "You already know, don't you?"

She gave a shrug. "It's Estes. Of course I do."

For what seemed like the billionth time, considering my feelings at Prime Slice with Leo, and then interactions with Watson, guilt slammed into me yet again, and I grabbed Katie's hand. "I'm sorry! I should've called you last night." The thought hadn't even entered my mind—not to call my best friend, my mom...

"No! *I'm* the one who's sorry." Katie shook her head, her brown spirals bouncing. "*I* should've called *you*. To congratulate you about your engagement, to make sure you were okay after the fire. I just didn't want to intrude on such an important night. And by the time I heard, it was late."

"Ah, Estes." I couldn't help but laugh. "I suppose I should be thankful I didn't find out Leo was going to propose before he actually did, especially since he bought the ring here in town. That's a rather large miracle in and of itself."

Katie gasped, let out a little squeal, and all apologies were forgotten when she twisted my hand around and pulled it up toward her face. "Speaking of. Let me see the—" Words fell away, her face paled, and she blinked. She twisted my hand slightly, causing the light to catch the diamond and set it ablaze. Her lips moved soundlessly for several seconds, and for one of the few times in our friendship, Katie Pizzolato was speechless.

My cheeks heated, and I imagined I was beet red.

"Did Leo rob a museum?" Before I could answer, Katie twisted my hand again while she cocked her head. "Wow! Fred, it's absolutely gorgeous." In what looked like a concerted effort, she peeled her gaze away from the ring and looked up at me. "It's absolutely beautiful."

I never enjoyed too much attention on me, despite that Susan Green would attest otherwise, and I sought to lighten the moment. "I thought the first thing you would do would be to rattle off a whole bunch of diamond trivia."

She cocked her head again, her expression shifting from awe to a scowl. "I actually don't have any knowledge about diamonds at all, other than they're formed from heat and pressure and the whole business around them hurts the environment and fosters the slave trade and—" That time *her* cheeks went pink.

The laugh that burst from me sounded a little bit unhinged, though it relaxed me somewhat, and I pulled her into a hug. "I love you. Of course, the only trivia you'd know about diamonds *would* be those sort of things."

"I didn't mean any judgment by it." She sounded worried. "Plus... knowing Leo, I bet he checked to make sure it wasn't one of those kind of diamonds."

"I'm sure you're right." I pulled back from the hug but held her gently at the shoulders, not letting her look away. "Beyond that, though, the point of all this isn't the ring or the diamond or anything. Neither of us have ever been jewelry types of women."

"Exactly." She brightened and leaned nearer with a conspiratorial whisper. "The point is, you and Leo are getting married."

"We're getting married!" I whispered back, and a happy thrill shot through me again.

"*Finally!*" Her next whisper was barely audible.

We both gave way to fits of laughter before she clasped my hand and led me across the bakery. "Come on. Let's get you your first dirty chai as a newly engaged woman. I think that calls for an extra shot of espresso."

"Or two!" Nick Pacheco, Katie's assistant and Ben's twin brother, smiled through blushing cheeks as he pulled a large knife through a tray of what look like caramel-colored fudge. "Congratulations, Fred."

"Thank you, sweetie."

Before I could say anything else to him, Katie released my hand and went behind the marble counter to snag one of the delicacies from the tray. "And one of these oaty ginger crunch bars to celebrate too. A new recipe—you're gonna love it." She gestured toward the espresso bar in front of the large window that overlooked downtown Estes Park. "Go sit. We have ten minutes before we open, and I want to hear all about it. I already know where Leo proposed, and that it had a rather fiery conclusion, but how did he ask? I want all the details."

"Well, thanks to the fire, that's about all the details there—"

A pounding on the door below promptly followed by a bark from Watson cut me off, and a second later Ben's voice traveled up to us. "It's Anna! Do you want me to let her in?"

Katie waggled her eyebrows at me. "Apparently I'm not the only one who wants all the details." Then she raised her voice. "Yes, Ben, let her in before she knocks down the door."

There was a momentary pause as Ben unlocked the door, and then a voice called up, "I heard that Katie Pizzolato! *Rude!*" In what was an impressively breakneck speed, especially considering Anna Hanson was quite a bit shorter, rounder, and decades older than myself, she made it through the bookshop and up the steps as if she'd been flying. Both her white poufy hair and her billowing gingham dress fluttered around her with her movement, and whatever offense she might've felt at Katie's comment seemed to have been burnt away. The scroungy white dog in her arms was wide-eyed, clearly not used to the accelerated pace. "Fred! Katie! I had to come over first thing. I'm so excited that—" Anna halted to a stop parallel to Nick and looked down at the tray of oaty crunch bars. "Oh! Pop two of those out for me." She started to continue, then paused once more, looking from Katie back to Nick and cleared her throat. "Sorry. What I meant was... Nick, would you mind getting me two of those"—she flitted her fingers at the tray—"things. Please."

"Of course, Ms. Hanson." As was so often true, Nick's cheeks blushed yet again at the attention. Katie had confronted Anna recently about her rudeness toward Nick and treating him as if he were less than an equal human, among other things.

"Thank you, dear." Anna smiled, a genuine little thing, and then hurried toward us once more. "Now, tell me *everything*! I want to know—"

As she drew nearer, the little dog in her arms let out several high-pitched yips and began to writhe.

"Why, Winston!" Concern flashed as she barely managed to hold onto the little diaper-clad dog. "What in the world is the matter?" Her question was answered as he tried to lunge toward me, and her eyes narrowed. "Oh." For a second it looked like she might turn on her heels and storm away. Then with an annoyed grunt, she thrust the dog toward me. "Fine."

The wire-haired terrier mutt was one of the worst-tempered animals I'd ever met, snarling and trying to bite everyone within reach. However, at some point, he'd decided that he loved me. Even so, I couldn't help but still feel a bit of trepidation as I accepted the little monster with his crooked fangs lunging toward my face. But yet again, he began to lick in affection, instead of offering a small werewolf bite. I scratched his head as he did so, my own affection for the little guy growing once more.

"I'll never know what he sees in you." Anna tapped her short nails on the marble impatiently.

Over her shoulder, I noticed Watson emerge at the top of the stairs. He hesitated, taking in the scene and glaring my direction as ruefully as Anna had done.

Proving that Watson might have learned some of his tricks from his mama, I moved a little further into view and increased my snuggling with Winston. To date, every instance Watson had seen us together, he'd gotten jealous and promptly made certain that Winston knew *I* was *his* mama. It was the only time he ever acted as if I was on par with Leo, Ben, or my stepfather, Barry.

For a second, it looked like Watson was going to rise to the occasion once more, but then he chuffed, in what was a clear *I know your game, woman*, and trotted toward his little apartment and out of view.

At the sound of the doggy door once more adding insult to injury, Winston gave a final lick to my face and wriggled, trying to get down—he loved Watson even more than me.

Obliging, I bent and placed him on the floor, and raised my voice in a false whisper "Okay, but be warned, Grandpa Watson is in a *mood*." I gave Winston a final scratch, and Anna gasped as he tore away at a frantic speed the Tasmanian devil would've envied.

Though I'd assumed Anna gasped because of Winston's excitement, she proved me wrong by grabbing the hand I'd used to scratch her little dog and yanking it into view. "Well... *that* I hadn't heard!" She twisted my hand this way and that, a little painfully, and didn't let go, nor did she look away. "I didn't know Leo was wealthy." She finally glanced up and gave an approving nod. "Winifred Page, you do beat all. Tall, handsome, *and* rich!" She glowered with a sigh. "I tried to get my Betsy to follow those rules, but no, she had to marry—" She fluttered her hand in the air again, then focused on Katie. "Never mind all that. How big is your diamond, let me see?"

Nick stiffened, Katie paled, and I did a double take.

Anna wriggled fingers. "Well, come on. Hold out your hand. Let's compare."

I thought Katie was speechless again. "Anna Hanson, how in the world did you know—"

Another snap. "Don't be daft. Let me see your ring."

"Your ring?" For the second time in just as many days, I struggled putting together the obvious puzzle pieces as I turned to Katie. "*You're* engaged too?"

Katie shot an annoyed glare at Anna and refocused on me with a cringe. "I didn't want to steal your moment. You and Leo have been together so much longer than Joe and me. I thought I'd wait, tell you this afternoon."

"You're *engaged*?"

Anna shoved my shoulder. "Good grief, Winifred. What's wrong with you? Catch up."

"Anna!" Katie hissed, looking at me again. "Joe asked last night. Remember a couple weeks ago I said I thought he was going to do it soon..." She shrugged. "Well... I was right." She chuckled. "Barely half an hour later we heard about the fire at Prime Slice and about you and Leo being engaged, otherwise I would've called you. Apparently, Leo didn't talk to Joe in advance about it since—"

I cut her off with what was probably the biggest hug I've ever given Katie. Then, surprising both of us as I pulled back slightly, my eyes filled with tears, and my heart—which was already so happy—nearly burst. "This is even better. I love it."

"I didn't think you'd mind, but..." Tears brimmed in Katie's eyes as well. "Like I said, I just didn't want to steal any of your moment."

"This is *our* moment!" Some of the nerves I'd been feeling mixed in with the excitement faded. "I love that we get to experience this together." Remembering protocol, I grabbed her hand as she had done me. "Let me see."

Her ring finger was bare, and Katie shrugged before heading toward the cash register. "I was going to tell you this afternoon and then put it on." She darted behind the counter once more as she glared yet again at Anna. "I suppose I should've known better with all the *busybodies* in town."

"You really should have, considering how smart you *think* you are." Anna preened at the busybody compliment. "Really, the two of you are rather disappointing."

With the ding of the drawer sliding open, Katie reached in and slid the ring on her finger. At the sound of the breakfast rush entering below, she hurried back over and held out her hand for my and Anna's inspections.

"Oh no." Anna gave herself a little shake and adjusted her tone. "I mean... that's very cute, dear." She cast her gaze my direction. "Engagements or rings *aren't* competition. I'm sure Joe meant well."

Neither of us paid her any mind. "Katie." I was smiling so wide it felt my cheeks might crack. "It's absolutely perfect."

Just as the first bakery parishioner arrived up the

stairs, I twisted her hand slightly as she had mine, allowing the light to glint off the tiny pink heart-shaped stone set atop a tiny gold cupcake, which was held on either side in the mouths of two hippopotamuses, whose bodies made up the rest of the band. It was the most Katie-like thing I'd ever seen.

With kids back in school, tourist season had been over for a few weeks, so the breakfast rush in the bakery above didn't apply to the bookshop below. The only customer visible as I reached the end of the stairs was Myrtle Bantam, who barely spared me a passing glance before returning to point at the computer screen over Ben's shoulder. Doubtlessly, the owner of Wings of the Rockies and founder of the Feathered Friends Brigade was hand-selecting which ornithological books should be grafted into our wildlife section.

No one required my attention. Relishing that fact, true to form, I entered my favorite spot in the bookshop, the mystery room. The river rock fireplace blazed invitingly, and the antique sofa beckoned for me to choose one novel from the recently refilled and reorganized shelves and get lost for a while.

"Don't mind if I do." I patted the arm of the sofa

on my way past, thanking it for its kind offer and headed toward the shelf of witch-themed cozy mysteries. There'd been a lot of drama and turmoil over the past several weeks, so it felt like a good idea to chase the upturn of happiness of twin engagements with complete escapism. Plus, with the leaves already beginning to turn a beautiful gold, I was in the fall mood.

I'd just cozied up by the fire and cracked a book by Molly Fitz, with a witch with flowing pink hair on the cover, when I felt a gaze on me. Peering over the pages, I found a pair of large chocolate eyes staring from the doorway of the mystery room. One of Watson's stubby legs lifted, and he paused midstep, glowering at being caught.

Knowing my little grump as I did, instead of just looking back at the words, I physically lifted the novel up a couple of inches to cover my face from view. After a few silent moments, save for the crackle of the fireplace and chatter from the bakery overhead, Watson's nails clipped over the hardwood and stopped as he jumped onto his ottoman.

That was a good sign. Maybe I was going to be forgiven for my litany of offenses sooner than predicted. I knew better than to let on and forced myself to read the first couple of pages. Proving that miracles truly did exist, there was a soft grunt as Watson made the narrow leap from ottoman to sofa and plopped down beside me. While he didn't curl against my leg, neither did he sit out of arm's reach.

I forced myself to finish the first chapter before slowly lowering my hand to rest on his flank. When he didn't pull away, I began to stroke. Watson tensed, then let out a little belch, grunted, and relaxed.

It took all the maturity I'd acquired during my first forty-one years to not make a snide comment about being forgiven so easily, and simply relished being absolved, or at least temporarily pardoned.

By the time chapter five rolled around, Watson was snoring against my leg, and I'd been transported into a fuzzy haze of contentment. I was in the mystery room with a delightful book, by the fire, had reestablished good graces with my corgi, my best friend was engaged, and most wonderful of all... though I'd known the outcome for a long time, I was going to spend the rest of my days with the love of my life.

Sinking into that feeling, I lowered the book, letting it rest in my lap, and stared into the flames, allowing myself to retravel the journey that had brought Leo and me to this place. As he'd started to say in his interrupted proposal, it really had begun with a feather, one found in the very building I was in now. And what started out as friendship had slowly bloomed into something so much more—more powerful, more consuming, and more lasting.

I had no idea how long I was lost to that gentle revelry when a cackle from the bakery brought me back to the moment. At some point, I'd released the book and rested my arm on the edge of the sofa, and as I moved my hand to grasp it again, the engagement ring slid easily off my finger, hit the floor, and bounced three times, directly toward the fire.

I screamed—which wasn't something I did very often—and flung myself from the sofa, accidentally shoving it backward. Having never been athletic, it wasn't all that surprising that as I hit the ground, stretching as if to catch a baseball right over home base, I missed the ring entirely. Even so, fate or Cupid was on my side, and the ring came to a stop less than an inch from the embers.

Snatching it up, I repositioned to a sitting position, holding it tightly to my chest as I leaned against the river rock, trying to catch my breath.

From his spot on the shuffled sofa, Watson once more looked thoroughly offended, having gone on such an unexpected ride across the mystery room. To my surprise, though I hadn't caught my breath enough to apologize, he didn't scurry up the stairs and disappear into his apartment once more when he jumped to the ground but padded my way. He even went so far as to sniff me to make sure I was all right, or maybe checking to see if any treat might have fallen out of the pockets of my skirt.

It was a cheap lesson; who knew where the ring might fly off the next time? I supposed the fire wouldn't have hurt the diamond as it had been forged through temperatures much hotter, but still. Less than ten minutes later found Watson and me up a block and on the opposite side of Elkhorn Avenue by the giant waterwheel. Maybe feeling like I'd been through enough stress at my near heart attack, Watson hadn't fought against the leash, or walked at a glacial pace through town.

Gold, diamonds—all smaller than the one on my ring, other assorted gemstones, and jewelry of all kinds glittered from the large square window of Aspen Gold. While the outside of the building itself matched the majority of the shops, with its 1960s mountain style, the door of heavily carved wood had been painted a deep bloodred and finished with an overlay of gold lacquer. When I pushed it open, a little bell dinged out a high, clear note.

As Myrtle had been in the bookshop, I was the only customer in the jewelry store. Well, *me* and Watson. Thanks to the slanted portion near the back of the left wall, the shop was a small pentagon. The store on the other side of the slanted wall was Alakazam, a little magic shop that had been shoved between other stores. While it had painted every one of its oddly angled walls a different color, Aspen Gold had gone a different direction. The entirety of the small place was wallpapered with a vertical striped design—alternating black and faded gold, each with columns of embossed flowery starburst embellishments. It gave the tiny shop the feeling of being extraordinarily tall, which was just an illusion. Though I was aware the effect was to be glitzy and glamorous, or maybe high-end romantic, the stripes always made me feel like I'd entered a gilded jail cell. A quick scan over the cases of jewelry made me reassess my take on the aesthetic. If not a jail cell, then the interior of a pirate's treasure chest.

Watson gave a tug at the end of his leash, pulling my attention, and I nearly laughed. Once I moved so he had more slack, Watson shuffled to his destination —a *literal* pirate chest. Actually, the brown leather box with gold hinges was too small to have belonged to a genuine pirate, or maybe one with less grandiose ambitions than most. Unlike the glittering glass cases around, the chest appeared filled with items to tempt children—Mardi Gras beads, large plastic rings with glittery glass stones, and gold doubloons. Watson stuffed his nose under a tiny plastic golden crown, tipped it over, sniffed, then lost interest.

He'd just turned his bored gaze on me when the door sounded in the back, promptly followed by the sound of voices. "I'm telling you, she's paranoid. She's not at all the kind of woman you think she is."

"No one's ever good enough for you." A woman's voice answered the man's that had come before.

"She's definitely not good enough for me." Though the words weren't yelled, or even all that loud, the bite of anger was clear in the man's clipped tone. "It drives me crazy that you're so gullible to give anything she says the slightest credence."

A door sounded again, and a second man's voice joined in. "There was no need to slam the door in my face."

"I didn't slam the door." The original man's volume was a bit louder that time. Though I'd only heard it once before, I recognized it—Julian LaRue.

"All I'm saying is you need to give her more of a

chance. Win her over." The woman's plea held bit of a whine. "I want us to stay in her good graces."

That didn't take any amount of shuffling of puzzle pieces for the picture to form easily enough, given what Leo had said the night before. The other voices were obviously Julian's parents, the owners of Aspen Gold. I'd stumbled into a family argument of some sort. In a moment more, all of them were going to walk into the front and catch me eavesdropping.

My theory was confirmed with the next comment. "Son, you know we trust you. You know that we don't see you as a disappointment. It's just that—"

I opened the door and closed it once more, causing the bell to chime, and the voices to stop instantly.

Though I succeeded in ending the awkward situation, I'd earned myself yet another glare from Watson, who'd darted toward the door clearly ready to get on with whatever part of the day came next, only to have it shut in his face.

Vivian LaRue emerged through a heavy-looking gold-embroidery-curtained doorway in the back, promptly followed by her husband, Roger. I'd met them a couple of times during my years of sticking my nose into various murders and questioning the storeowners downtown.

The couple, in most respects, matched their shop in style. Though Roger's thinning hair was slicked back in a Ken-doll fashion and Vivian's was piled high with hair-sprayed curls, they shared a matching shoe-polish black hue. Each of their combined twenty fingers sported at least one ring, and while Vivian's neck supported string upon string of pearls, Roger had one solitary thick chain of gold visible through the sharp color of his starched white shirt.

They both paused as they saw me, as if experiencing a glitch, then as one, continued to the back of the jewelry case in front of the curtained doorway. "Ms. Page." Roger glanced down at Watson. "And..." He blinked a couple of times.

"Watson," I provided.

At his name, Watson looked up hopefully, then plopped down on his haunches with a sigh of surrender, realizing we weren't going anywhere nor receiving treats.

"Yes," Roger agreed. "Watson."

"Has there been a murder, dear?" Vivian paled as an arthritic hand seemed to lift of its own accord to grip the mass of pearls around her neck. "I was hoping now that the Irons family was run out of town, we'd have a reprieve."

"No!" I forced a laugh. "No murder. Sorry. I should realize what showing up unannounced indicates to a lot of people."

Vivian relaxed and offered a tight smile. "What can I do for you, Winifred?"

I held up my hand, which clutched the ring as I hadn't trusted wearing it on my finger. "I need to—"

"Winifred?" Julian tossed open the curtain and hurried in. His questioning gaze cleared instantly at the sight of me, and he hurried my way, casting his parents a glance as he rounded the display case. "Fred!" He infused welcome in his tone, but the strain didn't disappear. "I didn't expect to see you again so soon."

Though Katie had accused Anna of being a busybody—rightly so—it took me a second longer than was polite to respond, as I was pondering if Julian and his parents' disagreement had something to do with Alessandra and their date at Prime Slice. I was unable to follow that bunny trail any further before remembering social niceties. "Yes, good to see you again, Julian." I pivoted slightly, now holding the ring toward him. "I'm afraid I need to get this resized. It seemed a little loose last night, but even more so today. Maybe it's just the cold, but it literally flew off my finger and nearly landed in the fireplace."

"Oh!" Vivian sighed in adoration. "Winifred. That ring. It's gorgeous. Where in the world—"

"*Here*, Mom," Julian snapped, his teeth clicking at the sharpness of his words. It softened quickly enough as he looked back at me. "Leo got it here. A custom order."

"Custom?" If I'd been wearing pearls, I might've clutched them myself. I hadn't really let myself think about how much the ring had cost, as the mere notion caused a gurgle of anxiety in my gut. But *custom?*

"I didn't know Mr. Lopez—"

"Dad!" Julian snarled toward his father that time, then turned back to me, flashing yet another smile.

In that heartbeat, an image of my ex-husband, Garrett, tried to superimpose itself over Julian once more. They were similar, to be sure, uncomfortably so, especially considering I was holding out my new engagement ring to him. In his mid-forties, Julian was older than Garrett had been when we'd divorced nearly a decade before. In addition, as I'd noted the night before, Julian was more classically handsome than Garrett. And... though things had ended horribly in our marriage, there was a quality about the man in front of me. Garrett had been controlling at times, selfish, and a very different man by the time we divorced than he'd been when we'd married, but he never had the empty cold look in his eyes that Julian LaRue possessed.

When he reached out and took the ring from my palm, I nearly snatched my hand back before he could. Julian didn't seem to notice. "Come with me. Let's get you measured." He headed toward the cash register, then paused by a glittering amethyst geode that was as big as my forearm. Once more, he glanced toward his parents, and this time he cringed and sounded as if he'd stepped into a confessional. "Alessandra and I bumped into Leo and Fred at Prime Slice last night, right before the fire." His gaze returned to me. "I'm so sorry. I was afraid I ruined Leo's proposal." Whatever emptiness I'd noticed in his eyes was gone then, filled with genuine remorse, or maybe just embarrassment.

"Oh... Julian!" Vivian whimpered and started to head around the jewelry case as well.

"It's okay." I attempted to shrug and gave another false laugh. "As you can see, since I'm here with the ring, nothing was spoiled." I gestured toward the diamond. "I just don't want to lose it, or damage it, or..." That time, my laugh held no humor, only stress.

"Honestly, I'm a little terrified I'm going to shatter it or something."

"Good luck shattering a diamond, Ms. Page." Roger appeared beside us, like a vampire forming in a mist. And while not complimentary, with his dyed-black hair, fancy clothing, and waxen complexion, that was kind of who he resembled—Dracula turned into a septuagenarian jewelry store owner. He took the ring from Julian and examined it. "It's stunning. You're a very lucky woman, Ms. Page." He cast a quick glance toward his son. "I'll make sure it's perfect for you."

"*I* insist." Julian snagged the ring back. "It's the least I can do after my faux pas last evening. I'll fix it myself and have it ready for you by the end of the day. In fact, in way of amends, if you should see earrings, a necklace, or some other—"

"Oh no." I motioned to the corgi-shaped pounded-silver earrings I always wore—a gift from Leo long before we'd started dating. "Between these and all the strings of crystals my mother and stepsisters force on me, I have all the jewelry I need."

"Crystals." Vivian shuddered as if I'd suggested I was wearing slugs, but leaned forward, narrowing her eyes behind her half-moon diamond-encrusted spectacles. "But those earrings. Those are lovely. I do believe Leo purchased those here some years ago."

"He may have. And I love them." I reached down to pet Watson, who dodged my hand. "One can never have too many corgis."

Roger chuckled and gave Watson an amused grin. "We'll have your ring ready for you quickly, Ms. Page. This time it will be done correctly."

"And congratulations!" Vivian chimed in, a little too enthusiastically.

FIVE

Though traffic was as light as the number of tourists in town, I paused at the intersection of Elkhorn and Moraine to lean against the corner of Shutterbug. I spared a glance into the darkened windows of the camera shop, whose owner had been killed a couple of weeks before, and my thoughts got sucked into the void. Not about Benjamin, his camera shop, the Irons family, or the chaos that had sent Estes Park into an upheaval.

Leo. He was all-encompassing.

In the sheltering interior shadows of Shutterbug, my thoughts finally went to puzzle pieces I'd pretended didn't exist since they'd started to appear at Prime Slice.

Actually, *Prime Slice* was one of them. A fancy restaurant, even one that wasn't on par with the elaborate prices of Pasta Thyme, was the last place I ever would've expected Leo to propose. In and of itself, maybe not a clue. In and of itself, it could be meaningless. Proposals often happened at fancy locales—it was expected, traditional. But Leo wasn't typically impressed by such things.

The other piece, the one I *really* had mentally locked away had appeared when I'd seen Katie's ring.

Anna was right, at least her words were right—engagement rings weren't a competition. Clearly her feelings revealed she didn't really believe that to be so, and also that Katie had gotten the shorter end of the stick.

She hadn't. Though impeccable in its detail, the ring was understated. The smallest chip of whatever the pink stone may be and the cupcake-hippo design was the most Katie thing that had ever existed. It was perfect, not only for her, but for what I'd learned about Joe Singer and their short, but intense, romance. The ring demonstrated how well he knew her.

The ring Leo offered me? It didn't. The part of me that felt guilty for allowing myself to go there finally had to admit there wasn't one aspect of the ring that said Winifred Page. Not a solitary one. I might not care about jewelry, fashion, or expense, but I did hold intention and thoughtfulness dear. It was one of the things I loved most about Leo. He was always thoughtful, always intentional. That engagement ring didn't say either of those things.

That was the part that kept my feelings from being hurt. I chuckled at the realization. How many people would have their feelings hurt when presented with the layman's version of the Hope diamond? But my feelings avoided that hurt, due to one fact—just as much as that massive rock didn't say a thing about me, neither did it say a thing about Leo, even if it was custom. Which meant that for whatever reason, Leo not only hadn't considered me in his choice of ring, he also hadn't considered himself.

I thought I knew why, and the empty dark windows of the camera shop demonstrated what that reason was.

Watson's grunt and tug on his leash pulled me from the darkness and into the beautiful soft light of the September morning filtering over downtown. The little glowing white man affixed to the stoplight began to blink, announcing I'd been lost in reverie for at least one walk cycle.

Before I could give in to Watson's urging, I moved out of the way of three beautiful women stepping onto the curb. "Get out of the way, buddy. We don't want to get people tangled in—" I released the slack in his leash as a pair of blue eyes flashed toward me then darted away, and I realized it wasn't three beautiful women, but three beautiful girls. "Britney?"

My sixteen-year-old niece flinched and turned back with a sigh. "Sorry, Fred. I wasn't trying to be rude. We're just in a hurry."

I had to bite my tongue to keep from pointing out that she had utterly failed in the not-being-rude department. Britney had been struggling for several months, rebelling and giving her parents fits. I didn't want to add to it.

"Oh!" The girl with long brown hair knelt. "He's sooooooo cuuuuuuute!" She didn't sound the least bit in a hurry. "You're Watson, aren't you?" She reached out delicate brown fingers and scratched his head.

Watson grunted again, and though he glowered, he allowed himself to be the center of attention as the redhead knelt as well and stroked his back. "I've heard about you. You're a detective."

I laughed. "Not really, unless there's beef jerky, potato chips, or some rotten meat hidden among clues." I laughed a little harder as Watson sent up a side-eyed glare my direction. Whether he didn't appreciate my disparaging of his detective skills or was offended I didn't save him from the indignity of receiving lavish attention, I wasn't sure. "But you're right—he does a fine job." The continued side-eye indicated he hadn't been overly concerned about my disparaging remarks.

"Come on." Britney didn't offer commentary about Watson as she motioned toward her friends. "We've got to go." She moved away before either of the other girls stood. "Good to see you, Fred, Watson."

As if summoned, the redhead stood instantly and followed. The brunette lingered a moment longer, patted Watson, then with a sigh, stood, offered me a flash of a smile, and hurried to catch up with the others.

I watched them go, my concern about Britney washing away any thoughts of Leo, proposals, or rings. While she'd been struggling, Britney had never been overly rude to me until then. In fact, I thought things had been getting better. She and Barry had been spending more and more time together.

Barry! Thinking of him brought things full circle, and Britney disappeared from consciousness, replaced by a giant diamond, and I searched my purse for my cell phone as if it might explode.

"Your timing is perfect, Fred. Almost." Mom answered on the first ring, and though her tone was cool, I caught the hint of humor. "I literally set a timer, and I was going to call you at the end of ten minutes. You had two left."

"Mom! I'm *so* sorry." There was no point in pretending she hadn't already heard—as Anna expertly demonstrated, it was Estes Park, after all. But might as well try. "I'm engaged!"

She sucked in an exaggerated gasp. "Really? I can't believe it. Tell me all about it." Her voice went breathy. "Was it romantic? Were there fireworks or just... fire?"

"You're terrible!" Barry's cackling from somewhere in the background came through the line so clear that Watson looked up and cocked his head, sudden hope flaring in his eyes.

"When did you become so sarcastic?" I couldn't help but chuckle along. "But yes, to all of it. Well, no, not the fireworks, but it was romantic..." I glitched for a second at that. Between Julian and the chaos, it hadn't been romantic, not really, at least not until we got home and settled into it. "And there was fire."

"Was there also a murder?"

Despite the remaining humor in Mom's voice, I halted. "What?"

"Well..." Mom drew the word out. "Surely that's the only reason a daughter wouldn't call her mother on the very same night she got engaged, or *at least* the very next morning."

With a grunt of defeat, Watson gave up trying to find Barry, decided it was well past time to return to the Cozy Corgi, and pulled me across the intersection.

Thankfully tourist season really was over, as neither one of us looked both ways or even checked to see if there was a walk sign. Barely noticing, I continued. "Mom, I'm so sorry. Really. It was a crazy night, and this morning I needed to get the ring sized and—"

"Oh, you know I'm only kidding."

"*I'm* not!" Barry yelled from the background once more, and they both gave way to more laughter.

"I don't care about how soon you call, darling. I'm just so happy." Before I could think of what to say, Mom's voice went serious, warm, and quiet. "It's not like anyone is surprised. We all knew it was a matter of time. You and Leo were written in the stars, literally. Just because it's as sure a thing as gravity doesn't mean we shouldn't celebrate it."

As I had with Katie, I felt tears burn in my eyes. The ring didn't matter, and if I was correct with the *why* Leo had chosen it, those reasons didn't really matter either. The gravity comparison was apt. That's how Leo felt, he was a grounding force, steady and strong, and we'd already been through so much I knew if the world shook and walls crumbled, *he* wouldn't. *We* wouldn't.

"Thanks, Mom." I paused that time to look both ways before moving on to the other crosswalk to get to the same side of the street as the Cozy Corgi. "And don't worry, I'll make sure you're invited to the wedding and not hear about it the day after." I nearly paused at that. *Wedding*. I hadn't even thought. Good Lord. Wedding!

"You'd better." Mom laughed yet again. "I hear congratulations are in order for Katie and Joe as well. I'll call her in a little bit. I wanted to wait to hear from you first. I also thought I'd see if you and Leo could come over tonight. I'd love to make a celebratory dinner."

"Yes, we'd love to. That would be..." The insights that had come to light in the darkness of the camera shop windows illuminated once more, and I paused. "Actually, could we do it tomorrow evening? Things were so crazy with the fire and all last night, it would be nice for Leo and me to have a little time on our own."

"Of course, darling." Mom's voice lilted in a warning. "However, you might want to ring up your uncles promptly. If Percival calls you first, you'll never hear the end of it."

The intention of calling my uncles flitted away as Watson and I reentered the Cozy Corgi. Tourist season over or not, several people milled about the bookshop, and Ben had his hands full in the children's section with a young mother and toddler triplets.

Watson and I fell into our respective roles as if they were a second skin. I headed to an older couple waiting by the cash register with a pile of three Carla Hall cookbooks. As I checked them out, Watson meandered, giving wide berth to anyone, lest they deemed themselves worthy of offering him affection.

As the older couple left, I headed to our rather small section of horror, where a man wearing a Donald Duck hat stood looking overwhelmed. I guided him to Dean Koontz's *From the Corner of His Eye*, which was a frequent reread of my own and an easy gateway to the genre. When I explained that *Phantoms* was a touch more traditional in spook factor and gore, he purchased that as well to test his resolve. Watson, who emerged from the mystery room, apparently changing his mind as to where he wanted to be, offered a growl to the duck bill bobbing over the man's head before the man left.

I often prided myself that I could predict if not what kind of book a customer might want, at the very least the correct genre, so I was a little surprised when the prim, conservative-looking woman asking for a romance novel turned down my suggestion of Francine Rivers novels and requested something a little steamier. By the time she walked out with a copy of Roan Parrish's *In the Middle of Somewhere*, Watson was sprawled on the hardwood floor, snoring away in his favorite ray of sunshine pouring through the window.

After all of that, Ben was *still* helping the young mother, sorting through a growing pile of picture books with one hand while supporting one of the triplets on his hip with the other. He offered me a quick smile when I shot him a questioning glance. Once assured he had all the help he needed, I decided it was high time for the next infusion of my addiction and headed up to the bakery. Watson stayed where he was, snoring so deeply it sounded as if he hadn't slept in months.

The breakfast rush was long gone and while there were a couple of patrons sipping lattes while engrossed in their computer screens spread across the Art Deco-styled expanse, Katie and Nick were busy in the kitchen, finishing up the next round of pastry items.

"Have time for a dirty chai?" On most occasions I wouldn't have needed to ask. It was just an assumption that when I appeared, so did a dirty chai—proof I had the best business partner and premier best friend in the world—but even as I approached the marble countertop, a heaviness radiating from Katie was nearly tangible.

"What?" Katie looked up from where she was portioning out dough to form into baguettes, flour covering her hands and swiped across her left cheek. "Oh. Chai. Um, of course." Her gaze didn't meet mine when she turned quickly and headed toward the espresso machine. If her mood wasn't clear enough, the rest of the proof was offered when she didn't bother to wash her hands and ended up getting flour on the espresso machine handles.

I shot Nick a concerned glance, and he cringed in response.

Yes, something was clearly wrong.

I took my typical seat at the espresso bar and glanced out at the shops below, wondering if someone had said something negative about her engagement, about her ring. Surely not—the townspeople might love the gossip, but they weren't mean. Anyone who knew Katie would realize her hippo ring was utter perfection. Anna's words came back to me as my gaze fell on her shop, Cabin and Hearth—*It's not a competition.* Unfortunately, not everyone would see it that way. I turned back to Katie. "Did someone say something to you about getting engaged on the same night as Leo and me? You know I don't care about that, right?" I started to reach out a hand to touch her, but she continued making shots of espresso. "You know that I meant it, that it makes it even better."

She sighed, poured the espresso into a large mustard-colored Cozy Corgi mug and then began making another shot. As it streamed into the small clear glass, Katie cast me a quizzical expression. "No, no one said anything... Why would they?" She shook her head and sighed again, a long one. "No. Everyone's been very nice. I just..." She poured the next shot into the mug and started another one. "Well, I don't want to believe it. I want to be wrong, but I'm not." As her hands continued to work, she glanced over her shoulder toward Nick.

He offered her a supportive nod.

With yet another sigh, she refocused on the espresso, poured it into the mug, and then finished up the dirty chai, not responding until she pushed the mug toward me. "I don't want to get her in trouble, and I don't want to make things tense between you and your sisters, well, Zelda, specifically. But I also think things should be faced head-on." She swiped the back of her hand across her right cheek leaving another trail of flour in its wake. "I can go over to Chakras and talk to Zelda without getting you involved."

The flitting confusion at her rapid-fire explanation cleared before I could take my first sip as my niece's hurried and rude demeanor came back to me. "Britney?"

Katie balked with an exaggerated blank. "Good grief, Fred. I know you're good at solving murders, but that was near telepathy worthy."

"Hardly." I grinned at her. "I ran into Britney and a couple of her friends on my way back from Aspen Gold."

Katie brightened. "Oh! Good. I'm sure they said there'll be no problem resizing your ring?"

"Yes. It should be done today, I think." Still, I didn't take the first sip of dirty chai. "But back to Britney, what's wrong?"

That time when she glanced over her shoulder, Katie seemed to look past Nick. "Well, she and her friends were over there, by Watson's little apartment and the Cozy Corgi merchandise." She refocused on me and her tone took on an apologetic quality. "Shelly Patel's daughter ordered their drinks. They also got a lemon bar to split." She bugged her eyes. "*To split*, Fred. *Three* girls, *one* lemon bar. I know there's a lot of pressure to be the size of a stick, but that's barely even a taste." At my chuckle, she sighed out a little breath. "And that's beside the point, but still. On with it... I didn't recognize Shelly's daughter, like I said, she looked so much more grown-up than the last time I saw her. It wasn't until I noticed Britney that I realized they were three high school girls in the bakery."

That time, when Katie didn't offer the punchline, I wasn't quick enough. "That's a problem?"

"School is back in session, Fred." She knocked on the marble as if trying to wake me up. "*Hello*, playing hooky, and in Britney's aunt's shop, flaunting it."

I relaxed, though surprised Katie was making that big a deal of it. "Why in the world would you be worried about that causing drama between Zelda and me? She's not going to be upset at me because Britney came in here when skipping school."

"Well, that's not the big part. I probably would've just kept that to myself, as kids will be kids, after all. The Patel girl and the other friend looked embarrassed when I confronted them about skipping school, but Britney was pretty rude and..." She leaned forward, lowering her voice, though none of the other customers were near enough to hear. "Well, when they left, the new little solar-powered corgi bobble head with the bakery logo on it was gone."

"Gone?" A sinking stone dropped in my gut. And here I thought Britney had been getting better. "She stole it?" It wasn't really a question. Not only was it clear what Katie believed, the way Britney had acted when she bumped into me on Elkhorn was practically a confession. I didn't wait for Katie to confirm before I pushed on. "On the one hand, that little corgi was probably less than ten dollars, and skipping school, like you said, it's just kids being kids, even though I never did that sort of thing."

Katie snorted. "Of course you didn't, and neither did I. But I'm not sure that says too much about *normal* kids."

I couldn't disagree with her there. "But stealing,

even something small, that's different." I considered for a moment. "Typically, I'd go directly to Britney, but..." I could see how that would unfold after our interaction on the street. "I can't keep this from Zelda." I didn't think my stepsister would blame me, but you never quite knew with Zelda, or her twin.

"Sorry, Fred." Katie shrugged. "We can just ignore it for now. No reason to dampen this wonderful day."

"No. Might as well get it over with. Besides, it's not like it's a murder. This is nothing compared to what we normally have to do." As true as that was, I didn't relish the thought of it and finally took a large swig of dirty chai—and choked. It took a couple of seconds to catch my breath, and I stared into the mug. "Good Lord, Katie. How many shots of espresso are in this thing?"

She halted, and then a smile grew. "You know, I have no idea. Let me make you a new one."

"No." I took another tentative sip. "I can't bring myself to throw away a dirty chai. I'll just sip it slowly, lest it causes a heart attack from all the caffeine."

. . .

As I reached the front door of the Cozy Corgi, Watson sprang up like his ray of sunshine had burned him. From the accusatory glare he shot my way, somehow it was my fault. Before I had time to either defend myself or ask what exactly was wrong, he shuffled over and headbutted my shin before looking at the door and then glaring once more back up to me.

I followed where he glanced. "What? You want to come with me?"

Watson, of course, didn't answer, only continued to glare, but I thought I was right.

"Okay..." Testing the theory, I hurried to the counter and retrieved his leash under the cash register. Sure enough, Watson remained right where he was as I bent to fasten it around his neck. "I have to say, I wasn't expecting you to switch from giving me the cold shoulder to clingy and needy so quickly, but"—I pressed a quick kiss between his eyes, which he didn't even pull away from—"I like it!"

As the Cozy Corgi sat directly between Ark and Whale, my brothers-in-law's shop, and Zelda and Verona's Chakras, the path Watson and I had to take on the sidewalk consisted all of making a right turn and about ten steps to get to the front door. It was around step five when my phone buzzed with a text message. Pausing, I retrieved it, Watson stopping right beside me, and glanced at the screen. Though I hadn't saved the number in my phone, it was clearly from Julian of Aspen Gold.

Your ring is ready and perfect. Swing by anytime this afternoon. We close at five, but if you can't make it down, just shoot me a text and I'll deliver it personally. Sorry again!

Granted, I had no clue how long it took to resize a ring, but it had barely been an hour since I'd left the jewelry store. I hadn't expected that, nor would have predicted such expediency or genuine regret from Julian. Although, it wasn't every day a guy ruined another man's proposal. I was tempted to turn around and head to Aspen Gold that very moment. While I thought I understood why Leo had chosen the ring he did, perhaps I could squeeze a few more details of the customization from Julian that would clarify things before I asked Leo about it.

Watson, his clinginess not overriding his impatience, tugged at his leash. As he continued on our previous trajectory, I let him make my decision and finished the last five steps to Chakras.

The new-age shop seemed void of customers, but I couldn't quite tell through the thick smoke that billowed toward us as Watson and I stepped inside.

For a heartbeat, I thought I was in the middle of another fire, but then I choked on the cloyingly sweet aroma of incense.

At my feet, Watson whimpered, then sneezed.

Typically, Chakras was sparkly and glittery with beautiful lighting and crystals everywhere, but at the moment, I could barely make out the silhouette of the main counter in the center of the room. And though I didn't hold any of my twin stepsisters' beliefs in the supernatural, metaphysical, and whatnot, it didn't take a psychic to feel the oppressive energy in the room.

Before I could call out, a form materialized like a specter through the mist, its arm moving up and down causing the fog to billow. Another figure appeared from the opposite side, its arm moving as well. Only when I noticed the little flecks of glowing ember did I realize the smoke was coming from them. "Verona? Zelda?" I nearly choked. "What are you trying to do? Burn the whole block down with sage?"

The figure to my left gasped and hurried forward, her long blonde hair coming into view and identifying her as Verona. Moving in tandem, her brunette twin, Zelda, emerged from the other side.

"Fred!" I couldn't tell which one said my name

as they rushed me, both wrapping their arms around me and squealing at the top of their lungs so loudly my ears rang.

At their wild embrace, which consisted of jumping and thrashing along with the squealing, a small earthquake seemed to enter the world of smoke and fire. With a howl, Watson took off, lurching forward so quickly his leash popped right out of my hand. A moment later, a loud crash that sounded suspiciously like crystals hitting the ground reverberated, followed by another howl. A clinking of beads meant Watson had made it to his favorite spot in the shop, a beautiful crystal room sporting a waterfall and pool.

The twins didn't seem to notice, judging by their continued thrashing.

Trusting Watson would be fine, I focused on staying upright as I was thrashed back and forth between them. "Zelda! Verona! What in the world? Calm down, breathe, if you can in all the smoke."

"You're engaged!" Verona squealed in my left ear.

"Finally!" Zelda squealed into my right.

They pulled back as one, though each of them still gripped my arms as they squealed in unison, "We told you it was about to happen!"

Verona took over. "We've actually been making you a necklace most of the morning to bring over, one that enhances love, commitment, and passion. We were just about done when... well... we needed to sage."

"And to burn Satya incense," Zelda clarified, gesturing back to the smoke to where I assumed an incense burner set. "It helps with anxiety and stress."

"But don't worry about that." Verona waved a hand toward her sister, shushing her. "Fred's *engaged*!" That time, her squeal was a little more forced.

"Thanks for being excited for me and for making me a necklace." I dared to attempt a small breath, managed not to choke, and considered requesting them to crack open the door. I didn't, nor did I point out that if I ever wore all the crystals given to me between them and my mother, I'd be crushed under the weight. Better to just rip off the Band-Aid and get to the point. "I'm actually here about Britney."

Both of their shoulders slumped, but it was Zelda who spoke. "She's why we needed to sage and Satya. Got a call from school, she's skipping again. She's not answering her phone."

"*Again*," Verona added with an unhelpful glare. "We have no idea where she is."

"I do. Or at least where she *was*." Maybe it would help soften the blow that they already knew part of the bad news. "I ran into her and two of her friends a while ago when I was walking back from Aspen Gold. Before that they were in the bakery at the Cozy Corgi—"

"What! Britney was *right there?*" Zelda screeched before I could finish, turning to Verona as she flung her hand toward the wall shared between the bookshop and Chakras. "She's just rubbing it in my face, taunting that she's not going to do a thing that's expected."

"And she was with her friends." Verona adjusted the sage in her hand and crossed her arms, giving an *I told you so* lilt to her tone. "Doubtlessly, her cheerleader buddies. This is what you can expect."

Zelda turned her temper on her twin. "Can it with the cheerleading criticism. This is bigger than your views on—"

"It's more than that, I'm afraid," I jumped in, knowing that once the two of them got going, it could continue indefinitely. "Britney... or maybe her friends..." I didn't want to point my finger directly at her, in case she wasn't the one responsible, but if she wasn't, the way she'd treated me on the street confirmed that she'd taken part. "They stole a little trinket from the Cozy Corgi merchandise in Katie's bakery."

"Stole." Zelda took a step back, stunned. "She... stole?"

"Oh..." Verona let out a deep sigh. "We should've been burning juniper. It protects against theft."

For once, Zelda wasn't pulled into the powers of crystals or incense and seemed to deflate. "She stole. I just..." She shook her head, tears brimming.

Verona leaped into action instantly, wrapping her arm across her twin's shoulders and pulling her in close. "It's those Ananya and Dawn girls, and the rest of the cheerleaders. I'm telling you."

Zelda didn't argue, but instead met my gaze. Now that the billowing smoke of sage was fading, she was easier to see—and looked every bit like a tired mother nearing fifty, who was worried sick about her child. "Is that who she was with? Ananya and Dawn? They're nice girls. But—"

"I don't know." I couldn't remember if Katie had said the girls' names. "I know one is Shelly Patel's daughter." I assumed it was the beautiful girl with long dark hair and brown skin, given Shelly's Indian heritage. "And a redheaded girl."

"Yeah," Zelda confirmed. "That's them. The

three of them have been inseparable since Britney joined the squad last year."

"And *that's* when she started changing." Verona didn't miss the opportunity to prove her point and did so by pulling me in with a knowing look. "It was shortly after she joined that she started that whole TikTok Diva nonsense and posted poor Athena nearly getting killed in your bookshop."

"Dad says she's fine, that she's simply being a normal teenager and we need to give her time." Zelda addressed her twin, and from the lack of force behind the words, I got the impression it was a conversation they'd had about Barry and his oldest granddaughter before.

"I know. But we weren't in Dad's life at Britney's age." Verona was suddenly gentle. "He doesn't really know what's normal for teenagers and what isn't. And stealing... well, it isn't."

"But Britney wouldn't..." Zelda started to protest, but then her shoulders slumped even more. "Yeah. You're right." Suddenly a little smile curved the corner of her lips as she looked down. "Well, hi there. I forgot you were here."

Following her gaze, I realized Watson had appeared. Most of the sage smoke had dissipated, and though the incense was still thick in the air, he braved reemerging from the back room. My heart warmed. As was so often the case, Watson proved that despite his grumpy, stubborn demeanor, he was attuned to when people were hurting and might be in need of comfort from something fat and fuzzy.

Sure enough, Zelda knelt and began stroking his sides, letting out a long sigh before addressing Verona without looking away from Watson. "Go see if we have any of those fancy bison treats he likes. It's been a while, but I think there's a few left."

"I believe you're right." With a pat on her sister's shoulder, Verona turned and headed deeper into the shop.

Watson watched her go but stayed where he was, proving two things—he had the heart of a softy, and he was no dummy where treats were concerned.

The approach of closing time found Watson and me, unsurprisingly, curled up by the fire in the mystery room. After several laugh-out-loud moments, I closed the final page of *Witch for Hire*, finished the spicy dredges of the dirty chai in my mug, and commented to Watson with a contented sigh, "Owning a bookshop really is the best, isn't it? *Especially* during low tourist season."

Watson didn't so much as bother cracking open a solitary eye but gave a yawn. A little thing at first, but it quickly morphed into the wide, fang-baring variety, followed by a cute little sneeze.

With the fuzzy floating feeling that often accompanied the finishing of a good book, the stress of Britney and my theories around Leo and the ring seemed lighter. Everything would be fine, everything would get ironed out. I stood, gave a stretch similar to

Watson's—without the fangs—and felt a smile form as my heart fluttered, thinking about the ring. No, it wasn't perfect, the proposal hadn't been either, but the end result was the same, and that was... *perfect*. I was a little surprised. Leo and I had been so certain about our future together for so long that I wouldn't have predicted being engaged feeling so different. Pleasant, to be sure, but nothing more than expected, like dessert follows dinner. However, expected or not, the growing commitment between Leo and me was better than any dessert. And that was saying something.

In that frame of mind, I left the Cozy Corgi and headed back down Elkhorn Avenue—partially walking, partially floating on a pink cloud. While Watson didn't particularly seem in the floating type of mood, he was happy enough trotting along beside me, enjoying not having to weave through the typical tourist traffic on the sidewalks. The fact he'd already forgiven me for the offense of being left in his comfortable home during Leo's and my dinner out the night before added a golden shimmer to the edge of that pink cloud.

As we approached Aspen Gold, I studied my finger. It didn't matter if the large diamond was what

I would've pictured there or not. A thrill shot through me at the imagined sensation of the ring, a constant little weight of assurance, of belonging. And with that hand, I reached out to pull open the red-and-gold lacquered door, only to be stopped short in my tracks. I started to pull again and noticed the Closed sign.

They must've gone home early. Strange, considering the text Julian had sent. Hoping they'd just locked the door, I knocked. After a few seconds, I moved to the large window and pressed against it with my hand above my eyes. The lights were off, though the early evening sunlight was bright enough to illuminate the small jewelry shop. Everything was in place, but no one was milling about.

I tried not to be rude, I truly did, despite my proclivity of sticking my foot in my mouth at inopportune times, but I never wanted to come off entitled. Even so, the desire to feel the weight of the engagement ring on my hand made me pull out my phone and text Julian, hoping he was close by and could return. Proving I did have my entitled moments, when he didn't answer within about thirty seconds, I called. After several rings, I left a message when his voicemail picked up.

Hoping he'd respond quickly, I decided to kill two birds with one stone—I'd wait close by while finally telling my uncles in person about the engagement. Watson and I crossed the street to Victorian Antlers, and I grinned down at him as we approached the door to the antique shop. "Gary will be sweet, of course, but Percival is going to give all kinds of corgi attitude that we didn't come down first thing this morning, you just watch. He's about as big a diva as you."

Watson simply cocked his head, one ear twitching, not offering offense or agreement.

Unlike with Aspen Gold, I could tell Victorian Antlers was closed before I started to open the door. With another unanswered knock, my afternoon reading by the fire seemed to feel less indulgent. Apparently lots of the storeowners were taking advantage of the break in tourist season. In actuality, that was probably only part of it. With the drama and stress of the weeks before—where multiple murders had occurred and the Irons family came crumbling down, revealing that a few of the businesses had been part of the crime syndicate— everyone was trying to come to terms and regroup in their own ways.

That thought brought me back full circle. It wasn't only the storeowners who had felt that weight, and not just those murdered like Shutterbug's Benjamin. If my theory around the ring was correct, Leo had been experiencing the fallout of all that had occurred as well. While I might not have my engagement ring, I *did* have my fiancé. And maybe I'd been slow to realize that over the past weeks or so, but clearly, he needed some reassurance. That I could do. The ring could wait, not that I had a choice.

No one would ever confuse me for Martha Stewart or Donna Reed, not even a little bit. Nor with Katie Pizzolato, for that matter. Still, while my specialty in the kitchen was grilled cheese and tomato soup, I wasn't exactly a candidate for the *America's Worst Cooks* show. As I prepared a pork loin, with carrots, onions, and potatoes, I intentionally dropped more crumbs than normal, keeping Watson prancing in delight at my feet as I hurried around the kitchen—to reward him for his expedient forgiveness and an unabashed bribe to ensure his pleasant attitude remained.

Unlike the storeowners, Leo's schedule had grown more intense with the absence of tourists.

Now that they were able to work more unencumbered, the renovations the national park service was doing to Chipmunk Mountain had moved into full swing. He'd taken off early the night before for our dinner, which had been my first clue that Prime Slice wasn't just a typical Friday fare. By the time he walked into the cabin around eight o'clock, his park ranger uniform rumpled and his dark hair disheveled, he looked dead on his feet.

The door hadn't even closed before he was nearly bowled over as Watson crashed into him. "Hey, buddy!" Simultaneously regaining his balance and kneeling, all tiredness fled from Leo's expression as he beamed at Watson, then looked up in pure astonishment. "After last night, I didn't expect a greeting like this for another week. Possibly two."

"I think he's been doing corgi yoga or meditation or something." I brushed my hands on the apron as I walked in from the kitchen. "His mood completely flipped on a dime about halfway through the day. Of course, it doesn't hurt that I've given a lot of *accidental* food-dropping reinforcements as I cooked."

"As you..." Leo sniffed and gave a final scratch to Watson's head as he stood, his gaze traveling over my body before settling on the Cozy Corgi logo over my chest. "You're wearing an apron." He sniffed again.

"And you're cooking." Another sniff, followed by his eyes narrowing even more. "That doesn't smell like cheese or tomatoes."

"Shut up." I smacked his shoulder as he smirked. "Just because you're a better cook than me, doesn't mean I don't know my way around the kitchen." I smoothed out the stiff fabric once more. "As for the apron, Katie finally got one in mustard, so really, this may become my new accessory for every outfit, whether I'm cooking or not."

Leo chuckled. "Percival will *love* that, a mustard-hued apron is exactly what he's been harping about for years." His honey-brown gaze flicked toward my hand, and some of that exhaustion returned. "I take it *that* particular accessory is still getting resized?"

"It's finished, but by the time I went to the shop they were closed."

"Fred, about the ring... I've thought about it all day." He cleared his throat, as Watson reared up to pound with his forepaws on Leo's thigh, he didn't even seem to notice. "I could tell you—"

"I was so disappointed when Aspen Gold closed early." With a flash of Leo's hurt and regret, all my thoughts about talking about the ring vanished. "I even texted and called Julian, hoping he'd be willing to come back down so I could pick it up."

"Really?" Doubt mingled with hope in Leo's tone, and he dropped a hand to Watson's bouncing head. "I thought maybe—"

"I can't wait to feel it on my finger at all times." The back of my mind whispered that we should have a conversation right then and there, that he'd opened the perfect door. But I couldn't. Leo looked so tired, so defeated. And he'd been so crushed the night before with the botched proposal. I couldn't add to it. I just couldn't. So, I kissed him long enough that Watson grunted in disgust, gave up his plea for attention, and padded away. Finally, I pulled back, barely enough to meet his gaze. "Just because we won't have the ring for another night doesn't mean we're not still engaged, and nothing could make me happier than the promise of marrying you." I forced a laugh, feeling self-conscious. "Which is why we have a pork loin that's probably shriveling to the size of a dried-up raisin as we speak. I wanted to... I needed to—"

His kiss swept my words away, while his arm wrapping behind my waist and pulling me to him as his other hand cupped behind my head, ushered all thoughts of rings, diamonds, and insecurities away with it.

No, I would never be Martha Stewart or Donna Reed. I didn't want to be, and just as wonderfully, I knew Leo didn't want that either. But if roasting a pork loin prompted the brightness that surged through him in that moment, I'd do it every single night.

Well... maybe every single week.

EIGHT

The envy I experienced as Katie crafted my breakfast chai the next morning had very little to do with the Katieness perfection of her ring design, and instead on the fact it was on her finger. I'd been engaged for a little over a day and had only worn my ring for a hot second. I was ready to slip it on and settle into the excitement.

I didn't have to wait long. By the time I finished the dirty chai and an apple turnover, Ben had unlocked the front door to the Cozy Corgi and the morning breakfast rush began, which meant all the stores up and down Elkhorn Avenue would be opening that very minute.

As I only planned on a quick back-and-forth, I hurried past Watson's little apartment without bothering him, and was surprised to hear the clatter of his paws scurrying behind me down the steps as we passed people on their way up to the bakery. With a haughty tilt of his head, he allowed me to fasten his leash before we made the well-worn trek down the sidewalk toward the waterwheel.

In my excitement, I made the same mistake I had the night before. Only that time when I attempted to open the door of Aspen Gold, I jerked so hard it actually stung my fingers as they slipped off the handle. Shaking my fingers from the sting, I glanced at the Closed sign, then at the time on my cell, which was silly, considering the Cozy Corgi had just opened. Repeating my actions from the night before, I stepped in front of the window and peered in, preparing to knock the second I saw Julian or his parents moving inside. Entitled or not, I was ready for my ring.

I blinked a couple of times, the sensation of my heart sinking indicating it understood what had occurred before my brain could quite make sense of what the morning sunshine illuminated.

Lowering my hand, I shot a questioning glance to Watson. Typically, he growled, stiffened, or seemed uneasy during these types of situations. But he just sat there, grinning up at me with his tongue lolling from his smiling jaws. Then, as was second nature by that point, I refocused on my cell phone once more and hit speed dial to call Detective Susan Green.

She answered in her typical manner. "Let me guess, you went back to Prime Slice and rifled through the conflagration. You're calling to tell me that despite neither the fire nor police department discovering any bodies, you happened to pull out... how many... five, six victims from the rubble? And that they were all stabbed before the fire began." She offered a gruff chuckle. "Maybe you called to tell me you're hanging up your amateur-sleuth hat to join Ethel Beaker as part of one of the ladies who lunch?"

Despite what I could see through the jewelry store window, I balked at that, completely thrown off. "What? Ladies who lunch?"

"You know..." Susan lowered her tone to a false whisper. *"The Real Housewives of Estes Park* crowd. I saw that diamond."

I couldn't help but groan and at the same time feel my cheeks heat from embarrassment. "No. Unfortunately, you're right with the first guess."

Susan must've been drinking something, as she choked. "No way. Fred, there were no victims at Prime Slice. You do not find—"

"Not at Prime Slice," I cut her off. "Aspen Gold. While I can't be certain, I'm willing to bet there's only one victim—Julian LaRue."

. . .

In less than five minutes, Susan and Officer Cabot parked their cruiser directly in front of Aspen Gold. Campbell offered a smile to me and a scratch to Watson's head, which was accepted with minimal annoyance. Susan skipped over pleasantries, getting right to the point. "I just spoke to Roger and Vivian. They're in Denver at—"

"An antiquing and costume jewelry exposé that's happening this weekend at the Merchandise Mart," I finished for her without even thinking.

She shot me a glare of exasperated admiration. "How in the world do you do that?"

"I called Percival and Gary last night to tell them about Leo and me, as the antique shop was closed before I could see them face-to-face. He told me they were down there for the weekend, and he mentioned that the LaRues were there as well." I left out that he'd sounded annoyed at their presence.

"Oh." Susan shrugged that off and pulled out a lock pick from her pocket and got to work on the door. "I got permission from them to enter. I simply told him we had a report of a burglary at the jewelry store and they might want to return home."

"They'll probably be worried when they call their son and can't get ahold of him." The timidity in Officer Cabot's tone suggested they'd discussed this on the way over and had a differing of opinion—which was rare.

"Well, I couldn't very well tell them their son was murdered when I didn't have any details, could I?" Susan didn't bother to look over at her partner as she finished working on the door. With a click, she pulled it open, casting me a glare after she stepped through. "Wait just inside the door. It's not like you're official or anything, and we don't need dog hair covering up yet another crime scene."

Campbell locked the door behind us—as was typical in any small town, maybe anywhere, a small crowd started to gather outside, this one made up of mostly other storeowners who'd noticed the police arrive.

Susan pulled a gun and announced her presence. After a few moments of silence, the two officers carefully weaved around the rubble in the tiny shop, trying to make their way toward the counter without disturbing anything.

Aspen Gold was in shambles, with overturned cases and shattered glass spread over the floor intermingled with rings, necklaces, and some loose stones and gems. While I couldn't be sure, it didn't look like enough jewelry among the chaos to account for what I'd seen the day before. Either the destruction had happened after the majority of the merchandise had been safely locked away in a vault, or it had been stolen. Despite the wreckage, the store itself seemed intact, so whatever had prompted the robber to overturn cases, they'd stopped there, not bashing walls or cutting through the black-and-gold wallpaper. When Susan and Campbell disappeared into the back room, I refocused on Watson.

He'd been studying them curiously. After he could no longer see them, Watson padded toward the end of his leash and sniffed at a large crystal that had gold feet on one end and a gold rabbit head on the other, making it look like a sparkly fat bunny. Only then did I realize Watson's ears hadn't flattened, nor had his hair risen on the back of his spine. He hadn't issued so much as a growl.

Watson missing the signs outside, while unusual, was understandable. Him missing them once we were *inside* Aspen Gold, with him sniffing around... no way.

I knew what Susan and Campbell would find before they reentered the main room. Susan's pale blue eyes narrowed in accusation. "I thought you said you saw Julian's body. Though I'm clearly slow on the uptake, as he would've been out here in the main room for you to be able to—"

"No." As I spoke, I tried to put the puzzle pieces together to form a new picture, but nothing was clicking. "I said he'd been murdered, not that I saw his body. But I was wrong, wasn't I? He's not back there."

"Thanks to you, I didn't even attempt calling Julian before I contacted his parents." She glared in way of response and pulled out her phone. "Let me call dispatch to get his number and—"

"I have it." I tapped his name and lifted the phone to my ear as I addressed Susan. "He was so adamant about getting the ring back to me yesterday, that with him not responding last night and then seeing the destruction in here this morning, I just assumed." When the phone went to voicemail once more, I hung up rather than leave a message. "He's not answering. I'll give you his number so you can try."

Susan didn't respond for moment, instead glancing slowly around the wrecked jewelry shop, her gaze settling where Watson sniffed another gold-and-crystal animal, this one the shape of a bear. Then she looked to her partner. "Given recent complaints, what's your guess, rookie?"

Officer Cabot's body slammed into stiff attention though he beamed like his favorite teacher had singled him out from a large class. "Given the lack of blood, that there was no alarm sounded, my first theory would be that Mr. LaRue, the junior, that is—" At Susan's eye roll he sped up. "My theory would be that he figured we'd question him again, so he cut and ran, making it look like a robbery gone bad."

"Feasible." Susan didn't sound convinced. "Although if he was going to go that route, why not leave some blood, a ransom note, something to indicate foul play or kidnapping. Otherwise, this was obviously him."

Campbell started to respond and then halted, stumped.

Susan didn't offer a theory of her own, not that I gave her a chance.

"What do you mean *again*?" I looked back and forth between the two of them. "You already questioned Julian? Why?"

Though she held on to her typical exasperation, Susan proved yet again that the two of us had reached heights in our relationship that neither would've ever predicted a couple of years before, as she didn't hesitate in answering my questions. "We've had a bevy of complaints about Julian over the past couple of days from residents in Aspen Grove." She gestured toward the slanted wall that was shared with the magic shop. "My brother's idiot fairy-lady assistant, which was why I didn't take it too seriously. But I also got a call from..." Susan halted, catching herself. "An anonymous source... suggesting that we should look into Julian LaRue, that he was up to no good. Though they didn't offer anything specific enough to warrant our attention. I... we did follow through on crazy fairy-lady's accusations yesterday, not that they amounted to much."

Though I'd seen Julian exactly two times, for probably what added up to less than ten minutes in total, a rush of snippets flooded through my mind, begging for attention. The dinner with Alessandra—*he* was at Prime Slice when it caught on fire. The argument I'd overheard between him and his parents. Him being adamant about returning my ring to me so promptly—perhaps it hadn't just been guilt about ruining Leo's proposal. Before I could think through any of those, I found myself staring at Watson, who moved on to sniffing a crystal mouse before giving up and settling down with a bored sigh, propping his head on his crossed forepaws. "You're right. If Julian was trying to steal from his parents, but making it look like someone else, that hardly works if he disappears at the same time without any signs of—" I jumped back to one of the memories and looked at Susan. "Unless Julian isn't trying to make it look like someone else. When I was in yesterday, I overheard a disagreement between him and his parents, and there was definitely tension with his father when I asked to get my ring resized. Maybe he's not trying to make it look like a robbery at all, at least not one performed by someone else. Maybe he was just mad and"—I gestured around the rubble—"wanted to add insult to injury on his way out of town."

Susan snapped her fingers, causing Watson to sit up in alarm. Not offering him an apology, she pointed at me. "It's annoying how quick you are, Fred." Without missing a beat, she whapped Campbell's shoulder. "Quit making me wish I had the irritating bookseller for a partner, would ya?"

"How do you outdo yourself every single time?"

"I can't be sure what you said exactly with your mouth so full of the oaty ginger crunch goodness, but I'm willing to bet it's a compliment." Puzzlement flitted over Katie's expression from the other side of the espresso bar as humor filled her tone. "So, thank you."

I hummed out my affirmation and focused on chewing while I stared in appreciation at what remained of the dense little square, with its thick crunchy bottom and caramel-colored fudge-like top. After finally swallowing, I took a sip of the dirty chai and sighed in a way that caused Katie to laugh. "This might actually be the most perfect combination yet."

"That only makes sense. There's enough ginger in the shortbread crust and in the topping to match the spices in the chai." Katie tapped the Cozy Corgi mug. "And the chai helps balance the super sweetness of the golden syrup I use."

"I don't need to know how you work the magic, just keep it coming." I popped the remainder of the little bar, cookie, whatever into my mouth and forced myself to savor, otherwise I'd reach for another and another until I finished off what remained of the tray.

As I returned to chewing, Katie swiveled away, taking the order—a cheese croissant and nonfat two-pump vanilla latte—from one of the many who'd gathered to gossip and speculate in the bakery. I'd left Susan and Campbell at Aspen Gold less than half an hour before. As was normal, Katie's bakery had turned into the main hubbub for the local gossip, even more so since the other major coffee shop downtown, the Koffee Kiln, hadn't reopened since one of its owners had been murdered recently.

Though tiny, the pink heart of Katie's engagement ring caught the light as she plated the pastry, pulling my attention. A quick shot of jealousy flashed into my mind and ushered in a new concern. What if my ring had been one of the items stolen? The thought made my heart sink. Of course it didn't mean anything about the engagement, there would be another ring, but it would be one more shot to the eye of all Leo had planned.

"Fred?" My name pulled me back to the moment, and I turned to see Zelda's furious face from where she stood at the corner of the bakery counter. "I'm sorry to bother you." She gave a dismissive flick of her wrist toward the crowded bakery. "Apparently there's been *another* drama downtown, and you're probably deep into solving a murder." She sniffed. "Wait... was there a murder?" She gave another flick of her wrist, batting it away as if someone getting killed was beside the point. "Either way, this won't take much of your time."

"No, there wasn't—" I started to explain about Aspen Gold, then saw the small entourage standing awkwardly over Zelda's shoulder.

Her husband, Noah, had his arm draped protectively over a scowling Britney's shoulders. Near Britney huddled the two girls I'd see with her the day before—both looked on the verge of getting sick all over the bakery floor. Beside them, the fire chief, Shelly Patel, and her husband, Ajay, stood near a crestfallen woman who I'd not met before. She was a carbon copy of Britney's redheaded friend, except twenty years older and thirty pounds heavier, so it didn't take much to put the pieces together.

Their clustered mass and the waves of tension rolling off them pulled the focus of the gossipy crowd, and people quieted, clearly expecting a show, maybe hoping it had something to do with the drama at the jewelry shop.

I snagged my half-filled mug of dirty chai and slid off the stool. "Let's... um... let's go down to the mystery room where we'll have some privacy."

"Thank you." Zelda gave a tight-lipped nod, started to head in that direction, then paused once more before pointing rudely at Katie. "You too." She flicked a long strand of brown hair over her shoulder and seemed to remember herself. "Please. Sorry, this isn't *your* fault. Will you join us too, please?"

After a quick glance toward Nick to make sure he was okay on his own, which of course he was, Katie joined us as we left the bakery and headed down the steps.

The mystery room was large enough to house several hundred books, the antique sofa and matching ottoman, the ornate lamp with the dusty purple portobello shade, and a river rock fireplace. It was cozy, charming. However, with ten people—especially when nearly all of them were vibrating with heightened emotions—the space felt rather confining. I nearly suggested we go downstairs to the storeroom, but with its low ceilings that would feel even more claustrophobic. After considering all of us squeezing into the back alley, I decided where we were was our best bet, even being crowded and not all that private.

"These three girls have an official apology to make. And there's no time like the—" Zelda halted as Watson padded in from where he'd been napping near the front of the store in his morning ray of sunshine. With his nose in the air, he meandered catlike through people's feet and leapt onto his ottoman, where he gave an exaggerated yawn, followed by a matching stretch, before curling up to resume his nap.

The redheaded girl chuckled and sent an adoring smile Watson's direction. That was wiped away quickly enough as Ajay Patel turned on her. "Really? You find something funny?"

"Dad!" The brunette grabbed Ajay's arm. "Don't be mean to Dawn. It's not—"

"Be *very* careful, young lady." Ajay wheeled on her next. "You're not in any place to be telling me how to act."

Shelly and the redheaded mother both looked like they were getting ready to interject, but Zelda beat them to it. "I should say not." After an annoyed glare toward Watson, Zelda refocused on me and Katie. "Again, I know you've had quite the morning, but so have we. It definitely wasn't in my plans to spend the last hour in the principal's office." As she had in the bakery, Zelda made another sweeping gesture with her hand, encompassing the three girls and the rest of the parents. "After yesterday's little crime spree, Britney, Ananya, and Dawn are all suspended. *And* at risk of losing their place on the cheerleading squad."

"I still say that doesn't make any sense." Noah, as usual, spoke in a voice that suggested half of his mind was floating somewhere else, probably dreaming up some cockamamie invention. "Why would a school have a three-strike policy of suspending students who skip classes? If that's the case, why doesn't every kid skip school, it's a free pass."

"I agree." Dawn's mother spoke for the first time, her voice soft and timid. "It's more like a reward, plus, we all have jobs to do. What are we supposed to—"

"It's called a consequence," Ajay snapped, his teeth gritting together so hard it sounded painful. "There are rules. And our girls keep breaking them. If we haven't raised them better, then it's on us to fix it, even if it means missing work. Your lack of discipline where Dawn is concerned is—"

"Ajay!" As her daughter had before, Shelly grabbed Ajay's arm. However, her husband halted at the reprimand that time. After a moment, Shelly looked at Dawn's mother. "Sorry, Becky. He didn't mean anything by it. We're just stressed."

Dawn's mother, Becky, apparently, offered a nervous smile in way of acknowledgment. If she was going to respond, once more, Zelda didn't give her a chance. "Who isn't?" She pointed to Ajay as she had to Katie earlier. "But you're exactly right. And it's *all* of our daughters. We adults have all put up with too much. It ends *now*." She turned to Katie. "We decided to come here first. Skipping school is one thing, but what they did in your bakery yesterday is a completely different issue. Stealing will never be tolerated and is never okay." She shot a glare toward Britney. "But even more horrible when done against someone we know and love, someone we count as family."

"Britney would never—" Noah attempted to wrap his arm over his daughter's shoulders once more, but Britney sidestepped.

"Noah!" Zelda gave a snarl that matched Ajay's,

loud enough that Watson lifted his head with an irritated grunt.

"Please." Katie stepped forward, lifting her hands. "It's okay. It was just a little trinket. And we all made silly choices when we were kids..." She forced a laugh "Honestly, it's a worldwide issue. I was recently reading a story about a nine-year-old Ukrainian boy who stole four thousand dollars from his parents and spent it all on candy. I mean, really, with candy involved, who could blame him?"

Dawn and Ananya both chuckled at that. Britney, on the other hand, matched her mother's tone and added a teenaged drawl. *"Really?* More random trivia?"

"Britney!" That time, as Zelda and Noah spoke in unison, there was no lack of unity in the admonishment.

Britney actually blushed. "Sorry, Katie."

Katie seemed to attempt a smile but didn't quite succeed.

The whole thing was making me feel completely out of my element. While the students I'd had when I was a professor were challenging at times, they never involved stealing or attitude tantrums. Though really, the conflict between the parents was more awkward than what the girls had done. All in all, it made me appreciate only having to deal with corgi stubbornness from time to time, and I simply wanted the scene in the mystery room to end. "We appreciate you owning up to it. How about we return the corgi and call it good?" Beside me, Katie nodded fiercely. "We'll trust that it won't happen again."

"That's just it. No one has owned up to anything," Ajay snarled at Ananya, then narrowed in on Dawn. "And what's as bad as the act of stealing itself is staying quiet and letting your friends take a fall."

Becky seemed to find a bit of courage as she sputtered, "Are you trying to imply that *Dawn* is the one who stole?" She pointed at Ajay's daughter. "What about Ananya? Or is *she* so perfect that—"

"I did it!" Britney yelled—loud enough that Watson jumped to all fours and looked like he was about to leap off the ottoman to hide under my broomstick skirt. "I did it." Just like that, all her bravado vanished in a whimper. "I stole the corgi."

"No!" Shock sounded in Noah's voice as he shook his head. "No, Britney. You didn't. You wouldn't."

Britney darted a glance toward her dad, and a tear rolled down her cheek, before she looked at Katie. "I'm sorry. I'm sorry, Katie."

"See!" Becky snarled toward Ajay. "It *wasn't* Dawn."

For their parts, Dawn and Ananya kept their gazes trained on the floor.

Ajay didn't offer an apology but looked relieved, as did Shelly.

Zelda, for once, was silent and stared at Britney, stunned. In all her anger, it seemed she really hadn't believed Britney would've crossed that line. Finally, she found her voice. "Then, the first thing you'll do is return it."

Britney's mouth moved wordlessly. Finally, she shook her head and her gaze followed that of her friends. "I... don't have it. I... threw it away."

"You..." Zelda's volume began to increase once more. "All that and you *threw it away*? Why in the —" She huffed out a furious breath, then snapped her fingers. "Fine, then. You're going to work, right up there in the bakery, or the bookshop, every day after school for the next month. *Without* pay." She looked toward Katie and me, and I thought she was getting ready to ask for Katie's or my approval. "Make sure she doesn't sneak out the back door or some such nonsense."

"Mom, wait. I—" In those three words, Britney no longer sounded like the defiant sixteen-year-old and more like the child I remembered from what seemed just a few short months ago. That vanished as her expression hardened, as did her tone. "Fine."

"Actually..." Zelda trembled in her rage. "You'll start today. Right now."

Britney sank onto the ottoman, hair falling around her slumped shoulders. After a bit, Watson nudged her hand. After another moment, she lifted it and stroked his head.

I might have been wrong about Julian being murdered and that we'd find his body inside the jewelry shop, but I was certain about one thing—while Britney had known the corgi had been stolen, she hadn't been the one to take it. She was either covering for Ananya or Dawn—or both.

Less than a quarter hour later, the mystery room was empty, save for Katie, me, and Watson. My fuzzy companion had fallen back to sleep without a care in the world while Katie and I sat on the antique sofa shell-shocked.

Finally, Katie turned slightly, speaking slower than her typical cadence, as if she was choosing her words carefully. "I love your family, Fred, I love them as if they were my own. And I love Britney. But I don't want children. Especially a hormonal teenager." She scrunched up her nose. "Joe could talk me into having a baby or two, dressing them up in adorable Halloween costumes, like little hippos or cupcakes." A surprise chuckle burst from her as she glanced down at her engagement ring, a soft smile growing to her lips, clearly the examples unintentional. After a second, she refocused on me. "Babies, Fred. *Babies*. After that, ship them off to boarding school, trade them in for a new car, offer them as prizes for raffle tickets, but—" She gestured to where Britney was helping Ben unbox a small shipment of children's books. "—a teenager. Really?"

"I know, but..." Katie's sentiment caught up with me, and I barked out a laugh. "Raffle tickets, really? Who in their right mind would buy raffle tickets in hopes to win a *teenager*?"

She pointed at my nose. "Right you are." Growing serious once more, Katie lowered her voice. "You know I wouldn't actually send kids off to boarding school, right?"

"Of course I do." I patted her knee but couldn't help myself. "But I do think you'd trade them in for a new car."

Katie brightened. "Oh, definitely."

We chuckled again together as we watched Ben and Britney work, before I too lowered my voice. "Did you get the sense Britney was covering for her friends?"

"Yeah." She nodded. "And while I don't have teenagers, nor do I ever want one, I went through that particular phase myself a while ago. And if I recall correctly, the surest way to make Britney double down on her claim is to challenge her about it."

"You're probably right. Maybe it doesn't matter. At the end of the day, even if Britney didn't steal the corgi herself, she was there, she knew it had happened. Still, I wish—" I paused to glance at my cell phone screen when it buzzed, prepared to ignore the call. I halted when I saw Susan Green's name. With a flash of it toward Katie in way of explanation, I hit Accept and lifted it to my ear. "Did you find Julian or his body?"

Beside me, Katie blinked and did a double take at that question.

"No. Actually I am back at Aspen Gold." A false brightness in Susan's clipped tone announced she was about three heartbeats away from exploding. "Mr. and Mrs. LaRue have returned from Denver. Not only are they requesting to not have to go down to the police station, they've also informed me that they will only answer any questions if *you* are present."

"What?" I choked on the word and nearly asked if she was serious, then recalled her tone. Once more I lowered my voice as if the LaRues could hear me on the other side of the phone. "Why in the world do they want me there? We've hardly had any interactions over the years."

She cleared her throat. "Well then, chances are

those occasions have been more pleasant than what has been experienced with me."

"Why? What's happened between you and—"

"Fred!" Proving the reception was crystal clear, at Susan's bark, Watson popped up once more and growled. "Get down here. And might as well bring Detective Fleabag. Maybe they have a soft spot for dogs."

There was no longer a crowd around Aspen Gold as Watson and I arrived, though I noticed Myrtle Bantam across the street, peering out the windows of Wings of the Rockies. Instead of slinking away at being caught, she merely offered a little wave and continued to stare. I waved back and glanced toward the windows of Victorian Antlers, expecting to see Percival and Gary doing the exact same thing. The antique shop was still dark. They must've remained at the convention.

"Gossipy old crow!" Susan snarled from behind, startling me, and thrust her hand over my shoulder to wave exaggeratedly at Myrtle, who scowled and turned away. "I swear, I need to move to the city where crime can happen without being the talk of the town."

I lifted my eyebrows at her as I turned. "Now *there's* a goal."

"I bet city cops don't have to deal with people requesting nosy booksellers to join in on an investigation." Susan offered a welcoming sniff down to Watson. "Probably have more scrounging mutts there, though. But surely they wouldn't shed as much as you." Without waiting for more of a reply, she stepped aside, making room for Watson and me to enter, then closed the door and locked it behind us.

Though it had only been a couple of hours, the change in Aspen Gold made me realize I'd made a mistake about other things as well. Now it had been cleaned up, only one case had been turned over and broken, with the glass and jewelry scattered everywhere—earlier it had looked like so much more. Officer Cabot stood in the far doorway, holding the curtain to the back room apart. At his beckoning, I headed that way.

Watson moved casually with me, sniffing here and there but not pausing at anything interesting, which further suggested we were in the middle of a robbery, not a murder scene.

The back room was about a fourth the size of the showroom, and its walls were shoved together at odd angles, like the magic shop next door. Unlike most back rooms, it was decorated as thoroughly as the front. While lacking the gold-and-black wallpaper, every one of the angled walls had been painted the deep red of the door... but without the golden lacquered finish. The large safe, behind where Vivian and Roger LaRue sat at their twin antique desks, however, was gold. I assumed it was only painted that way and not the genuine article, but... who knew?

"Thank you for coming." Vivian stood, worry and fear in her eyes. She moved easily around the desk, reaching out her hand for mine as she approached. Her skin was sallow, making her look older than she had the day before. "We need your help finding Julian before something horrible happens." She cast a brief glare toward Susan, then returned her attention to me. "We know your reputation. If anyone can find him before it's too late, it will be you."

"Oh." Not for the first time that day, I wasn't exactly sure what to say and looked to Susan for help. "There's been word from someone? A kidnapper? What do they want... some sort of payment?"

Campbell cleared his throat uncomfortably.

"No." Susan crossed her bulging arms over her chest and offered Vivian's glare right back at her.

"Apparently it's inconceivable that Julian is behind this himself. There has to be foul play."

"This is just like the other day. You only want to see the negative in Julian." Vivian twitched and gave a little shake of her head. "You only want to *make up* the negative in Julian, which is why we need Winifred here. *She'll* actually help." Moving with smoother grace than I expected, judging from her appearance, Vivian knelt to meet Watson right in the eye. "Do you smell anything? Can you lead us to him?"

Watson took a step back and cocked his head this way and that as he studied the tight black curls of Vivian's beehive. After a moment, he chuffed and slipped beneath my skirt.

Susan smirked but stayed silent.

"I... ah..." Stalling for time, I glanced back and forth between Vivian and Roger, trying to figure out the best way to be supportive while not stepping on Susan's toes. "Of course I will help in any possible way I can, but I don't really know what I have to offer. And Watson, as clever as he is, isn't exactly a bloodhound. He won't be able to sniff the trail from here to wherever Julian is."

"Oh." Vivian was crestfallen for merely a second

before she pressed my hand again. "But you'll look. You'll help us find whoever took him."

There was such surety in her tone, it seemed she must have a suspect in mind. "You really think someone took Julian? Why? For revenge? Does he have enemies?"

That time, the uncomfortable clearing of the throat came from Roger, who finally stood from behind his desk. Unlike his wife, he merely looked sad and tired. "I wouldn't say—"

"Of course not." Vivian thrust her chin skyward, causing long icicles of diamonds dripping from her ears to sparkle. "*Julian* doesn't have enemies. No one would want revenge on him." She faltered, but not long enough for anyone else to get a word in edgewise. "It's probably like you said—they want a ransom, money, jewels."

"He's not a child, darling." Roger put an aged hand on Vivian's shoulder, and though she stiffened, she didn't pull away. "No one kidnapped him like that."

"They did. They must've." Fire lit Vivian's words, and she shot them toward Susan. "You're blaming him without any proof, just like you did the other day, upsetting him so. Upsetting all of us." She turned to me, going soft and pleading. "Detective

Green wants us to believe Julian would steal from us, tear up our shop, and run away. He would *never*."

Over her shoulder, it was easy to see Roger wasn't as convinced as his wife.

Clearly reading my train of thought, Vivian sidestepped, bringing herself back into view. "A mother knows, Winifred. Please. Help find my son before it's too late."

The pleadings of parents were too close together to keep from blending in my mind. How Noah so adamantly defended Britney, just as Vivian was with Julian, only to be crushed when his faith in his daughter had been shattered. Although... Katie and I both thought he'd been right about Britney, regardless of what she'd admitted. That had a different feel as well. For one, Britney was sixteen, Julian a man I figured was in his forties. I got the sense this wasn't the first time Vivian LaRue had refused to see the obvious where her son was concerned.

The solution came to me suddenly and was so obvious I wondered how it hadn't been... well... been obvious to the police. "We know it happened between closing time last night and early this morning, because I looked in when I came to get my ring, and everything was in order. I'm sure you have security. What do the cameras show?"

"Thank goodness you're here, Fred." Susan's snarl told me all I needed to know as she turned to her partner. "Quick, check the security. Why didn't *we* think of that?"

"See?" Vivian clutched the pearls—literal pearls—around her neck. "You're treating this as a joke, all your sarcasm." She looked back at me and gave a sorrowful shake of her head. "Unfortunately, whoever took Julian knew about the security system and stole the videotapes as well. Everything for the last three days is gone."

That was even more proof against Julian. As I looked for a kind way to say so, a little detail nagged at me and I faltered. "Videotapes? As in... your jewelry store security system is—"

"Don't worry, Fred." If anything, the sarcasm in Susan's tone increased. "They were VHS, not beta, so we haven't completely returned to the dark ages."

Vivian's cheeks went as red as the walls. "I'm going to report you to—"

"Do it! I'll ring up the chief this very minute." Susan truly was on the verge of losing her temper. "How many times have I come down here and told you to get an up-to-date security system? I've indulged you too much, including with asking Fred to join. I don't know why I bother." She turned to me, the sarcasm fading. "I'm sorry to have bothered you, Fred. We won't take any more of your time. If the LaRues aren't going to fully participate—"

"We haven't hopped on the digital bandwagon. We don't trust it. The government spies and tracks through those sorts of things." Roger cut Susan off and looked at me, the pleading in his eyes matching his wife, though it was different somehow. "Whether Julian did this or not, please help us find him."

"Roger!" Vivian sputtered. "How can you—"

He turned on her, and though firm, his tone wasn't harsh. "As long as Winifred finds him, what difference does it make what people think now? When he's home, he can explain." When she still started to argue, Roger adjusted. "Again, it doesn't matter what they think. The sooner Winifred and the cops find who took Julian, the safer he'll be. The semantics aren't important at the moment."

Vivian considered, looking like she was going to argue, but didn't. "Will you help, Winifred, please?" Before I could answer, she bent once more, demonstrating an astounding lack of boundaries, and picked up the hem of my skirt, peering underneath. "And you too?"

Though I couldn't see him, I could only imagine Watson's expression at having someone invade his safe place in such a manner for the first time. Clearly it was something, as despite her mood, Susan smirked and looked on the edge of laughter.

"Yes." I pulled the material from her hands, letting it shelter Watson once more. "Of course I will." Remembering myself, I glanced toward Susan. "If that's all right with you?"

She shrugged. "Like you require permission."

"Okay then..." I jumped right in. Truth be told, if the rest of the morning hadn't been taken up with Britney and her friends stealing from the Cozy Corgi, I would've been trying to put these puzzle pieces together anyway. "First off, do you mind explaining why you two were arguing about Alessandra yesterday? Is there any way this could be connected?" Realizing how that sounded, I rushed to correct myself. "Obviously, I'm not saying that she kidnapped him or anything like that, but maybe there's a connection."

Susan and Campbell both perked up at the new information.

The LaRues blanched as one, but it was Roger who spoke. "You... think you heard us arguing with our son?"

"Yes." His confusion was so genuine it nearly threw me off. "When I came in yesterday to drop off my ring to be resized. I didn't mean to, but I heard you tell Julian that he needed to give her more of a chance, and that—" I realized my mistake. "No. I assumed that, didn't I? You weren't talking about Alessandra but about someone else. Who?"

"Oh, of course," Vivian responded before her husband had the chance. "You heard that. Yes, you are correct, on both counts. We were arguing about Ms. Costa. We've encouraged Julian to... pursue her. To settle down. And no, she would not have kidnapped him or been involved."

Roger's paper-thin cheeks had gone scarlet as Vivian spoke, and for a second I thought in anger, but then realized it was embarrassment. I tried to recall more of the details of what I'd overheard, as something was about to break for Mr. LaRue. Then it came back. "I also heard him say that she wasn't good enough for him. Were there other women you've been trying to set him up with?"

"While Ms. Costa is a beauty—" As he spoke, Roger didn't meet my eyes. "—perhaps Julian was correct that she isn't good enough for him. I do agree with Vivian, however. She would not be involved."

I studied them silently for several moments, exchanged a glance with Susan, then pressed on. "Mr. and Mrs. LaRue, what's going on? What are you not telling us? Was Julian involved in something and got in over his head? We'll help you, but you have to be honest. Was he in a relationship with someone who—"

"You're doing it too," Vivian snapped but looked on the edge of tears. "Now you're blaming Julian, just like the police. I hoped you'd..." She turned toward her husband, cutting off the rest of us. "We'll hire a detective... a real one, not like her over there." She didn't bother to look toward Susan as she insulted her. "*They'll* help us find our son."

Katie let out a huge sigh as I walked back up into the bakery after locking the front door at closing time. She waited, clearly for dramatic effect, until Watson and I were nearer before she sprawled her upper body over the surface of the Velluto marble and sighed again as if the world was ending. "The Cozy Corgi may never be cozy again."

I tried not to laugh but failed. "There was a hint of a gray cloud hanging about this afternoon, wasn't there?"

"*Hint* of cloud?" Katie shot back up, her normal perkiness returning. "Fred, there was no hint and nothing gray about it, for that matter. It was storm-cloud broiling black billows of hurricane-worthy..." She snapped her fingers and her brows furrowed. "See, I've been so pulled down into the doldrums that I can't even remember what I know." After a couple more snaps, she brightened once more. "Oh, right... Hurricane-worthy cumulus congestus clouds of despair."

"Really? *Cumulus congestus?*" I cocked an eyebrow.

Watson had been on trajectory to curl up under one of his favorite tables, but pivoted, trotting back the way we'd come and disappeared into his little apartment.

That time, Katie burst out laughing. "I think he decided he didn't have the energy for us."

"*Us?* That was entirely *your* fault. After cumulus congestus, who can blame him?" I gave her a wink and plopped down on one of the stools at the edge of the espresso bar... far enough away, or I would be tempted to request a dirty chai. "And Britney wasn't *that* bad."

"Yes, she was." Katie offered another sigh, though that time it seemed more in sympathy. "That girl is glum. And it may or may not be because she's a teenager. Nick and Ben were still teenagers when they started here, and they weren't ever like that. Granted, there's a big difference between having just graduated high school and being in the middle of it."

"Even the twins seemed affected by her. By the time they left, they looked full-on depressed." Though Katie and I were making light of it, I hurt for

Britney. She was clearly miserable. "Maybe she'll be a bit lighter tomorrow. Spending the evening with Mom and Barry will help."

"I hope so." Katie touched my hand. "But I am sorry your dinner with them got postponed. You all should celebrate together."

I waved her off. "No, it's actually good. Britney needs time with them, and honestly, I'd be distracted, thinking about what in the world is going on with the LaRues." I glanced down to Katie's hand, staring at the hippos on either side of the sparkling cupcake. "Plus, it will be more fun to celebrate the engagement after I have the ring back."

"I'm sorry about that, too." She hummed sympathetically. Then she leaned forward, whispering conspiratorially, "But, on that note, I've been thinking. Your night is freed up, Leo's going to be up on the mountain for at least another hour, and thanks to Britney's mood, we didn't really get a chance to go over things this afternoon, so..." She tilted her head toward the remaining pastries. "Why don't you help me *clean up*, and we can discuss."

"I do love your version of cleanup. I definitely wouldn't say no to another one of those oaty ginger bars." A car splashing through a puddle left from the afternoon rainstorm pulled my attention down toward the street. As I started to turn back to Katie, another movement behind the glass door of Paws caught my attention. It seemed Flotsam and Jetsam had heard the loud splash as well, or maybe the water had sprayed and hit the front of the pet shop, as they were both frantically licking the inside of the door. Sudden inspiration struck, and with a mental apology to Watson, I shared my idea with Katie. "How about we make a night of it? We haven't gotten the Scooby Gang together in a while. We'll see if Paulie and Athena want to help us look into Julian."

"I love it!" She clapped. "In fact, I'll invite Joe too. We'll order pizza or Mexican or something. Let's do it up. It'll be a—" She shimmied. "—Scooby Gang superfest and double-engagement celebration extravaganza."

Perhaps it was horrible of me, after Britney being so miserable that day, after the LaRues' clear betrayal by their son, but my spirits soared. "Yes! That sounds so fun!" I actually giggled. "That shouldn't sound fun, should it?"

She made a dismissive snort. "Oh please, we'll be together for a noble purpose doing what we do best." Katie held up one of the oaty bars. "Well, *one* of the things we do best. And this time, we're not even looking into a *murder*. Let's enjoy it to the hilt."

. . .

A little over an hour later, not a single one of the LaRues had been mentioned, and the bakery was filled with as much noise as the morning breakfast rush, which was impressive given there were only five people. The four dogs helped make up the difference... well, two of them, anyway. Flotsam and Jetsam, from the moment they arrived, sped in laps as if they were part greyhound, running circles through every room of the bookshop, then galloping like a two-headed Cerberus up the stairs to the bakery, where they wove in and out of the legs of tables and chairs, only to half gallop, half tumble down the steps into the bookshop to repeat the entire process once more. Watson and Pearl had both given the chaotic corgis a judgmental glare as they disappeared into Watson's apartment.

"They get like this in Paws sometimes." Paulie grinned. "I wish we had this much space, it would go a lot better. There they run into the fish tanks and hamster cages. More than once they've turned over the birdcage holding the finches. Here, it's a lot safer and they can—" A loud crash below caused him to cringe.

A muffled warning growl came from the little

apartment under the Cozy Corgi merchandise, which made me chuckle.

"You were saying?" Athena offered Paulie a knowing look before turning to Katie, holding out her hand. "Let me see it again, sweetie."

With her cheeks blushing as pink as the stone on her ring, Katie offered her hand for inspection.

Athena tsked. "Never in a million years would I think I'd find an engagement ring with hippos on it elegant. Charming, maybe. But elegant?" She shot a glance up at Joe, who had a large arm resting across Katie shoulders. "You did good, Joe Singer, you did good."

He shrugged a shoulder, and the blush that was Katie's twin turned the features of his asymmetrical face to a wash of beauty. "It was either that or offer her a real live baby hippopotamus to get her to marry me."

Katie went wide-eyed and turned to him. "Seriously? I can get a baby hippo? I've never even thought about that." She whipped back toward Paulie. "You have pet shop connections. Can we get a baby hippo?"

"You do remember that my fiancé is a park ranger, right?" I reached across the table and teasingly smacked Katie's arm. "Pretty sure he would frown on wildlife trafficking, no matter which continent the wildlife is from."

Katie's expression went crestfallen, causing everyone to chuckle.

Below, Flotsam and Jetsam went wild again, and there was the sound of the front door opening before Leo hollered up, "Anyone order pizza?"

"Leo!" Katie leaned back in her chair, causing Joe to have to readjust as she raised her volume. "Leo, can I get a baby hippo?"

There was a pause filled with nothing more than Flotsam and Jetsam's barking before Leo's confused voice sounded once more. "Get a *what*?"

"Oh... never mind." Katie grumbled to herself, causing the rest of us to burst out laughing once more.

"Why is the display of knitting books spread all over the floor down there?" Leo soon emerged up the steps, carrying the three pizzas he'd picked up from Rocky Mountain Pie. He was having to take large careful steps to avoid either tripping on or squishing Flotsam or Jetsam.

"You're stepping over the *why*." Athena smirked.

At his appearance, Watson tore out from the apartment—the fact he hadn't the second Leo had spoken was proof of how distracted he'd been by

Pearl—and charged at Paulie's corgis, snarling with fangs bared.

Both of them yipped and fell back.

With a chuff, Watson returned to Leo and took his place, frolicking around Leo's feet until Leo delivered the pizzas to us and he got the greeting he demanded.

"This time I don't know if you're happy to see me, or if you're bribing me for a piece of pizza." Leo knelt and ruffled his fur. "And I don't care." Sneaking one of his hands free he offered it to Flotsam and Jetsam, who hurried over to get more Leo attention.

After a second, Pearl emerged as well, tiptoeing over, giving the three corgis a wide berth, and returning to her mama. Obliging with a smile, Athena leaned down and lifted Pearl into her lap.

Finally, Leo stood. "You all have no idea how much I need this tonight. It was crazy up on the mountain today, all the—" He stopped as his gaze traveled around the table and landed on Katie. "Katie Pizzolato!" He threw his arms wide. "Get over here. I haven't seen you since I heard the good news."

Giggling, she popped up and wrapped her arms around him. "Ah, thanks, Smokey Bear."

He pulled back. "Now, let me see this ring everyone's talking about." Before he had a chance to look, a knock at the front door set Flotsam and Jetsam into hysterics again before they tore away and rushed back down the stairs to confront whoever was there.

"I... uh... um, that's Campbell." It was Paulie's turn to blush. "I sent him a text a little while ago to invite him. That okay?"

"Of course it is!" Leo reached out and smacked Paulie on the shoulder, then turned. "I'll go let him in."

Almost another hour passed before the LaRues were mentioned. It was nearly that long before I even remembered them. I hadn't realized how much I needed a night like this, maybe how much all of us needed a night like this. And while I didn't have a ring on my finger, it truly did feel like a celebration of engagements with our friends. Katie and I eating pizzas with the men we were to marry by our sides, and the easy camaraderie among us was heightened just a little bit with the emotional glitter of something special.

We'd pulled several small tables close for the seven of us to gather around to devour the pizzas, and when Julian's name was finally mentioned, the empty cardboard boxes had been replaced by—unsurprisingly—an array of pastries ranging from the remaining oaty ginger bars, brownies, lemon bars, chocolate chip cookies, and even a couple of cupcakes with pink swirled icing that just happened to resemble the one on Katie's ring... which I doubted was accidental.

Athena lowered Pearl to the floor to once more to join the other dogs, then ushered in a more serious tone. "From what I understand, we're not thinking Julian's been murdered, correct? Vivian and Roger are odd... but harmless, I think. The thought of them losing a child is horrible."

"Odd..." I tried out the word. "That's a good way to describe them." I settled into mystery mode easily enough. "It sounds like you spent some time with them?"

"A bit." Athena made a noncommittal expression. "Though they're more part of the Ethel crowd, if you know what I mean, but more on the fringe. They've always been a little bit reclusive since they moved to Estes. But they've been here..." She considered. "I don't know, fifteen years at least."

"I hadn't met Julian until the other day, when I bought Fred's ring," Leo spoke up. "He wasn't there when I got her earrings a few years ago. Vivian sold me those."

"No, you wouldn't have." Athena nodded sagely.

"Julian's only been here seven or eight months, I believe. Helping his parents at the store."

"Somehow, I don't really get the impression that's how it's going." I glanced toward Campbell. "Tell me if I overstep my boundaries, of course, but were the police getting complaints about Aspen Gold *before* Julian arrived?"

Campbell shook his head, took a moment to swallow whatever pastry he'd been eating, and cleared his throat. "I talked to Detective Green on my way over to make sure she was okay with me sharing the stuff we found out this afternoon." He spared a quick glance toward Athena. "We're definitely not looking at a murder." Then back to me. "While the LaRues' security tapes were stolen, we *were* able to check the recordings from the traffic cameras and such. Julian drove downtown around one in the morning, then left again about forty-five minutes later."

"Could you see him going to the jewelry shop?" Katie leaned forward, excited.

"No." Another headshake from Campbell. "There's not a camera facing the entrance to Aspen Gold, but judging from which way his car was going, it's not exactly a stretch to believe he was driving to and from there. And..." He lowered his voice, not so much to a whisper as an announcement he'd arrived at the important part. "Just a few minutes after the shot of him heading out of downtown, the traffic camera caught him once more crossing where Elkhorn Avenue becomes Big Thompson Avenue."

"Heading out of town through the canyon."

"We're assuming, yes." Campbell nodded toward Joe. "We have a request in to see what we can find from other traffic cameras through the canyon, then see if he went all the way to Loveland, or if he turned onto the interstate to get to Fort Collins or Denver."

"I bet Denver," Paulie chimed in. "If he stole all the jewelry, then he's probably going to hop on a plane."

"Good thought." Campbell smiled encouragingly at Paulie. "But he hasn't yet. Detective Green already checked—no record of him flying out."

Half my brain was listening, the other half jumping ahead, but got caught in one detail and returned to Leo. "I didn't get the ring back. Maybe it's still there. Couldn't very well ask Vivian and Roger about it, given the situation, but if Julian took it, then all the money you—"

He slipped his hand over mine, giving it a squeeze. "Don't worry about that. If he took it, he took it." He squeezed my hand again. "That ring doesn't make our engagement or marriage."

My heart melted a bit, and I probably would've leaned in for a kiss if Watson hadn't shoved his head up between us at that very moment, using his nose to wrench our hands apart and whimper.

"You really have become the world's worst beggar." Leo ruffled his fur affectionately.

Not to be outdone, Flotsam and Jetsam did the exact same thing to Campbell and Paulie, apparently taking the divide-and-conquer route. Paulie just laughed. "Nope, I think my boys win that competition."

Athena pointed one of those French-tipped fingers toward Watson. "Don't you dare teach my darling such bad manners. I won't have it!" The warning in her tone was only half teasing.

Katie stood and hurried to the bakery counter. "Let me get some treats, you all. It's only fair that the pups get them, after the feast we've had."

All four dogs, including Pearl, frolicked around Katie. She held a finger to her lips before she turned back toward us, and they followed her inside the actual kitchen portion—where dogs weren't allowed—and then one by one exited, a large all-natural dog-bone treat gripped in their teeth. Katie emerged a few seconds later, her trusty laptop in her hand. "Let's see what I can dig up on Mr. Julian LaRue."

As she settled back in by Joe, her fingers instantly flying over the keys, I dove into speculation. "So then the question is, do we know how much merchandise he took? And if he stole from his parents and left town, why now? I still don't understand why he would attempt to make it look like a robbery, except to simply add salt in the wound if he was angry at his parents." I posed to the group at large but narrowed in on Campbell. "You said there's been complaints. Could any of those have prompted the need for him to leave town?"

"Or maybe," Leo jumped in before Campbell had a chance to answer, "someone came in the shop the past couple of days, just like I did, and had some altercation or threatened him over something." He grinned. "That sounded wrong. I'm not saying *I* threatened him." He started to laugh then, and his eyes narrowed at the thought. "Although, he was acting strange when I bought your ring."

"He was?" That surprised me.

"Well..." He shrugged one of his broad shoulders. "I wouldn't have classified it as strange at the time, but hindsight and all." Leo brought the others into our conversation with a glance around the table as he spoke. "As I said, I'd never met Julian before, but he was in a really, really good mood, almost hyper, and was crazy excited about me buying an engagement ring." Leo returned his focus to me. "It honestly felt right at the time, as I was really excited about it too, but now..."

"Maybe a little *too* excited for some reason?" I offered.

"Maybe." Leo shrugged again.

"We were thinking along similar lines, Fred." Campbell shifted in his seat so he could pull out a pad from the back pocket of his jeans. He unfolded it on top of the table, revealing his small, neat handwriting—I'd noticed before that he was a thorough notetaker, and this time was no different, as he flipped through several pages. "We have a list of most of the customers who have come in over the past few weeks, the ones the LaRues could remember and the receipts for the items they purchased." A glance toward Leo. "You are on here." Then back to me. "Also, I have a list of the complaints we've gotten. And..." He turned another page. "A couple of calls from people in town with their own theories about why he left. I think Detective Green is going to see if you want to join her for a couple of them tomorrow."

"Really?" While that didn't totally surprise me, I

was pleased. I also realized I was having fun. I took just a heartbeat for some self-reflection and decided that was okay. These particular puzzle pieces didn't add up to murder. It was okay to enjoy them. "Okay!"

At Leo's chuckle, I realized I was rubbing my hands together in excitement. He leaned over and pressed a kiss to my temple before whispering, "You're adorable."

"Well!" Katie clapped, causing all of us to jump and look her way. She didn't notice as she didn't bother to look up from her computer screen. "Whether he got on a plane or not, I can tell you where Julian isn't going. *Vegas!*"

"That's where Vivian and Roger moved from." Athena's tone switched from confirming to judgmental. "Which, in my opinion, explains some of the more... gaudy decisions in the store and fashion." She cleared her throat. "And hairstyle."

Paulie laughed and gave Athena a squeeze. "You're horrible, and I love you!"

Athena grinned before prompting Katie, "What have you found out?"

"Well..." She continued to scroll as she drew out the word before answering, and finally looked up. "After over a decade living in LA, trying *unsuccess-*

fully to be an actor, singer, model, and a whole list of other things, from what I can find, Julian returned home to Las Vegas." She nodded toward Athena in way of confirmation and then gave a side-eye to me. "From the way you described Vivian defending him this afternoon, I'm assuming he ran back to Mommy and Daddy when everything else failed."

"That fits." I still wasn't seeing the connection, though. "Why are you sure he won't return to Vegas?"

She snorted out a laugh. "Because of why he moved to Estes to begin with, which was once more running back to Mommy and Daddy when he burned all of his bridges." As was so often the case, her tone took on that know-it-all Hermione Granger cadence. "From what I can find, it sounds like Julian was quite the blackjack dealer for several years, going from casino to casino to casino. *And* that he—"

"Yeah." Campbell winced when he realized he'd interrupted, but kept going. "There is litigation against him that he was embezzling from a few casinos and that he was helping some guests cheat the system and then splitting the profits with them. Detective Green got that information this afternoon, but no real details as they're still building the case from what we understand."

When we all stared at him dumbfounded, Campbell blinked.

"What?"

"You don't deserve this." Katie stood, leaned over the table, and snatched the brownie off his plate. "Why didn't you *lead* with that?"

He blinked again. "Oh. I... don't know."

Joe burst out laughing so loud, Flotsam and Jetsam, who'd snuck off downstairs, rushed back up barking, as if playtime had begun, only to cause Watson to storm out from his apartment with a reprimanding growl.

As we all gave in to fits of laughter, finally joined by Campbell, I decided it was the best impromptu, unofficial engagement party a girl could ever want.

The drive up the side of the mountain the next morning suggested Aspen Grove—the combination retirement and nursing home—could've stolen the name of Aspen Gold from the jewelry store, despite its collection of precious metal. With the leaves of the white-barked trees starting to turn their golden hue, there was really no comparison about which was more beautiful. I supposed that proved it was only right I was engaged to a park ranger, as I found the splendor of leaves more compelling than that of jewelry.

My pleasant mood was a continuation of the night before. And though we'd stayed up late in the bakery in a combination of tossing around theories and celebrating engagements, even my tiredness offered a pleasant buzz—one that would be burnt away in an even more pleasant manner by some dirty chais when I went into the Cozy Corgi as soon as this little errand was achieved.

Even the errand added to my good mood. At this point, it wasn't uncommon to team up with Susan to question people, but it was rare for her to plan my presence in advance. The small but genuine smile she offered from where she waited on a bench near the entrance, as I pulled my Mini Cooper to a stop beside her cruiser, suggested that perhaps we were turning a corner into an even more harmonious relationship.

While not floating on cloud nine, Watson was also in a pleasant mood and hopped out to trot along contentedly—until he noticed Susan when she stood at our approach. Catching me off guard, he bolted toward her, ripping his leash right out of my hand.

He was less than two feet away and clearly preparing for a happy leap when both of Susan's hands moved simultaneously, one of them pointing a finger with a swordlike thrust toward his face, and the other seeming to move of its own accord to the pistol holstered on her hip. "Stop!"

For the first time ever, Watson obeyed a command without even a moment's hesitation, or at least attempted to. With the speed he was going, his abrupt attempt to slow and end his preparations to leap, caused him to stumble. He tripped, part falling, part crashing with a roll, coming safely to a stop on Susan's shoes.

She glared down with a sneer, and though her gun remained holstered, she shoved her finger downward, gesticulating with each word. "If you ever try to jump on me again, you deranged fleabag, I will toss you in the air and use you for target practice."

Not intimidated in the least, Watson rolled once more, regained his footing, and glared up at her, clearly blaming Susan for this great humiliation. He chuffed, chuffed again, and then turned with the grace evidence of the royal canine breed that he was, and met me as I approached, allowing me to pick up his leash.

Susan looked at me baffled. "What in the name of all that is decent was that?"

"I'm not entirely sure, but if I had to guess..." It was all I could do not to burst out laughing, but the sight of Susan's hand still resting on the butt of her pistol helped me stifle it. "Well... you made me swear to never mention it again, not even to you."

Susan blinked and opened her mouth, her expression suggesting she was getting ready to tell me to quit being weird, when her pale blue eyes widened in realization. "Oh..." She glared back at

Watson and barely breathed the words to him. "Those tre—" She cut herself off in time from uttering Watson's favorite word. "Those *things* I bought you. Do you see my office anywhere, Sherlock? Do you think I carry around fake bacon strips for you, mutt?" She bent, her hand finally leaving her gun, so both her fists could rest on her hips. "Just for that, when I get back to the station, I'm eating them all myself. I swear on every nasty shedding hair on your body."

Watson offered her a silent but fang-revealing snarl.

"This was one of my dumbest ideas. Although..." Susan muttered to herself as she straightened and turned toward the oversized ornate doors of Aspen Grove, then paused. Finally, she looked back at me. "Might as well see it through. When we go in here, do your normal nosy, questioning thing."

If I wasn't used to her directness, her tone would've been insulting, but as it was, I jumped over it, realizing the buddy-buddy situation I'd been envisioning on my drive up to Aspen Grove wasn't exactly on point. "Why do you want me here instead of Campbell?"

"It's not about Campbell, it's about..." Susan stopped herself with a sharp shake of her head and needlessly crammed her already formfitting hat down to hit her pulled-back miniature ponytail. "Just do your thing. Ask questions, be nosy. What you need to know is we've gotten complaints from the residents here of being swindled by Aspen Gold. Considering the sources, I hadn't given them too much credence, but... things have changed."

I wanted to push, get more details, but knew better, so simply gave an affirming nod and followed Susan as she opened the door with one hand—a task I couldn't do without grunting while using all my strength—as if it weighed no more than a feather. When she didn't hold it open for us, Watson and I darted through behind her before it closed.

"I need to speak to—" As was her normal, Susan didn't offer any form of greeting or announcement and jumped right in, issuing commands as she stomped toward the welcome-desk. She'd been heading for the new receptionist—who I noticed, unlike the previous Martha Booger, didn't have soap operas playing on the nearby television set—but halted. Susan had already been ramrod-straight, or so I thought, but as the recently appointed executive director turned to face us from where he'd been speaking to the receptionist, she somehow found another couple of inches to her height and thrust her shoulders back to the width a 747 would envy.

Mario Toscano boasted giant-sized muscles and was as handsome as he was tall. His deep olive complexion paled slightly. "Detective." There was a slight, almost pain-filled sigh to his deep voice. "I'd appreciate when you come here on official business that you give us advance notice. Any forms for documents you require, we'll happily prepare for you to pick up." He shot a glance back at the receptionist. "Or, we could even have someone drop them off at the station for you."

"It's Detective *Green*, Mr. Toscano." Susan crossed those impressive arms of hers over her chest.

"Seriously?" Mario cocked one of his thick brows as he twisted his head slightly to inspect her.

If I wasn't mistaken, Watson and I were making similar expressions as we looked back and forth between the two, and the puzzle piece of why I'd been invited clicked into place.

"Fine." Mario sighed, and Susan didn't answer him, only lifted her chin. "We'd appreciate, *Detective Green*, a formal heads-up when you're here on business."

"Noted," Susan quipped. "Unfortunately, when I'm here on official police business, your convenience is not my concern." As she spoke, though there was no weakness or waver in her voice, one of her hands had traveled behind her back and tucked excess material beneath her belt.

I'd noticed it before, but I wasn't going to make the mistake on this particular morning of pointing out to Susan once more that she liked Mario Toscano. Was attracted to him, or... something. Her reaction to Mario and how she handled that sensation was rather cute, in a terrifying manner. And though I was adequately skilled in reading people, I couldn't tell if Mario was aware of the reason for her disdain.

"As you may have heard..." I jumped in and paused just long enough to cast a quick glance toward Susan to see if I'd put the puzzle pieces together correctly, and when she didn't cut me off, I decided that I had, indeed, been brought along merely to handle this situation. "Aspen Gold was recently robbed, and the owners' son, Julian, is believed to have taken the merchandise and skipped town."

I was halfway through the explanation before Mario's gaze finally left Susan to refocus on me. There was a flicker of annoyance as that gaze traveled from me to Watson and back to me again.

Though we'd interacted during a murder a month or so before, I expected him to push against me, ask why I—a bookseller—was there. Maybe deciding to get through things quickly, Mario didn't go that direction. "I try to stay out of the gossip circuit, but I've learned that's impossible here in Estes, so... yes, I've heard about Julian." As if he couldn't keep himself from it, he refocused on Susan. "What does that have to do with me?"

She bristled, and the fingers that had been pushing in the back of her shirt seemed to be traveling to her gun holster once more.

I took a couple of steps as I spoke, moving slightly between them. "Some of your residents have made complaints regarding the service they had at Aspen Gold. That their jewelry didn't return to them in the same condition in which they'd sent it."

"I've not sent any jewelry in myself, so I don't have that complaint." Though he started to speak to me, once again he looked over my shoulder toward Susan. "I'll leave you, then, and Nancy can help get you to whomever you need to see." Without waiting, he turned on his heel, squaring his shoulders as Susan had done before, and started to head off down the hallway.

"Don't go anywhere," Susan barked out before

he barely made it five feet. "You need to stay on premises in case your name comes up and there are questions you need to answer."

He paused, and though he didn't have a gun holstered, both hands curled into fists at his side, and he growled through gritted teeth, "Whatever you say, *Detective*."

To my surprise, maybe to hers, Susan didn't reprimand a second time about her name, though as I turned to face her, I thought I saw a blush rise to her cheeks. She stepped around me, blocking off the view as she approached the receptionist. "Nancy, is it? First off, we need to speak to Charlene Sweitzer." She thumped a hard finger beside the bell on the front desk. "Get me a room number. Now."

While Mario had been a puzzle piece of why Watson and I had been included, another piece answered the door of Charlene's room.

"Winifred! Watson." An old, tiny fairy positively glowed at the sight of us. She ducked out of view for a heartbeat, then returned, lowering in a gossamer billow of pale yellow fabric and holding out a clenched hand toward Watson.

As he had the first time we'd met Glinda, Watson sniffed her knuckles and then gave her a lick.

With the twittering chuckle causing her glitter-covered lace wings to tremble on her back, Glinda turned her hand over, unfurled her bony fingers, and revealed the dog treat.

Watson scarfed it up, chewing so rapidly that crumbs went flying. Before the old fairy stood once more, he proved an efficient vacuum by dragging his tongue all over the floor to "clean up" after himself.

Glinda sent me a wink and tilted her head toward something out of sight. "We keep a jar by the door for when Paulie brings his darling boys to visit."

"Ah. That's sweet of you." I was almost disappointed in her explanation—as Glinda rarely provided one when it seemed she was doing actual magic.

"Sooooo sweet." Susan's tone revealed the eye roll even if I couldn't see it. She was forever annoyed with the older woman who was her brother's assistant at his shop, but after her encounter with Mario, it was even better that she'd brought me to mediate. "Shouldn't you be getting along to open Alakazam instead of playing dress-up and feeding mongrels?"

"Dress-up?" Again, Glinda tilted her head in

genuine confusion but didn't pause for an explanation. "The wizard doesn't require me at the magic shop as of yet. We've moved into our winter hours, if you recall."

"Right…" Susan groaned. "My brother, the laziest wizard who ever was."

Unflustered and sharper than most people would expect an elderly woman dressed as a fairy to be, Glinda offered a smile and stood aside, gesturing entry with her hand, the fabric of her sleeve fluttering nearly to her waist at the movement. "Doubtless you have come to inquire upon my dearest Charlene. She'll be most pleased you've arrived… Finally." The last word was thrown in a couple heartbeats after the rest and was perhaps the first dig toward Susan I had ever heard the fairy make, despite plenty of opportunities.

"Oh, Glinda!" I sucked in a breath, which was both a genuine reaction and an attempt to cut off any diatribe Susan was about to launch into. "This is the prettiest room I've ever seen here." I stepped in farther, having the pause to tug on Watson's leash as he sniffed around the table with the treats set overhead, and moved into the main living room. Large windows overlooked Estes Valley and the mountains in the distance, revealing just how many groves of

Aspen really were turning golden. "Although, I guess *room* isn't really the right term. This is like a little house."

"Thank you, dear." Glinda walked past an open door that revealed a bedroom with a canopy bed hung with translucent moth-green fabric—doubtlessly her own—and knocked on the closed door. "When Charlene moved in with me, between the two of us, we were able to upgrade to one of the nicer quarters here."

A moment later, the doorway to the second bedroom opened, and Charlene Sweitzer emerged. As the older woman rolled her wheelchair out into the living room, I was struck as I'd been the few times I'd seen her since I'd help solve her son's murder two Christmases before. She looked younger, happier, and healthier. Clearly living with Glinda had been an improvement from her previously over-controlled life—proving blessings sometimes did come from tragedy. "Oh! Fred and Watson!" She sounded just as happy as Glinda had been to see us, but without the breathy quality of her roommate. "How wonderful!" Her gaze traveled past us to where Susan still waited in the doorway, then flicked back to me. "Oh good. You're helping the police figure out what happened to my jewelry, aren't you?"

"Not quite." That got Susan moving, and she entered the rest of the way, closing the door behind her. As was to be expected when Glinda was concerned, the apartment was done in a mixture of soft, dusty jewel and earth tones, with an abundance of shimmery materials acting as curtains, blankets, and tiny pillows. Little statues of fairies, unicorns, mermaids, and a wide variety of mythical creatures littered shelves and tabletops. Looking as thoroughly out of place as a businessman walking into Narnia, Susan plopped down on a chair—after tossing a small poufy purple pillow to the couch—and spared a derogatory glance toward a cloudy crystal ball on the side table. "Fred's merely here to interpret your ramblings..." Susan paused as she looked back to Glinda, clearly cutting herself off from saying something cruel. "I don't speak fairy."

"That's okay, dear. As so often happens with siblings, magic does not lavish itself equally. The wise wizard was chosen to be blessed with the light of the ethereal." Glinda smiled sympathetically and looked like she was about to stretch out to pat Susan's hand, then thought better of it. "Conversely, *you* were bestowed the strength of the here and now."

Proving that her instincts to include me had been spot on, I jumped in before Susan either reached for her gun once more or gave in to an aneurysm. "So, Charlene..."

The older woman had been grinning in affection at Glinda, seemingly amused with her eccentric friend, and she retained that pleasant expression when she turned to me.

"What exactly is the problem with your jewelry?" Though I'd worn it all of two minutes, my thumb moved of its own accord and rubbed against where my ring should sit on my finger.

"It's not just Charlene's." Glinda's ethereal tone took on a touch of panic. "After she realized that her pearls were imposters, a few other residents checked and discovered their treasures had been altered."

"My family doesn't have much, we never have, not for several generations." Charlene joined in without more prompt. "But my great-great-grandmother was wealthy. Though, not to the extent that it could last all the way to me or my children and grandchildren. The only thing that remained of her wealth was a string of pearls." She grimaced suddenly and seemed to be speaking to herself then. "I meant to give it to Sheila when she finally gave birth to Tiffany, pass it down to my daughter and granddaughter, but..." Her hand lifted from where it had been resting on the arm of the wheelchair and trembled to her throat as if she could still feel the pearls. "But I just couldn't get myself to part with them, not yet. I made certain the will was updated so they would go to Sheila, and then Tiffany, after I pass."

"You..." I wasn't completely following. "You sent the pearls to Aspen Gold to get appraised? For the will or insurance?"

"Oh no, it was terrible." Glinda cut in again. "It was that dreadful day, when the town celebrated the anniversary of the flood and that poor Ebony girl was murdered. The stars and planets were off course for hours that evening. Charlene and I were partaking in tea before bed, and just as I extinguished the candles, Charlene's necklace snapped, and pearls went everywhere."

"It took a couple of days to find them all." Charlene took over the story once more. "I wouldn't let them vacuum that whole time. It was that sweet Mario who found the last two." She gestured toward the chair Susan occupied. "Somehow they'd bounced and landed between the cushions."

Susan stood, glaring at the chair as if it somehow offended her. As she began to pace, Watson darted out of her way and plopped down beside the wheelchair. Charlene reached a hand down to stroke his head, and Watson stayed where he was. "Good Lord, Glinda, get to the point. Charlene reported that the pearls she got back weren't the same as the ones she sent in. How do you know?"

"Well, you could *feel* them, dear, obviously." Glinda wasn't put off by Susan's harsh tone, but clearly thought the inquiry was a given. "Pearls, especially ones with the powerful magic passed down from generation upon generation, have a life force of their own, ancestorial memories, some protection. These didn't. They felt empty. Cold."

Susan halted, glaring at the fairy, though refraining from reaching for her gun yet again. "*This*, old woman, is why I didn't rush over the second you called." She looked toward me. "If Julian hadn't stolen and run away, I'd actually feel guilty about questioning him. Campbell didn't bother telling me—"

"It wasn't just the pearls," Charlene spoke up. "Other people's belongings were impacted. Cybil swears her brooch had its stone replaced with an inferior one. Albert said the same of his onyx cufflinks. And Bianca is certain the diamond in her wedding band isn't the same, either."

My blood went cold, and I couldn't find my voice.

"And all of this happened at once?" Instead of speaking to Charlene, Susan continued to address Glinda. "What? Some mythical energy smacked into the moon and caused all the jewelry to simultaneously morph into subpar materials, and this is Aspen Gold's fault?"

"What type of mythical energy would run into the moon?" Glinda shook her head in utter disbelief. "It's not an asteroid, dear."

"Every so often"—thankfully, Charlene stayed on track and addressed me as she continued to pet Watson—"since it's right next door to where she works, Glinda takes all the residents' jewelry to get cleaned or fixed. Typically, it's a lot more than just those pieces. But when my necklace had to get repaired, it was only the other three who needed to send any in at that moment."

"If Mario is so wonderful, why doesn't *he* take it in instead of making the residents do his job for him?"

I shot Susan a glare for missing the point. To my surprise, she blushed at the reprimand. As I turned back to Charlene, my thumb once more began to rub where my engagement ring should be. "You're saying..." I had to think back to pull the name. "Your friend Bianca claims the diamond in her wedding band was replaced?"

Charlene started to nod, but Glinda answered for her. "Not claimed, it *was*. Just like with Charlene's pearls, diamonds—especially those given in devotion and commitment—are imbibed with the energy of those who exchange such love. Bianca's ring doesn't feel like hers at all now."

Susan lifted a hand to rub her temples. "No wonder Julian ran away from this town. When I find him, I'll see if he'll let me join."

I barely noticed Susan's words as I glanced down and stared at my ring finger, where the massive diamond should have been sparkling. I didn't believe in mythical powers of pearls, diamonds, or the moon, for that matter. Neither, at least for the most part, did I believe in coincidence.

As I had done the morning after I received the ring, I stared at my hand, twisting the steering wheel as I drove Watson and myself back into town from Aspen Grove. That time, I wasn't mesmerized by the cut and sparkle of the diamond, nor overwhelmed by its unexpected size, but by its absence. The bare spot on my finger taunted, pulled my attention from the road. It had been a puzzle piece—and not only into Leo's psyche when he planned our engagement—to a mystery I hadn't realized was about to unfold. There was no question the ring had played a part, I just wasn't certain how.

If Julian started replacing precious stones and gems with counterfeit, then doubtlessly—despite its sparkle—my diamond wasn't a diamond at all, but cubic zirconia or the like. In a way, that fact eased some of my misgivings around the ring, knowing it hadn't been part of the dark diamond trade, or that

Leo hadn't spent... I couldn't even imagine how much for a diamond that size.

I looked up from my barren finger in time to see the stoplight, as I pulled nearer to town, change from green to yellow. Coming to a stop, I returned my attention to where it had been captured.

That was the point, though, wasn't it? No matter how much he had spent, Leo had gotten swindled, spending much more than the fake diamond was worth. Perhaps that matched Julian's overly excited attitude when Leo had been in Aspen Gold. It was part of Julian's sales pitch, the distraction of excitement, happiness, all smoke and mirrors. Another question arose... was Julian swindling customers on his own, or was it a family effort?

As the light turned green and I hit the gas, the answer to that question was obvious enough. He was doing it on his own. If the LaRues had been swindling their clientele, that would've come up long ago. The little jewelry store had been downtown for around fifteen years, if Athena remembered correctly, and it had a solid reputation. So, no. This was on Julian, not his parents.

By the time I parked behind the Cozy Corgi, I'd settled fully into that theory. If Vivian or Roger knew what their son had been doing to their customers, they wouldn't have been so adamant that we search for him. I didn't even think Vivian was covering for her son yet again, because surely she couldn't be that naïve that if she'd suspected what he was up to, he wouldn't turn on them and run away. No... She believed he'd been kidnapped or taken, or some such nonsense. She didn't know he'd been stealing from clients, and by default, she and Roger as well.

Maybe not nonsense. If Julian had swindled the wrong person, perhaps they'd gotten revenge? Possible, I supposed, but something about that didn't sit right. Not even close. Julian had been seen driving to and from the jewelry shop. There'd been no blood, no sign of a scuffle, a pure and simple robbery. Perhaps the wronged party would see stealing being a sort of payment, but that was a stretch. Further, if it was a case of switched diamonds, pearls, or whatever Charlene had said was in the cufflinks, why kidnap or murder, or even steal? That was nothing more than calling the police and making a report, and easy enough to prove, I would think.

Perhaps if Julian's crime had ruined something important... like an engagement? But even then, hardly justification for murder or kidnapping.

While the mystery of the missing Julian had been a pleasant buzz of snooping and acquiring of clues, it suddenly took on a more personal nature. At the end of the day, even more than the money that had been taken from Leo, was the insult of manipulation around his love for me, taking advantage of him wanting to start our life together.

Watson nudged my elbow roughly, bringing me back to the moment, and I blinked. I'd gotten carried away. How long ago had I parked? Long enough that the tourists walking by openly stared at the crazy lady sitting behind her steering wheel with her corgi glaring from the passenger seat.

"You're right." Laughing, I ruffled the fur on the side of his muzzle. "Not doing any good sitting here. Besides, it's well past time for dirty chai, don't you think?" When he just blinked at me, unimpressed, I laughed again. "What I mean is, how about a *treat* for me *and* you?"

Those chocolate eyes went wide in excitement, and he began to bounce on the passenger seat. He continued such an undignified display all the way from the car through the parking lot and into the back of the Cozy Corgi. Granted, he paused in his fixation long enough to rush Ben in an adoration-filled greeting, but he caught back up to me before I reached the top of the steps to the bakery.

We were late enough in our arrival that the

breakfast rush had died down, and only half the tables remained filled. From one of them beside the large windows overlooking Elkhorn Avenue, Katie saw us arrive and motioned us over.

Her elderly companion on the other side of the table followed Katie's attention and offered a bright, toothy smile. The pastor of Estes Valley Church was a round man and short enough that only the toes of his shoes reached the floor from where he sat. Though he wasn't wearing his robes, his billowing silk shirt was the same purple hue, and he looked like an adorable giant blueberry with a shiny bald head as he waved. I brightened at the sight of him.

I paused—I swear it was only for a heartbeat as we neared them—and glanced toward the espresso machine.

"Want me to bring you one?" Nick clearly saw the longing in my eyes. "Mine aren't quite as good as Katie's, but there's just as much caffeine." He finished with a shy wink.

"You are a godsend!" It was a sentiment I repeated frequently, about both of the Pacheco twins, and it still didn't quite capture how wonderful they were. "Oh, and would you mind bringing one of the dog treats for Watson as well?"

Nick actually met us at the table as we joined

Katie and Pastor Davis. "Here." He held out the all-natural dog-bone treat to Watson. "I know better than to keep His Highness waiting."

Pastor Davis had been reaching down to pet Watson's head but was thwarted as Watson snagged the treat and offered a grunt, which was either a *thank-you* toward Nick or a preparation to swallow it whole, then tore off toward his apartment.

"Be right back with yours." Nick grinned at me and turned away.

I chose the seat beside Katie, so I was across from the pastor, and gave her shoulder a squeeze in greeting. "You two having another quiche meeting?" Katie and Pastor Davis had bonded over their love of baking with unusual ingredients and had frequent brainstorming sessions. "What outlandish combination of flavors have you come up with now?"

"You tell me how outlandish this is." Though his full cheeks boasted a rosy complexion, Pastor Davis's smile faltered somewhat. "Fig, bacon, and smoked maple bourbon."

As Watson had in the car, I blinked, feeling a few steps behind, then promptly gave up. "I don't know why you look so disappointed, that sounds amazing."

Katie giggled. "That's what I said."

"It's not a question about being amazingly delicious." The pastor threw his hands up in surrender. "But those flavors are expected, nothing unusual about them. Utterly void of inspiration."

"And once more, I disagree." Katie tapped her finger on the tabletop as she listed ingredients. "Fig and bacon are often with maple *or* bourbon, not *both*."

"That's a technicality, as we're talking about maple bourbon, which is *one* thing." He scrunched up his nose as he considered. "Although, the smoked aspect helps, I suppose."

"And this is why my specialty is grilled cheese and tomato soup." I reached out and patted Pastor Davis's hand. "I think you've got a winning combination. But what do I know?"

Before I could pull my hand away, he grabbed it and offered another beaming smile. "I hear congratulations are in order." He reached out his other hand and grabbed Katie's. "I know I've already said it, but I'm just so happy for both of you wonderful women. Leo and Joe are fine, good, decent men. And..." He cleared his throat, lowering his voice. "While the Estes Valley Church doesn't charge for the use for those who attend our services—our event fee for weddings of nonmembers covers a host of repairs—I want to offer the church, free of charge, even though neither of you are churchgoers. You both do so much for the town."

"Oh, Pastor Davis!" I was a little blown away. While I hadn't thought of the wedding service yet, I never would've considered the church, since I didn't attend. The building was spectacular, like a small log-cabin version of a castle, and just as charming as the Cozy Corgi. "That's such a kind offer. Thank you."

"*That's* why you wanted to talk to Fred and me together, Stuart?" To my surprise, Katie leaned forward, hesitating. "We're not planning a double wedding."

"Oh no, I didn't mean—"

"Although," Katie interrupted the pastor, turning toward me, "I hadn't really considered it."

My heart rate increased at the thought of wedding planning, but Pastor Davis rescued me. "No, dears, I wasn't suggesting you could only have one service, though that would be fine, if not a bit crowded." He leaned back and patted his belly. "I'm not sure there's room for two couples *and* this mortal body overly filled with the Holy Ghost *and* a few donuts, but if that's what you want." He attempted a chuckle, but it dried up halfway through as he narrowed in on me. "I'm actually here to talk to you about what occurred at Aspen Gold. You're looking into it, of course."

That wasn't a question, but I nodded. Before he could continue, Nick delivered my dirty chai. I flashed him a quick smile of thanks then refocused on the pastor. "You know something?"

"I'm not clear if it's as much of a clue or gossip, or..." The rosiness to his cheeks deepened in embarrassment as he cast a glance around the bakery, then leaned forward with barely a whisper. "Lord forgive me if, possibly, it's merely me speaking out of resentment."

Katie and I exchanged a glance, and as I looked back toward the pastor, I lowered my voice as well. "Did you take in jewelry of some sort to Aspen Gold, or maybe one of the jeweled crucifixes, and some of the gems were replaced with counterfeits?"

Both of them sat up a little straighter, but Katie spoke first. "Wow, Fred. What have *you* found out today?"

"No, no." Pastor Davis waved a hand between us. "Please don't answer that, not in this particular circumstance. Not in front of me." Surprisingly, he reached up, snagged my dirty chai and took the first sip. After a deep, contented sigh, he peered into the mug. "Oh goodness. I didn't mean to..." He smacked his lips and then took another drink. "My heavens, this is wonderful."

Despite wanting to know why he'd come, I couldn't help but laugh once more and patted his hand. "It's a dirty chai, liquid of the gods. You keep that one."

"Now that's love, Stuart, when Fred gives up one of those." Katie laughed as well but got him back on track. "Now why in the world are you not wanting us to talk about it in front of you?"

Pastor Davis deflated and looked every one of his eighty-some years, which was unusual for the jovial man. "Because it's not just harmless gossip this time around." Without letting go of the mug, he lifted his index finger. "*Not* that there is such a thing as harmless gossip, mind you, but in this case..." He took another sip as if for sustenance and continued, a little bit of foam on his upper lip. "I've been praying over this for the past couple of days, and I can't get clarity on what I'm supposed to do. I think telling you or the police is correct, but I fear I would be doing so out of a sense of self-righteousness, and a good shot of personal indignation as well. But now that Julian LaRue has gone missing..."

I was already curious, but I perked up at that. Whatever was going on, Pastor Davis had been thinking about coming to see us *before* the drama at the jewelry store unfolded. "And it doesn't have anything to do with manipulating a piece of jewelry you or the church brought in?"

"No, dear. But I have to ask, why would you think..." He shook his head and spoke to himself. "No, Stuart, stop it. Just stop it." After another swig of the dirty chai, he let out a long breath and adopted a tone as if he had entered a confessional. "A week ago, Roan, the church's handyman, maybe you've met him, I'm not sure..." He didn't wait for response. "He drew my attention to the fact that Estes Park has a new church in town. As you recall, the last time a new religious organization arrived was the Holy Rapture Fellowship, and we all know how *that* ended up. So... he was concerned. Roan wasn't trying to gossip, he only wanted to preempt another Bible-throwing stoning attempt."

I waited for the punchline, but it didn't seem to arrive. Katie pushed him onward for me. "I can't say that I keep up on the opening and closings of new churches, but I take it that's unusual."

Again, the pastor looked around the bakery and lowered his voice even further. "In this case, it's a jewelry store masquerading as a church. A false prophet in priest robes, if you will."

Though it was clear what he meant, I struggled with the concept. "*Aspen Gold* is pretending to be a *church*?"

"Registered and licensed as one, yes." He gave a shrug of his shoulder in a suggestive way that the reigning gossip queens, Percival and Anna, would've approved of. "But it is a church in name only."

"The jewelry shop got licensed as a *church*?" Katie sounded as baffled as me. "They have services? A new religion that worships gold or something?"

He scowled. "Worshiping gold is hardly a new religion, but no."

I grabbed Katie's hand. "Taxes." It clicked, out of the blue, but it clicked, and I looked to Pastor Davis for confirmation. "Aspen Gold would have a tax-exempt status if it was registered as a church."

"Yes. Which would be appropriate if they were having services, acting as an outreach to the community in the name of... a higher power *other* than gold. But..." He finished with another shrug.

"Huh..." Katie once more tapped the table. "How could the jewelry store get registered as a church? Wouldn't it need a pastor or, maybe—"

"Julian." I nearly jumped out of my chair and held Pastor Davis's gaze. "Did you find out? Is Julian a minister? He was in Vegas. Maybe he got ordained to perform wedding services at casinos, and now he's using it to—"

"No. Not Julian." Pastor Davis cut me off that time. "*Vivian.* Vivian has only recently been ordained, at least from the license I found online." Guilt washed over his face. "And this is where I am not sure of the honest intention of my heart. It is not my place to question another's religion, their relationship with God, or how they see the world, but at the same time, getting ordained, becoming the leader of a flock, took years of sacrifice, study, and dedication on my part. I can find no proof that Vivian did more than apply online, which is all the rage these days. But to do so... here in this small town where we all are aware? Well, it's just such a blatant move. I don't understand the thought process. How she thought no one would notice..."

If the implication hadn't been so huge, I might've laughed at the notion of getting ordained over the internet being the new social fad, plus, I was struggling to keep up. "Vivian. Really?" I'd been so sure as I'd driven from Aspen Grove that Julian had been acting on his own. "Vivian?" Stunned, I grasped the mug of dirty chai and took a deep drink, before realizing what I'd done. I looked back up at Pastor Davis. "Oh, sorry."

"Completely all right, dear." His tone was serious. "I quite understand. Like I said, it's all very upsetting." He motioned toward Katie. "Which is why I can't seem to come up with a more inspired combination than fig, bacon, and smoked maple bourbon."

During tourist season, the large crowd of people walking down the sidewalk wouldn't have pulled my attention away from Pastor Davis's revelations, and as it was, it required a double take for me to find the entourage odd. After narrow-eyed, closer inspection—in which I accidentally bumped my forehead on the window—I made out Alessandra Costa leading the group to Madame Delilah's Old Tyme Photography, where they began to disappear inside. Though I didn't know any by name, a few of the people looked familiar, which led me to think they weren't tourists at all. Not that it mattered. I'd thought about visiting Alessandra at some point, so her showing up at that moment seemed like too much kismet to let slip by.

After a quick goodbye to Pastor Davis and Katie, I paused at the top of the steps and reconsidered. Alessandra never seemed overly fond of Watson, but Delilah was. His charm might be useful.

Doubling back, I retrieved a second all-natural dog-bone treat from Nick, and then threw decorum to the wind as I knelt on all fours in front of the doggy door into his little apartment and tapped on the one-way window.

At the knock, Watson jumped from where he'd been napping on his miniature sofa and glared at me. Though I knew from his side the window was a mirror and he was only seeing himself, it was clear he knew exactly what was going on and who had disrupted his slumber.

Proving I hadn't just been born as Watson's mama the day before, I lowered myself even farther and spoke through the crack at the doggy door. "Treat, Watson. Treat!"

Casting aside decorum as easily as I had, Watson flung himself from the sofa so quickly he skidded on the floor, his rump bumping into the mirrored glass before crashing through the doggy door so quickly it nearly smacked me in the face.

Rearing up on my knees, I lifted the treat slightly above my head, out of reach.

Watson whimpered up at the treat and then cast his gaze to me with a glare.

Without the slightest guilt, I looked from him to the treat and laid out the terms of our bargain. "Part now, part later." I broke the treat in two and offered him the smaller portion.

He swallowed it whole, then looked expectantly at the other half.

"Play nice and you'll get the rest." I stood and headed toward the steps, not looking back until I reached the first one.

He padded forward a few steps, glanced toward the bakery, doubtlessly considering demanding another treat directly from the source, then with a put-upon sigh, lumbered my way.

"Thanks, buddy. This won't be too painful." I bent to scratch his head as he drew near.

Watson sidestepped and trotted down into the bookshop ahead of me.

Though unintentional, as we entered the tintype photography shop, I was proven to be a liar. There were two feminine squeals as a couple of women and a man—the women partially dressed as saloon girls, the man already wearing black-and-white-striped prison garb—hurried toward us, hands outstretched to pet Watson.

Group attention, painful indeed.

"Hold up, you three." A tall voluptuous redhead

right out of the pinup days and dressed in her own typical saloon-girl apparel, sidestepped them and took the role of protector. "Watson here isn't a big fan of adoring crowds, and you need to finish getting dressed anyway." As the three disappointed people headed back toward the rest of the group, Delilah Johnson—owner of the photography shop and leader of the Pink Panthers—did a graceful combination spin and kneeling move that caused both her skirt and her long tresses to flare like she was on the silver screen. "Well hello, handsome."

Though she'd just reprimanded the others, Delilah thrust a hand toward Watson, but paused long enough for him to sniff. Satisfied, he licked her knuckles and allowed himself to be fawned over. As she cooed, he cast a side-eyed glance up at me, his expression unmistakable.

Obligingly, I retrieved the remaining portion of the treat out of my pocket, broke it in half again, and offered one of the pieces to him.

Delilah chuckled. "Ah, bribery. A favorite of mine with all three of my bassets." She stood once more and caught me completely off guard as she pulled me into a tight hug. Though we'd crossed the friendship line ages ago after a rocky start, hugging wasn't all that common. "I'm so sorry, I meant to come down yesterday to congratulate you, but I got a little carried away with chores and such." She pulled back slightly, meeting my eyes, letting me see the sincerity of her sentiment. "I'm *so* happy for you and Leo. While marriage, in most cases, makes me either want to run for the hills or place bets on how long it will last, you two are a perfect match, if there ever was one."

Her hug wasn't the only thing that caught me off guard, as Delilah's words caused my throat to constrict, and I could barely choke out a thank-you.

"Now..." When she pulled back farther, I thought Delilah was going to release me, but she clasped my left hand and pulled it up. "I've heard about this monster. Let me see..." Her deep blue gaze flashed up to me questioningly.

Though surprised that little tidbit of gossip hadn't been passed on, I knew it didn't require a full explanation. "It was getting resized at Aspen Gold."

"Oh no!" She looked truly crushed. "Fred, that's..." Delilah took a step back, confusion flashing suddenly across her features. "That means Julian took your ring?"

"Delilah. I know it's going to come out in black-and-white on the tintype, but I look absolutely horrible in this shade of green. Do you think—"

Alessandra, wearing a lace-bodiced gown worthy of the *Gone with the Wind* set, stepped through a curtain in the back, joining the small crowd getting dressed in old-time clothes, but halted when she saw me. After appearing to offer some sort of explanation to the people nearest, she headed toward us, having to lift the hoop skirt to move easily. Though she didn't appear confused, differing emotions seemed to cross her face. And though I wasn't certain of both, one of them was definitely annoyance.

At her approach, the green dress probably looking like some sort of bell-shaped monster, Watson darted beneath my skirt for shelter, as he so often did. In truth, it would probably be doing him a favor if I started wearing hoop skirts instead of the broomstick variety. He'd have more room.

"First off, Winifred." Alessandra didn't waste any time as she came to a stop. "I truly do feel horrible about Julian ruining Leo's proposal the other night. It was a bonehead move."

Delilah winced. "Oh, I forgot about that detail."

"Yeah, he really stuck his foot in his mouth that time," Alessandra commented to Delilah, before returning to me. "But even so, let him be. Granted, Julian's not my favorite person, but he's been through enough. Do you really need to stick your nose into this one?"

"Alessandra!" Delilah bristled. "Fred may have declined our invitation to become a Pink Panther, but must I remind you that she's not only a valued and trusted friend of my own, but to the group."

Her sentiment both surprised and touched me.

Surprising me further, Delilah wasn't done. "It wasn't her fault what your parents chose to do. And because of the way Fred figured it out, at least partly, you avoided all scandal and were able to keep the restaurant." She thumbed toward the back where the group had nearly finished getting dressed. "And is why you're able to do staff photos for Pasta Thyme today."

"I know." Alessandra's cheeks darkened, though I couldn't tell if in embarrassment or anger. Even so, she didn't pull back her accusation. "Like I said, Julian didn't have the kindest heart and had... a lot to be desired, but he had his reasons. Let him go. It's not like he killed anyone."

"He did have his reasons," Delilah agreed. "Julian wasn't my favorite person in the world, either, but I can't say I entirely blame him." Her eyes narrowed once more. "Except for taking your ring. Which, again, I hear was *spectacular*. I have to admit, I'm surprised Leo made such a lavish choice, at least without me or my girls' input."

Though the LaRues had been forefront in my mind, Delilah whisked them away. How had I not considered that possibility? Leo was friends with every member of the Pink Panthers. If I'd thought of him going to the group of women asking for engagement ring advice, it would've made sense, at least somewhat, for him to have selected the massive diamond. But clearly he hadn't, which brought me back to my belief that he—

I nearly had to shake my head to get myself back on track, and I looked back and forth between the two women. "What did you know? You're aware that Julian was going to stage a robbery at his parents' store and disappear?"

Alessandra snorted and gave an eye roll so annoyed that even with how beautiful she was, she was unable to pull off gracefully.

"Fred!" That time, Delilah's reprimand was for me. "Do you really think if we knew about someone planning a robbery, we'd keep it to ourselves?"

I didn't even have to consider. "Yes, I do. If you thought the reasons were just." Delilah's statement from a moment before echoed in my mind.

"Although... you both stated Julian wasn't one of your favorite people."

"No, he wasn't." As ever, Delilah didn't beat around the bush or pretend to be embarrassed to give her unfiltered opinion. "Julian was gauche, selfish, shallow, and an overgrown spoiled brat. And could be a little a cruel in how he treated people."

Alessandra snorted again, this time more daintily. "Tell us how you really feel."

I looked toward her. "You disagree?"

"No." She laughed. "Not at all. He was all of that."

One of the things I admired about Delilah was her bluntness, a quality that was true of myself, and one I was attempting to tame on occasion, but given the moment, I let it loose as I leveled my stare on Alessandra, hoping for some shock value. "I overheard Julian tell his parents that you weren't good enough for him. His father agreed."

Alessandra started to wave me off, then glowered. "That old man agreed?"

Delilah cast her friend a glance and chuckled before refocusing on me. "We're going in circles. How about we break it down for you?"

"Please." I was feeling more lost than I had the entire time, which was saying something.

From below there was a rustle of my skirt and Watson emerged, checking to see if the coast was clear. Apparently only partially satisfied, he folded his forepaws and rested his head.

Delilah grinned down at him in affection and then got to the point. "Like I said, Fred, Julian was gauche, selfish, shallow, and spoiled. However, his parents also didn't allow him to be who he was. And as you know, I don't believe anyone should be held down by society's expectations, so I encouraged Alessandra to go along with his ploy, buy himself some time where his parents are concerned."

"As pathetic as it is for a forty-three-year-old man to be worried about what his parents say."

"That's not our place to judge," Delilah reprimanded Alessandra but returned to the explanation without me needing to prompt. "I'd hoped we'd help him stand up to them in ways that really mattered. Never mind we're in the twenty-first century, Julian's parents are back in the dark ages. They demanded he date women when he has absolutely no interest. So, to keep them off his back, he'd go out with Alessandra from time to time. Or sometimes they'd join Mario and me for double dates, catch a movie... whatever. Just keeping up appearances."

"Julian is—" Again, Delilah's words played

catch-up in my mind, and I got hung up on them as I gaped at her. "You and... Mario?"

Delilah gave me a puzzled look. "Um... yeah. That wasn't exactly the point, but yes."

"Mario *Toscano*?"

She flinched. "Yes. Fred, is there something I should be concerned about? Do you know something about him? Granted, it's just a casual thing, but still. You were right about Jake. If Mario is—"

"No." I reached out to grasp Delilah's hand quickly enough that it startled Watson, who popped back beneath my skirt. "No, I don't know anything about Mario. I... wasn't aware you two were... seeing each other." I wondered if Susan knew. If she got wind of Mario ever being with Delilah, any attraction she felt would be burnt away as quickly as the steakhouse. That thought also held me up as a memory flashed unbidden, and I refocused on Alessandra, changing directions once more. "You were with Julian the night Prime Slice partially burned down."

"Whoa, you are scattered, girl." Alessandra gave me a less than flattering appraisal. "And you know that already. You were there. Julian literally spoiled your proposal with me at his side."

Not caring of her judgment, I pushed on. "I saw

you and Julian standing in the crowd as it burned. Right before you left, you laughed."

Alessandra balked, seemingly confused, but a blush rose to her cheeks before she lifted her chin in defiance. "So?"

I'd been right about her reaction that night, and her response confirmed it. "You seemed to enjoy watching it burn, or find it funny, or... something."

"Tom Colter is scum and an opportunistic pig. He did everything he could to steal Pasta Thyme right out from under me when everything happened with my parents. And he nearly succeeded, reported me to insurance, claiming I was part of what Mom and Dad were doing." Her chin tilted even higher. "You bet I enjoyed watching his restaurant burn. Too bad it was only half of it."

I gaped at her, stunned at the pure hatred dripping from her.

Ever attuned, Watson whimpered at her furious tone.

Taking the last portion of the treat, I lowered it to the floor as I spoke. "But... why in the world were you cating at Prime Slice if—"

"I didn't set that fire, and if that's what you're—" Alessandra stopped when Delilah put a restraining hand on her arm.

Watson's crunching sounded in the silence between us.

"No." I shook my head, I hadn't been thinking that, but now that she put the idea in my head... "It's just that, if he did that, and you can't stand him, why would you eat there?"

She smiled, a hard thing. "To rub it in his face, remind that little weasel Tom that he didn't get the better of me. Every time I go, I order the most expensive thing there."

I had no idea how that made sense, but a different possibility entered my mind. "Weren't you two in the grill room when the fire started?" I'd started to wait but rushed ahead as fury washed over her face again. "I'm not blaming you. But... did you happen to tell Julian about Tom and your past?"

Again Alessandra started to protest, but paused, mouth caught open midway, then she nodded slowly. "Yes, actually. We had a good laugh about it over dinner."

Delilah cocked her head. "Well, the plot thickens. Perhaps, as a thank-you, Julian burned all of his bridges on the way out of town."

"I doubt it. Granted, I wasn't exactly staring at Julian or anything, but I think I would've noticed if he set the place on fire." Alessandra considered, but seemed unconvinced. "Besides, it was Paulie and that new police officer playing around with fire like overgrown twelve-year-old geeks." She rolled her eyes for the third time. "Now *that* cringeworthy display, I saw."

It was something to ponder anyhow. For another moment I debated on how much to share but then decided it was Estes, word would get around either way, and trudged on. "From what you know of him, would you think Julian capable of replacing precious stones and gems that came into Aspen Gold with fake replicas?"

Both women flinched, and Delilah glanced down at the diamond bangle on her left wrist. "No..." She blinked a couple of times, her concern suggesting she'd recently taken the jewelry in for cleaning or something. "Well... maybe." Her upper lip turned into a snarl, as if she was quickly growing convinced.

"You know what... I actually *can* see him doing that. I've felt sorry for him, but..." Alessandra sounded equally disgusted. "It's one thing to steal from his bigoted parents, but from everyone else?" She shuddered. "I've dated some losers from time to time, but that takes the cake. Even if it was fake dating."

FIFTEEN

I thoroughly considered the consequences of my actions as I stepped out of Madame Delilah's Old Tyme Photography and looked back and forth from the Cozy Corgi to down the other side of the street where Aspen Gold was just out of view. At least, as thoroughly as one could in a matter of seconds. As I swiveled on my heel to the right—after giving a tug to Watson's leash, as he'd wanted to return and curl up in his sunbeam, on his ottoman, his little apartment, or a combination of the three—I took the remaining steps from the photography shop to the jewelry store to validate my impulse.

Vivian and Roger had made it perfectly clear, despite their insistence I be present at the beginning, that they no longer required nor wanted my input. So really, what more harm could I do? Similarly, they were hiding something. Chances were, lots of somethings. I'd discovered in the past that sometimes a surprise attack of launching all the bombs you had at one time gave the best chance of at least one of them hitting pay dirt.

One other aspect broke through my train of thought as I crossed the short distance, one that the absence of crowds of tourists seemed to highlight. Downtown Estes Park, with its blocks of shops done in 1960s mountain-style façades, was charming, cozy, and in many aspects right out of the pages of a storybook. Currently, there were several empty storefronts between the block that held my bookshop and the one with the stores curved around the waterwheel. Just in the past couple of weeks, after the Irons family crumbled, revealing its claws deep in the heart of Estes, the camera shop, scrapbook supply, and knitting store were no more, their windows dark holes piercing through the charm. It was that which offered me a momentary pause at the door of Aspen Gold. When this was done, when puzzle pieces were fitted together and questions answered, would this be one more barren location in the town I loved so much? I'd had a part to play in the unraveling of the others; was I doing that again?

That question took even less time to answer than I'd spent debating whether to walk down or not. The truth was what the truth was, and I'd not made the choices that would be responsible for the consequences. If the beautiful window displays were merely a cover for darkness and misdeeds, there wasn't real charm to begin with. Better to let them be empty for a while so they could be filled with something genuinely good.

For what felt like the billionth time, the door to the jewelry shop stayed closed as I attempted to open it. Though it was locked, there was movement inside. Vivian and Roger both turned to face me. After that spark of recognition, they exchanged glances, taking about the same amount of time as I had done to debate what they should do. Whether they spoke or not, I couldn't tell, but they suddenly moved as one. Roger heading toward the door, while Vivian went perpendicular toward the cash register.

After the click of the lock, Roger opened the door and stood aside, surprising me with granted entrance. "We were going to call you in a little bit."

Before I could make a comment about being glad they felt ready to confess about a few things, Vivian held out a miniature version of a padded manila envelope. "We found this while we were cleaning today."

"What—" I realized the answer to that question before I could finish forming it that time, and my body moved without any consideration or forethought. I even dropped Watson's leash without thinking as I hurried across the small space. "Thank you." I took it from her and glanced at it before I opened the little flap. My name had been written in cursive with blue ink, and it read *Fred*, not Winifred, so I figured I knew which of the three LaRues had written it. Tilting the envelope, my engagement ring tumbled out into my palm, the giant diamond sparkling in the light. Again, moving of its own accord, my right hand picked it up and placed it on the third finger of my left hand. The ring slid smoothly, fitting perfectly.

"Julian resized it for you quickly, like he promised." Vivian's tone was a combination of defiant and mournful. "It was right where it was supposed to be, with the rest of the orders to be picked up. We just didn't look, or think of it, honestly, with everything going on."

Watson snuffled around my feet, his leash trailing by him, probably searching for snacks or crumbs. I was too captivated by the ring to bother to stop him. Too many emotions were traveling through me as I continued to stare, too many to name or even come close to identifying.

"So, you see?" When Vivian spoke again, she

finally broke the spell, pulling my attention to her. "If Julian did what they're claiming, why would he leave a diamond such as that behind. It's worth a fortune."

"Because it's fake. Not worth very much at all." That answer was obvious, so obvious I was surprised she brought it up. Maybe she really didn't know.

"I *beg* your pardon!" Roger hurried over, full offense in his voice and over his features. "We only sell the best diamonds. They are inspected, certified, and—" His voice was growing louder and broke off suddenly as disgust marred his features. "How dare you."

His affront was genuine, at least I thought so. Perhaps it could've been overreacting, but it didn't feel that way. However, I couldn't help but notice he responded more vehemently to the insult about the quality of a diamond than he had defending Julian's reputation.

Vivian, it seemed, had also noticed, as irritation lined her words when she spoke. "And Julian would never—"

"Isn't that why you are irritated with Detective Green already?" I needed to push thoughts of my ring aside and launch all the bombs. Keep on track.

"She'd just questioned you about complaints from Aspen Grove? And there's—"

"Enough." Roger thrust a hand in the air, cutting off the next launch of bombs. "This is a witch hunt, prompted by people in an unfortunate situation, but I'll not allow decades of our reputation to be smudged by those on the edge of sanity in a nursing home. We are a stalwart of the community, and the pillars of the town come to us—Dr. Williams, the Hansons, the Patels, *Mayor* Sallee, the Beakers—for every anniversary, birthday, or Christmas. Even your man came to us because of our reputation."

The curtain to the back room moved as Watson hurried back in—though I'd not realized he'd wandered so far, coming to stand beside me at the sound of Roger's aggression. That had definitely earned him another treat when we returned to the Cozy Corgi.

"Nice list of names there, but I can't help but notice, Mr. LaRue, that you're extremely dogmatic about the reputation of your jewelry store." I'd already been determined to not back down, but Watson's move of devotion helped spur me onward. "You don't defend Julian's reputation with quite so much vigor."

He took a step back, soundlessly looking like he'd been struck.

Vivian cast him an accusing glare.

They made quite the picture, every shoe-black hair in place, from Vivian's coiled beehive to the plastered helmet of Roger's. Their clothes, while over the top in their finery, were pristine. Aspen Gold, though it was missing a display case, was already completely back in place, almost as if nothing had happened.

I debated for a second, wondering if I should keep launching bombs or wander down that trail, asking why they turned their attention to their store instead of their son, questioning if they'd really hired another detective. Or were they somehow in on what Julian had done and were playing a long game of some sort?

"Who were you arguing with Julian about that day when I dropped off my ring?" Maybe launch the next bomb. "The woman Julian said wasn't good enough for him?"

They both blinked, clearly thrown off by the question out of left field. "You said it yourself." Vivian found her voice first. "And he was right, that Alessandra Costa girl isn't nearly good enough for him."

"*She* isn't who you were talking about. I made an incorrect assumption, and you allowed me to go along with it, for some reason." As I spoke, panic ignited in both of their eyes, and... maybe anger? In that instant, despite plenty of confirmation that Julian was indeed shallow and a host of other qualities, I joined Delilah and Alessandra in feeling the need to defend him. "Is it really that horrible for people to find out your son, who's a full-grown man in his forties, by the way, isn't interested in women at all?"

The shame and repulsion that etched itself clearly in the lines of Roger's face was answer enough—both of his feelings and confirmation of the claim's validity.

"We shouldn't have asked you to get involved in the first place. You're too prone to give credence to idle gossip, as opposed to dealing in cold hard facts." Vivian, however, whether out of desperation or self-deception, didn't relent. "Julian and Rion were *working* together." She floundered somewhat, surely sounding desperate even to her own ears. "It was at my behest. I thought our stores could collaborate on a joint promotion. Wedding gowns and engagement rings. That's all they were doing."

It took me a few seconds to catch up, as no one

had mentioned wedding gowns at all. Though I'd never been at Day of Lace, I'd met the owner, Rion Sparks, in passing once or twice. Apparently he was Julian's real interest, not Alessandra. I didn't bother to argue with her. "Maybe that's why he stole from you and took off—you wouldn't let him be himself."

"Stole from us? *That* again? Then explain the geode." Vivian was nearly hysterical in her panic and flung a hand at a couple of hefty-looking stones that had been cut open to reveal sparking crystals inside. "Julian hates these geodes. He said we should leave the rock shop to carry things that look like they're from an archeological dig. The big amethyst one by the cash register is gone. He wouldn't have touched it. And these..." Snarling, Vivian rushed toward me. Watson barked, leaping between us, but the two of us had been wrong, as Vivian kept right on going toward the display on the far side of the room. "See these?" She gestured toward something on top of the case.

Watson was still growling. I retrieved the end of his leash before moving closer, just in case.

The objects were the crystal-and-gold animals that had been on the floor the day Julian had left—a bear, rabbit, and an elephant I hadn't noticed before. I looked up at Vivian, not sure of the connection.

"Julian hated these even more. Thought they were tacky and cheap." Vivian tapped one of the large crystals. "They're not real."

"And we don't claim that they are." Roger spoke up behind us but also headed our way.

"Not the point." Vivian shot him a glare and return to me. "Julian wanted us to quit carrying them, but they're very good sellers. A lot of tourists either can't afford high-quality jewelry or simply aren't in the market for it on their vacation. Items like this, however, sell like hotcakes."

I waited for more of an explanation, but none seemed to be coming, and in my confusion, I neglected to throw another bomb. "I'm sorry, I don't understand."

"Two of these are among the things that were stolen—a unicorn and a chipmunk." That time she tapped the crystal elephant so hard it fell over, not that she noticed. "*Julian* would never steal these. Not that he would steal anything, but if he did, why in the world would he take these? Not only did he hate them, he knew they weren't valuable." She finished with a gesture toward my hand.

"Likewise, why leave *that* diamond behind? And no, I'm certain it isn't fake!"

I disregarded that last bit; the diamond being

fake was the only thing that made sense, unless I found out Leo had... well, I had no idea how many thousands such a diamond would cost, but it wasn't something a park ranger could afford.

Instead, I narrowed in on the crystal animals. Vivian had a point. Why would Julian take those, unless it was one more slap in the face to his parents?

Since I didn't have an answer, I resorted back to the bombs, lifting my gaze from the animals to meet hers. "Does Julian's disappearance have anything to do with you being ordained and claiming Aspen Gold is a church?"

As her husband had done before her, Vivian took a step back. Then, also repeating what they'd done before, she and Roger exchanged a look. Unless I was reading her wrong, I'd seen genuine confusion, but whatever had passed between them seemed to offer some understanding.

Roger took over. "You need to leave. As I told you yesterday, we're hiring..." He cleared his throat. "We've hired a private investigator to help us locate who took our son. We won't be needing your inadequate services, and now that you have your ring returned, you no longer require ours."

My walk back to the Cozy Corgi was slow, not because I was formulating what steps to take next, or which person I needed to speak to about fake jewelry, fake romances, or fake kidnappings. I was caught in a haze of complete confusion. I had absolutely no idea what was going on.

Watson, on the other hand, had no such hesitation. He trotted along happily ahead of me, content in knowing there were both treats and multiple napping spots in his future—if he could just get his mama to hurry up and get him there.

After a quick but thorough greeting to Ben, Watson settled down where the late-morning sun poured through the front windows. He'd barely more than settled before he popped back up and trotted into the mystery room, where he did a similar circular dance on top of his ottoman. That position lasted a touch longer before he hopped up again with a grunt and shuffled into the main room to his sunbeam. He turned clockwise three times, counterclockwise once, as if he'd gone too far, then settled down. One of his ears twitched, his nub of a tail wagged then stopped, and finally he gave a long, contented sigh that indicated sleep was finally about to arrive.

Having watched the entire production, Ben and I exchanged glances. Though he chuckled, he kept his voice low, clearly not wanting to disturb our chubby little mascot. "Someone seems a little bit ungrounded today. Too many treats or not enough?"

"Are there ever enough?" On that note, I decided it was high time for another dirty chai but lingered with Ben for another second. "He's not the only one ungrounded. You know, sometimes I fancy myself pretty decent at putting together the pieces of a mystery, but this one has me spinning more than Watson just did. I quite literally have no idea what to do next."

"Maybe you don't need to do anything next." I'd started to head up to the bakery, but Ben spoke, holding me in place. "I mean, there's not a murder. There's no rush, right? You don't really think he was kidnapped, do you?"

"I..." After considering for a moment, I nodded. "You're right. I don't really think he was kidnapped, and you're also right about the urgency. I was actually thinking that last night, but somehow that got washed away in the bustle of the morning." I smiled, my frequent affection for him blossoming once more. "You're pretty smart, Ben Pacheco, thanks! I think for the rest of the day I'll merely be a bookseller."

His dark gaze twinkled. "And if I know you, probably one who hopes for no customers so she can curl up and read a book by the fire."

"See?" I chuckled. "You're pretty on your toes putting together mystery pieces as well."

. . .

I took Ben's advice and played the role of the owner of the Cozy Corgi, after filling Katie in on my interactions with the LaRues at Aspen Gold over a dirty chai and an oaty crunch bar... or two... of each. However, though the mystery room called to me, I didn't curl up with a book in front of the fire. I worked—rearranging shelves and entire sections, preparing for the soon-arriving holiday displays that would be needed in the next three months, and even going so far as to help the random customer who wandered in. All in all, a very unusual day.

Still, as was so often the case when my body and hands went to work, the narrow twist and turns in the back of my mind shuffled through things. Ben was right, I didn't think it was a kidnapping. We'd found that Julian had enemies, or at least people he'd stolen from or taken advantage of. But from what we could tell, those wronged parties were taking action, the legal way. Plus, the scene didn't feel like a kidnapping. There had been no sign of a struggle, jewelry hadn't been taken out of the vault, which if it had been a real robbery, as they'd had access to the combination thanks to the owners' son, emptying the vault would've been the first move. And there was no follow-through with threat or ransom. So that left me with fewer options. The easiest explanation was what Delilah and Alessandra offered. Spoiled by his parents though he might be, Julian had had enough of their demands and took off, adding insult to injury as he did so. Or the LaRues had a bigger endgame, which wasn't clear yet—parents and son working together on some sort of scam?

Even that nettlesome worry was pushed aside shortly after three in the afternoon.

I'd forgotten Britney was going to be ending the day with us for the foreseeable future. She came in with a huff, tossing her backpack behind the counter as if she was at a bowling alley.

Watson, who'd been in his unending nap, gave her his trademark corgi side-eye before booking it right up the steps to disappear into the bakery.

"Sorry!" Britney had the wherewithal to look a little embarrassed as she called after him. That remorse didn't go so far as to keep her from crossing her arms in an annoyed fashion and an irritation entering her tone as she looked back and forth between Ben and me. "Well, what do you want me to do today?"

"Um..." From the expression Ben shot me, he'd forgotten as much as I had that we were going to have a new employee. He skimmed over the bookshop, clearly looking for books in disarray or for items misplaced, but thanks to me being an actual bookseller, things were in tip-top shape.

In an effort to help, I scanned the bookshop as well, my gaze landing where Watson had been sleeping. The answer was so obvious any person who owned and loved a corgi would wonder why it took me so long. "Sweeping!" It was almost silly how excited I sounded about that.

"Oh! Yes!" Ben caught on instantly.

"Sweeping?" Britney dropped the gold pendant she'd been tugging on around her neck as she recoiled in such disgust no one would ever know she was actually a pretty girl underneath her revolted expression. "As in... a broom?"

"Sweeping." I gestured toward where Watson had been napping and then traced a line across the floor. "It doesn't matter how often we sweep, vacuum, or mop, or how much Watson is brushed. There are always tumbleweeds of corgi hair. They clump together and... well, tumble... anywhere the floor meets the wall, the bottom of the bookshelf, a boot if you stand too long."

"A boot?" Britney cocked an eyebrow.

"Yes." Trying to break her mood, I pulled up the

hem of my pale brown broomstick skirt and waggled a boot. "If you stand long enough, you *will* collect corgi hair."

Ben chuckled.

Britney? Not so much.

I let my skirt fall back in place. "If you'd sweep, that would be great."

Before she had a chance to comment, Ben motioned for her to follow. "I'll show you where the broom and the rest of the cleaning supplies are."

"Oh... fun." Though her shoulders slumped, Britney tagged along.

Feeling like I'd done my daily duty as bookshop owner, I wandered into the mystery room, picked up the next of the cozy mystery series I'd started the other day, and settled down to read. Before too long, Watson plodded back down the steps, jumped onto the ottoman, and after a couple of circles, settled down to resume his never-ending nap.

I only made it partway through the first chapter before I found myself constantly distracted. The glittering diamond on my finger kept stealing my focus every couple of words. By the time I reached chapter four, I had to admit I hadn't caught more than a modicum of the plot, as my psyche was more invested in the debate of whether to tell Leo he'd purchased a fake diamond or just keep it to myself. I didn't care if it was real or not, so what was the harm in letting things stay where they were? He'd feel like he'd gotten me a wonderful diamond and never need to know he'd been taken advantage of.

That wasn't a real possibility. Keeping things from him would eat at me, and if the roles were reversed, I'd want to know.

As I settled into that obvious fact, my attention was pulled into the main room by a sharp outburst of giggles.

Watson lifted his head off the ottoman, glaring at me as if the disruption was my fault.

After returning his glare, I turned to see Britney by the cash register, her friends Ananya and Dawn crowded close across from her. Ben was on the far side of the room assisting an elderly couple.

My first instinct was to remind Britney she was there to work and ask the other girls to leave, but instead I decided to just observe.

After murmured whispers, the giggles burst out again, and it was clear the loudest, highest one came from Ananya. She tossed her long dark hair over her shoulder, threw her head back, and let out a loud laugh—a pleasant sound, happy. Carefree.

The other two girls giggled along, but not quite to the same extent.

I narrowed in on my niece, studying her. And though she whispered back, I realized she was doing something similar to me. She was studying her friends, her keen gaze flicking back and forth between them. Something about her expression seemed sad or stressed. Maybe it was a case of three's a crowd? She felt like the odd one out. The other day when I'd observed them on the sidewalk, it seemed Britney had been the leader, but watching them... I didn't get that sense. In that moment, judging from the body language, Ananya was the *it* girl of the three.

There were more whispers—another joke, another tidbit of gossip, I wasn't sure—before another outburst of giggles. That time, I noticed Dawn flip back her long red hair in an identical way to Ananya, complete with throwing her head back in a similar fashion as well, though she didn't quite achieve the same easy grace the other girl had managed. Yes... Ananya was the *it* girl. Was that what had been causing Britney to be so dark the past several months, feeling that she didn't measure up? Was there bullying happening?

On the next outburst of laughter, I caught it. I

wouldn't have if I hadn't been staring, as Dawn moved so quickly it was barely noticeable. A flick of her long hair and she giggled, and her hand shot out, snagging the tiny silver coyote statue. In a blink, it disappeared into the pocket of her jeans.

My gaze flicked to Britney, and I realized she'd noticed it as well. Finally, feeling my attention upon her, she looked my way. Her cheeks flamed scarlet, and a hand lifted to cover the pendant at her clavicle —much as an older woman might clutch at their pearls—before giving just the slightest of headshakes. A wordless but clear pleading for me not to say anything, not to embarrass her in front of her friends.

For a second, I considered, but only a second.

Once more, Watson glared as I stood, accidentally bumping into his ottoman and disturbing him again.

I'd barely taken a step out of the mystery room when the front door opened and Ajay Patel stormed in. "You've got to be kidding me?"

Britney had been staring at me, and the other two facing away, so the sound of his voice made all three girls jump.

Ajay didn't slow until he was upon them, nearly looking like he was going to bowl them over. "Do you think this is a joke? That you can disregard what your parents say?" He glanced my way as I approached, anger flashing in his eyes. "Winifred." He sighed, shaking himself. "I'm sorry, bursting in here like this and that this is taking place in your shop to begin with."

"Dad! We wanted to—"

"What you *want* is the *last* thing on my mind right now." He grabbed Ananya's shoulder, giving her a solitary shake. "You're supposed to be with your mom at the firehouse, working, like Britney is here. When she called and said you blew her off, I..." His other hand went up and squeezed his temples, as if he was on the verge of an aneurysm. "I... can't believe it. And then the audacity to show up *here*, of all places."

I came to a stop beside Britney, on the other side of Ajay and the two girls, completely at a loss for what to say. Part of me felt like I should apologize that I'd just been sitting there watching; another part of me wanted to confront Dawn about the coyote.

"How is that fair, Dad?" Ananya helped me by filling that flash of silence. "Why should Britney have to work here, and why should I have to help Mom?" She gestured toward Dawn. "*She's* not in trouble. Didn't even get grounded. Ask her. *Her* mom is cool and not a—"

"Becky didn't give you *any* consequences?" Ananya's distraction worked, as Ajay turned to gape at Dawn. "Seriously? After all you three did?"

Dawn shrugged, her hand slipped into her pocket as if covering the little coyote. She took several small steps backward, toward the door.

"Oh no." Ajay still had one hand on Ananya's shoulder and used his other to point to where Dawn had stood. "You stay right here, Dawn Erickson. I'm calling your mom. Don't you even think of walking away and—"

"You can't talk to her like that." Britney found her voice suddenly, and it was laced with every ounce of her teenage fury. "*You're* not her dad, are you?"

Ajay flinched, taken aback at her rudeness.

"Britney! Watch your tone." I had always been extremely careful not to take on a parental role to my nephews and nieces. It wasn't what I wanted nor felt all that comfortable with—it would be too easy to step on toes or cause family drama. But considering Zelda and Noah had used my bookshop as the consequence, I didn't see what choice I had. "You don't speak to anyone that way. And definitely not in front of me."

Britney wheeled my way, eyes flashing, her

mouth opening like she was getting ready to shout or curse or scream how much she hated me. No words came, but the tears practically exploded, and she turned and darted away.

At the distraction, Dawn did the exact same thing, except in the opposite direction. As Ajay called after her, she exited the door and ran down the street.

Ajay let out a long, shaky breath and turned toward his daughter. "This is—"

"How could you?" Ananya captured the rage Britney hadn't been able to voice, the tears fell swiftly down her cheeks as well. "Do you know how embarrassing, how—"

"Enough!" Ajay barked the command, cutting Ananya off.

An answering bark sounded from the mystery room, though Watson didn't come running, to my surprise.

Ajay didn't seem to notice, all his frustration laser-focused on his daughter. "And act your age. Even your brother doesn't throw fits in public, and Sam is thirteen!" When Ajay looked back at me, it was like he'd aged twenty years in those two seconds and sounded utterly defeated. "I'm so, so sorry, Fred. This will not happen again. I'm so..."

"It's okay." And as before, it all made me grateful I was a mama to an overfed shedding corgi and not to human children, teenage or otherwise. "We all go through stages, right? This is part of it." That hadn't been true, at least not for me. While there'd been moments, I couldn't recall ever speaking to my mom or dad the way I'd witnessed Ananya and Britney speak to Ajay.

He smiled an apology and moved his hand from his daughter's shoulder to rest at the base of her neck as if she might try to flee as well. "Come on. Let's go see your mom."

As they left, I attempted to figure out what I needed to say to Britney, although chances were she'd locked herself in the bathroom and wouldn't come out until past closing. And honestly, I was okay with that.

To my surprise, I found her when I went to check on Watson. Britney had wedged herself in my spot on the antique sofa underneath the purple portobello lampshade. Surprisingly, Watson had taken sentinel beside her, and though he was an antisocial little grump, he allowed her to pet him, offering comfort.

I sat beside them, still trying to figure out what to say.

Britney solved that for me. "I'm sorry, Fred. I didn't mean to be rude to you. I'm just so... frustrated that Mom and Dad pulled you into this. They have a lot of stupid ideas."

"*Britney.*" Though I'd been touched by her apology, I couldn't help reprimanding her for calling her parents stupid.

"Really? You're going to pretend like they don't have a lot of stupid ideas?" Even with tears still brimming, she managed a perfect teenage glare. "Mom was upset that the Irons family *didn't* bug her store, remember? And she thinks all those crystals actually do something. Dad with his idiotic inventions. I mean, who even... It's so..." She didn't seem able to finish.

I knew I should reprimand her again, tell her she shouldn't say such things about her parents, but... she wasn't wrong. About any of it. Still... I dared to touch her knee, and she didn't pull away. "Your folks are eccentric and see the world through a different kaleidoscope than a lot of people look through." When she snorted in derision, I pushed on. "At the end of the day, they are good and kind. They love you with everything in them."

At that, after a few moments, she gave a nod of

agreement. Which appeared to be the most she could handle.

I squeezed her knee, daring to push a little farther. "I know you didn't steal the corgi from the bakery."

Britney flinched her gaze back up to me, panicked. "Yes, I did. I told you. I—"

"No, you didn't." I leaned nearer, hoping she saw both truth and affection in my gaze. "I knew it that night, I could tell. So could Katie. But seeing Dawn take that coyote was proof."

"Dawn didn't take—" She stopped the lie midway, knowing it was useless, and surprised me by being more aware than I gave her credit for. "It was Ben's, wasn't it? He's writing that book about the Ute coyote deity or something."

"Yes." I released her knee but only moved my hand to Watson, keeping it near.

Britney straightened, and in that moment, I could easily see the woman she was becoming. "I'll get it back for him. I promise."

"Why are you covering for Dawn?" I leaned a little nearer once more but didn't touch Britney. "Why would you say you stole for her? I know she's one of the cool girls, but—"

"No." She shook her head and gave a little laugh.

"Oh yes, she's cool, but... Dawn has... she's had a rough life, okay? She has her reasons."

I wanted to push, do my typical throw-all-the-bombs, be direct, but... this was Britney, and whatever her flaws, whatever her struggles, she was my niece; she was family. And maybe she was making poor decisions, but I believed her; they came from a place of softness, of friendship. I wasn't going to ask her to betray that, not any more than she had. Besides, I could find out myself.

After closing time, I decided to launch a different type of bomb in hopes of surprising out some answers. If not answers, at least pull out a clue or two. I momentarily debated letting Britney know my plans, even went so far as to consider inviting her... a peace offering, or a chance for her to earn some trust. Unfortunately, I wasn't certain that just because she'd admitted what I'd already known, she wouldn't throw a kink in however this confrontation went. The last thing I wanted was her shouting at me, or Dawn's mom, the same way she had at Ananya's dad. So instead of asking Britney where Dawn lived, I used the old-fashioned method to find Becky Erickson's address—the yellow pages. Well, not quite, but the digital version on my cell phone, so close enough.

After we bypassed the turnoff to our little cabin, Watson turned a suspicious gaze on me. He didn't get all huffy and pout but merely looked back out the passenger window with curiosity. Perhaps he'd decided I'd endured enough having to deal with teenage attitude and didn't need corgi disapproval piled on top.

As we neared the end of the almost half-hour drive toward Allenspark, we passed Estes Valley Church. Though silly, I offered a little wave, picturing Pastor Davis inside his tiny river rock castle, probably in his office leaning back in his chair with his feet on the desk, wearing his purple robes and reading one of his first-edition Agatha Christie novels. I ignored the impulse to swing by and pick him up, thinking that maybe a man of the cloth would help prompt Dawn's confession.

Cementing the choice to not disturb him, my cell buzzed. After a glance and seeing Leo's name, I pulled the car to the side of the road, both for safety reasons and to maintain cell service. "Hey."

"Hey." Even from the other side of the line, Leo's brightness was contagious. "Sorry to bother you, I just had to call."

"No need to be sorry, ever. Is everything okay?" My anxiety spiked a bit, despite his clearly good mood.

"Oh yeah," he chuckled. "I had to call because —" Another chuckle. "—well, Nadiya and I were talking about you, and she called you my fiancée. I suppose that's obvious, but I hadn't quite put that term with you yet. I love it."

The shimmery golden pink cloud settled over me, washing away that momentary worry, and I sank into its glow. "Pretty wonderful, isn't it?" I glanced toward the ring, shifting my finger so the light would cause the diamond to sparkle. "Funny, in reality, nothing's changed, we've known for a long time this is where we would be. But—"

"It feels different, doesn't it?" He sounded as if he was in a dream state as well.

"It really does." I sighed.

Watson whimpered, cocking his head toward the phone, obviously hearing his park ranger soul mate.

Proving he was ever attuned, Leo chuckled for a third time. "I heard that. Tell him I'll see him tonight. And to make sure you're safe at Dawn's house."

I'd texted Katie and Leo the address I was going to, just in case—not that I was expecting any trouble. "He will, though I can't imagine he'll actually need to."

"Me neither." There was a slight growl in Leo's tone. "Otherwise, I'd be driving down the mountain right now to join you."

"All will be fine." I reached over, scratching

Watson's head as he leaned nearer trying to get a clearer sound of Leo's voice. "See you tonight?"

"Of course." The growl left, or... was replaced by a different kind. "I love you, *fiancée*."

I laughed. "And I love you." After hanging up, I sighed, checked the side mirror, and pulled back onto the road.

Proving it had been the right decision to stay still during the call, the almost half-hour drive turned into just shy of an hour, and my reception kept flickering in and out the farther we wound into the mountains, continuing to make the map shouting out directions either freeze or get confused as to where we were. By the time we arrived at the Erickson house, we were deep into the woods, and the sun was getting low enough that if I'd been planning a surprise arrival for someone suspected of more than stealing a few knickknacks, I might've reconsidered.

Watson hopped out of the Mini Cooper without any angst of his own and trotted up the broken cement sidewalk, looking mildly curious as opposed to annoyed. He even went so far as to sit patiently at full attention, as if he didn't think he was the one in control and waited for me to ring the doorbell.

In a lot of ways, the Erickson house looked like my little cabin, and even had sort of a cozy feel.

Becky answered mere seconds after I rang. She must've looked through the peephole, as she didn't seem surprised to find Watson and me. With red-rimmed eyes, she sounded utterly defeated. "I already got the riot act from Ajay." She squeezed those puffy eyes shut and gave an exhausted shake of her head. "From Ananya's dad—because *she* can't do any wrong—letting me have it for not punishing Dawn enough. I promise you, I'm not going to take this lightly. I know the girls stole the corgi, but if you'll remember"—her gaze looked up at mine once more, holding it—"your niece is the one who stole it, not my Dawn."

That statement threw me off enough, it took me a second to reply as I tried to judge her sincerity. Did she really believe Britney's story? Was she trying to cover for her daughter? I couldn't tell. "I'm not here to... give you the riot act. And I'm not angry. I just..." I wasn't sure how this was going to go if Becky was the type of parent to refuse to acknowledge their child was less than perfect. Maybe bomb throwing wouldn't work. "I hoped we could chat."

Becky hesitated; it was easy to see the internal debate behind her eyes. One that I was certain revolved around what would get me off her family's case the quickest. After a few moments, she took a couple of steps back, opened the door wider, and offered a welcoming smile. "Of course, come on in." Apparently the strategy of indulging the nosy book lady and her corgi had won.

While the outside of our homes might have resembled each other, the interiors were nothing alike. The inside of the Erickson home had been updated; all semblance of cabin was erased, save for a three large log beams at the vaulted ceiling. The rest had been redone, sheetrocked, painted, and wallpapered. It was nice, everything good quality, family friendly, but thoroughly lacking in charm. It could have been a stock home from any suburb in the US.

"Have a seat." With one hand, Becky gestured toward a large cream-colored sectional, and with her other through a doorway that showed an equally updated kitchen. "I'm sorry, I don't have a lot of time, as thanks to that phone call, like I said, I'm running a bit behind. I was just finishing up preparing dinner when you rang the doorbell." Her implied accusation of me not calling in advance was clear. Not that I blamed her.

As I sat, Watson started to do his normal meandering, checking out every scent in a new location. However, at Becky's narrowed glare, I recaptured his leash, earning myself a glare from him as well.

"No need to bother looking for crumbs, you won't find any. Everything is spotless. I need to take lessons." If my commentary didn't earn me any corgi points from Watson, I did earn a couple of bonus ones from Becky. She seemed to soften a little bit at the compliment of her housekeeping. I decided to take advantage of that, as it might be the only breakthrough I found, especially since she'd made it clear this needed to be quick. "I'm not concerned about the cost of the corgi from the bakery, but I did want to address it, if you don't mind. I know Britney—"

"As I told Ananya's dad, I don't see why my daughter should have to pay for her friends' mistakes. And also, like I told him, there will be consequences because I do believe we are in charge of our own actions and *who* we hang out with. In that, Dawn needs to make better choices. As the events at your shop this afternoon, *yet again*, validate." As she spoke, a flush rose to her cheeks, and she sat a little straighter. "Furthermore, I know it was at your shop, but you're not Britney's parent, and if I'm correct, you're not a mother at all. So I don't really need any advice from you."

Despite myself, I flinched and felt that spike of temper that suggested I was either going to stick my foot in my mouth or say something hotheaded I'd regret. However, I got the sense Becky needed some power after being on the receiving end of Ajay's phone call, so while I stayed direct, I kept that flash of temper in check. "I don't plan on speaking to you as a mother—I wouldn't dream of pretending—but unfortunately, I am a storeowner, and this afternoon I watched your daughter shoplift right in front of my eyes."

When Becky flinched, I saw it then—just a flash, but it was there. She believed me, and it looked like a painful realization.

"Mom, tomorrow I'm going to go to—" Dawn emerged from the hallway into the living room, halting in a way that suggested she'd been moving fairly quickly over the carpeted floor. Her eyes went wide as her gaze flicked between her mother, Watson, and me.

With Dawn standing behind her mother's shoulders, it hit me, as it had when they'd been in the bakery, that despite the age and weight difference, the two of them were literal carbon copies of each other.

Becky swiveled slightly to look toward her daughter. "Ms. Page says she witnessed you take something from her shop today."

Even the flush that rose to Dawn's cheeks was

similar to her mother's, and her expressions were almost painfully transparent as they shifted from panic to defiance. "That's a lie."

Becky surprised me when she took it a step further. "Can you bring it out here, please, whatever it was."

"Mom!" Dawn hissed through gritted teeth, casting her glare once more toward me. When Watson whimpered, she glanced down at him and gave an uncomfortable grimace.

"Do you really expect me to believe that Ms. Page would come out here and lie about—"

"Ananya took it." Dawn tilted her head back, shaking out her long red hair. "I'm just keeping it for her so—"

"Dawn..." Becky sounded exhausted. "Please, bring it to Ms. Page. You and I can talk about—"

"It's true." The fury-filled glare Dawn gave her mother made all the ones Britney had offered over the last several months seem like cotton-candied hugs. "I had to keep it for her. *You* know what Ananya's dad is like. He'd ground her for a month."

"I know." With that, Becky relented. "I understand. Please go get it. I won't tell Ajay that Ananya took it, promise." She glanced toward me. "Will you? If you get it back, can you please let it drop?"

I sat dumbstruck for several seconds, unsure what to do and rather disgusted by the whole display. Deciding to jump over it, I addressed Dawn directly. "That little silver coyote wasn't part of the store. It belongs to Ben, who works for me." I might not be a mother, but I could use a mothering tool if I saw the opportunity—guilt. "You know him, right? He was only a couple of years ahead of you in school. That little figurine is important to him."

"*I* never knew him." Dawn was completely unfazed by my attempt, but for some reason her mother caught her flash of ire instead of me.

"Just go get it, Dawn, okay?" Becky's exhaustion seemed to be increasing.

"Fine!" Dawn disappeared once more.

"I watched Dawn take the coyote from the counter and put it into her pocket. With my own two eyes." Maybe I should let it go, but I always struggled with lies.

Becky started to shake her head, but instead cast a quick glance over her shoulder to the empty hallway and then back to me, lowering her voice. "I've homeschooled Dawn her whole life until this year. She finally talked me into letting her go to the public high school. She felt like I was depriving her. She wanted to try cheerleading, go to prom, all the things. And..." She waved a tired hand. "Dawn fell in with Ananya and Britney almost immediately. I'm sure they are nice girls. But... Dawn was sheltered, and they've not been a good influence."

"Here." Dawn was back. She hurried across the room and thrust the coyote into my hand. "And please don't mention this to anyone. Like I said, Ananya's dad would be mean to her." Before I could challenge Dawn, remind her I'd seen *her* slip the little statue into her pocket, she bent and patted Watson's head. He didn't pull away, nor did he lean into her touch. *"You're* why Ananya stole that little corgi from the bakery to begin with. She thinks you're cute." Though her voice took on a cooing sound, there was a hint of anger in it. "So really, this whole thing is your fault, *dog*."

Before I could react, she stood and disappeared once more down the hallway.

"Winifred, can we be done?" Becky pulled my attention back to her. "I'm sorry that you had to come all the way out here. I'm sorry for any inconvenience, any rudeness you might perceive from Dawn or me. Things are just... very stressful right now. Teenage years are..." Choosing to search for words, in that moment she reminded me of Zelda's frequent overwhelmed state due to Britney. "Anyway, can you please keep this to yourself. You've got the silver wolf thing back. I don't want another call from Ajay. I don't want to hear about how Little Miss Ananya is the state of perfection while Dawn can never measure up."

At another time, I might've questioned her on that, or at least offered a different perspective, as Ajay had seemed plenty harsh to his daughter to me and compared her inadequacies to her better-behaved younger brother, much the way Becky was doing right now. Something about the interaction with Watson, the way Dawn had reminded me of running into the three girls at the intersection when I walked back from Aspen Gold... I glanced toward the silver coyote in my hand. It wasn't that far of a leap to consider. Dawn had more than proven she had sticky fingers and was attracted to sparkly or cute things.

"Thank you for your time, and I'm sorry to have bothered you." Knowing I only had one shot, though not a very good one, I decided to take my chance. I jumped over Becky's request about keeping secrets. "However, do you mind if I use a restroom? It's a long drive back, and I—"

"Sure." Becky cut me off abruptly, sounding more tired than rude, and flicked her hand down the hallway. "Second door on your left. It's kind of hard to lock, but don't worry about it, neither one of us will barge in."

"Thank you." As I stood, I slipped the silver coyote into the pocket of my skirt and headed toward the hallway. Thankfully, Watson didn't pull a sit-down strike and followed along. When I reached the doorway to the bathroom, I paused, looking back in time to see Becky pass from the living room into the kitchen. There were three more doors in the hallway. The first one I came to had been closed, maybe a laundry room? The others were open, one dark, but with the shadow of a large fourposter bed just visible. From what I could see through the crack of the lit room—a pink faux-fur rug and the edge of white bedspread—made me certain it was Dawn's room.

Not giving myself any more time to consider, as I might see a whole host of issues with my spur-of-the-moment plan, I dropped Watson's leash.

He looked up at me, and glanced at his leash laying on the carpet, then back up to me again.

I gestured toward the light coming from the partially open doorway.

He glanced there too, then back to me once more.

"Go." I whisper-hissed the plea. "Come on, sniff

around. In there."

That time, he didn't even bother glancing toward Dawn's room.

Even a heartbeat before I did it, I knew I was a horrible, horrible corgi-mama. "Go on." I gestured toward the room again. "Go sniff around for *treats*."

His foxlike ears seemed to go even straighter as his chocolate-brown eyes widened.

"Yeah!" I pointed again. "Go look for treats." I wasn't *exactly* promising he would find the manifestation of his favorite word in there. Merely suggesting. Yeah... Watson was never going to buy that argument. But I'd make up for it with plenty of treats as atonement.

He waddled slowly down the hall, pausing near enough that he was able to stick his nose just inside the room and sniff. Clearly not smelling anything edible, he looked back at me.

"Treats!" That one word was both a little evil and barely qualifying as a whisper. But it worked.

Watson disappeared inside.

I waited until the end of his leash had just entered the doorway before hurrying down the hall. I knocked in a way that the door opened from the force and stepped right in.

Dawn let out a little yip and whipped toward me

with startled eyes from where she sat on the bed, yanking out one of the white earbuds. "What do you—"

"Sorry." I pointed to the floor. "Watson wandered in."

As Dawn leaned over the bed to find my corgi, Watson shot a glare at me.

I'd apologize later. I'd make sacrifices of mounds and mounds of treats later, but for the moment, I looked away from him and scanned the room, almost certain what I'd find.

It didn't even take a full scan. The gold-and-crystal animals sat on the far bedside table, the lamplight causing the unicorn and chipmunk to sparkle.

Dawn followed my gaze, and for the first time, it took her a heartbeat to come up with a response, and she didn't look back at me until she had one. "I bought those."

As responses went, it was lackluster at best. "No, you didn't. I talked to the LaRues themselves. They were stolen, along with a lot of other things."

"No they weren't." There went that chin thrust and a shake of her long hair. "I bought them."

"Dawn, seriously?" I took a step forward. "Did you take the amethyst geode as well?"

"What's a geode?" Genuine confusion crossed

her face.

"Never mind." I didn't bother explaining, plus I couldn't imagine how the girl could've snuck the large stone out and not get caught. The thing had to have weighed twenty pounds or more. "You don't really expect me to believe the very same crystal animals—"

"What are you doing in here?" Becky entered the bedroom, her voice spiking.

"He gave them to me." Dawn shifted tactics, too caught up to worry about her mom entering. "It's not my fault if those old people were too busy arguing with that taffy lady to remember him giving them to me. I *didn't* steal them."

"Who gave you *what*?" Becky looked toward her daughter, but she halted at the two animals, instantly figuring it out. Maybe she hadn't been in Dawn's room in a couple of days or simply hadn't noticed them.

"What do you mean they were arguing with the taffy lady?" I pushed on before the inevitable happened, caught by another detail. "Who's the taffy —" I didn't even need to finish before it clicked. The old people were Vivian and Roger, of course. And the taffy lady was doubtlessly Dinah Zuckerman, who owned the saltwater taffy shop on the other side of Alakazam. "The LaRues were arguing with Dinah? Why? Did you hear?"

"You need to go, Winifred." Becky stepped between me and her daughter. "Now, or I'll call the police."

A little guilt bit at me for that, knowing I'd crossed the line walking into her daughter's bedroom, but it burned away easily enough when my temper returned. Though, considering, I managed to keep the threat out of my tone when I spoke. "Go ahead. And when you do, make sure you tell Detective Green to expect a call from me about those. Surely you heard about the robbery at Aspen Gold. Those two were among the missing items."

Becky paled, and all bravado fled with a whimper. "Just go. Please."

"He gave them to me!" Dawn shouted, full of fury, making Watson scurry to me.

There was more than anger at being caught in Dawn's tone, in her expression. "What do you mean? Who gave them to you?" Maybe I was being gullible to even indulge. "Julian? Did he—"

"Leave." Becky stepped between us. "You need to leave right now."

I was halfway back to Estes before my reception was strong enough to call Susan myself.

EIGHTEEN

At home—after making good on my penitence of treats—I finally curled up in front of the fire. Susan was going to handle Dawn and the crystal animals. As annoyed as she was, Susan and I exchanged info and tossed back and forth more questions and theories than we had answers.

Neither of us believed Dawn had stolen the other items from Aspen Gold and then kidnapped Julian. Maybe Julian really had given her those animals. If so, it all gave more credence to Julian being behind it all. I thought I believed Dawn, though she was far from reliable, trustworthy, or anything. Believable or not, she had the items in her possession, so maybe Vivian would come to terms now that the crystal animals' disappearance didn't have anything to do with her son.

As I knew he would be, Leo was working late on Chipmunk Mountain, and as I'd been spinning much of day around the ring and Julian, I decided to parse through some... emotions? Memories? Ear worms? ...of my own that had very little to do with the LaRues that I'd not given myself time to indulge in. So after retrieving a few things from the closet, I settled down in the overstuffed armchair by the fire in my living room.

With his belly full, Watson, proving that naps were just like treats and one could never get enough, curled up on the hearth and promptly began to snore.

So with the shadows of the forest gradually growing longer outside the windows, I sank into things I'd been dreading but knew I needed to sift through.

After the divorce, even with Garrett's cheating and the rough last years of our marriage, I hadn't been the type to set all of our memories on fire. I also hadn't been the type to fawn over them crying, so this occasion would be the first time the wedding album had been cracked open in a long, long time. I hadn't been sure which set of pictures I dreaded going through more—the wedding album or the stack of loose photos I'd received from my mother barely two weeks before. As they were the ones I started to parcel through, I supposed that answered the question of which I dreaded seeing the most, and that said something, didn't it? When the photos documenting over a decade of privacy invasion, being spied on, and used as a pawn to manipulate my mother were easier to look at than what had been promised, at the time, to be the happiest day of my life.

I looked at the picture that had been sent to my mom of Garrett and me coming out of a restaurant on the Plaza in Kansas City. They had captured us leaving the meal where he'd told me he wanted to divorce, where he confessed his infidelity. I studied myself for a bit. I looked younger, naturally, shell-shocked, numb, and maybe a bit relieved. Garrett looked hard, guarded, and also a little bit relieved. However, now I was looking at his face, he less resembled Julian than I'd thought. There was a similarity in that all-American male kind of way, but Julian was much more handsome than Garrett had been. More polished, more eye-catching. However, and maybe it was just because I knew Garrett so well, even in that picture I could see a confidence in Garrett I hadn't felt in Julian. The jewelers' son had been arrogant and maybe a bit pompous, but thinking back, it seemed a bit forced, as if he was trying to convince everyone and himself. That had never been a problem for Garrett. And despite how things ended with us, there was still a coldness I'd seen in Julian's eyes that Garrett never possessed.

There weren't many more of my ex-husband in the stack of those photos; the majority were stolen moments of me and Watson or other members of the family. Photos of Leo and me, many of those.

Perhaps it was unfair, given the circumstances, but I returned to the first photo of me and Garrett and compared it to one of Leo and me. Leo was holding open the door of the Cozy Corgi for Watson and me to walk through, so in that they were similar, both walking through doors. I studied Leo, studied Garrett. There was such a light that seemed to emanate from Leo, even in that grainy photo. He had strength and gentleness. That was lacking in Garrett's image. And again, I knew it wasn't a fair comparison—Garrett had literally just told me he wanted a divorce, of course he wasn't going to look light and bright. But had Garrett ever come close to the levels Leo possessed of those qualities?

It was that pondering that forced me to open the wedding album. I got caught on the very first page, the two of us, so young. While Garrett wasn't nearly as handsome as Julian, or Leo, for that matter, he was still handsome in his tux. And me? I barely recognized that girl, that young woman.

I ran a finger over my auburn hair I'd swept up into an elegant bun underneath the veil, then traced it down my gown. I'd forgotten. It was so long ago that I'd forgotten.

Ever since I was a child, I was the big girl, taller than all the rest, stronger than all the rest—not nearly as strong and thick as Susan Green, but still. I'd also been heavier than all the rest. My finger moved over my waist in the wedding gown. It was small, not model-thin, but small. I'd forgotten. I'd dieted for over six months for our wedding. Garrett told me how beautiful I'd looked and reminded me of that fact for years later when I stopped starving myself.

As I continued to trace over the photo, I came to the ring. A thin band of gold. No diamond, no etching, no hippos. Just a band of gold. While I had changed a lot over the years, I remembered how I'd felt when Garrett had proposed, cracked open the box, and there'd been no flash of diamond. I hadn't even noticed. I'd thought the ring was perfect.

I glanced back and forth between the photo of that ring and the diamond I had on, then between the photo of Garrett on our wedding day and the one of Leo and me leaving the Cozy Corgi. How did that make sense? How could the wrong man get me the right ring, and the right man give me a ring so, so wrong?

Ah... but I'd already figured that out, hadn't I? And part of the answer was in the stack of pictures on my lap. Another in the darkened windows of Shutterbug. The past weeks had been a torrent of revelations, peril, and death. They'd exposed how much danger had been around us, walking side by side with us, that we'd never realized. It was only natural to try to overcompensate for that.

It was a testament to how caught I was in the past and the emotions of the present that Watson's joyful barking didn't sink into my consciousness until the front door opened and Leo knelt, fawning over him.

He smiled over at me, stray corgi hairs floating up around him. "Hey. How'd it go with Dawn and her —" The diamond glinted, and he flinched. "You got it back. It wasn't stolen?"

"No." A flare of panic ignited as he stood and headed in my direction. I felt caught and had an impulse to slam the album shut and try to shove all the photos underneath the armchair, as if he wouldn't notice. Instead, I forced myself to stay exactly how I was. "The ring was at Aspen Gold the whole time. Vivian and Roger found it as they put the shop back together."

Leo bent to give me a kiss in greeting, then paused when he saw the pictures, the wedding album. Garrett. His honey-brown eyes flicked to me and held my gaze. "You okay?"

"Yes, of course." It rang hollow to my own ears, and I knew this was the time. We'd been so busy, and during the slow moments, I had pushed it off, for the past few days. But it was time. Where to start? With the ring being fake? Trying to assure Leo, even as I knew why he'd proposed the way he had? "I—"

"Fred, I—"

We both laughed as we spoke simultaneously and halted.

"Hold on." Leo flashed a quick smile, then darted, scooping a small footstool tucked beside the couch and then used it to sit beside the armchair. Watson squeezed in between us so he was pressed against both of our shins and rested his head on Leo's knee. After sparing him a quick glance, Leo reached for my hand, pausing. "May I?"

"Of course." I offered it to him, unsure what was about to happen.

Leo took it, turning it gently side to side. "The ring fits." He turned my hand again, then sighed—a sound almost like defeat, but when he spoke, I realized it was more of acceptance. "I planned on proposing to you at Prime Slice the other night."

I couldn't help it, I laughed. "You did propose." I twisted my hand in his grip, causing the diamond to flash. "Remember?"

He laughed as well. "Yeah, but I mean, I *planned* to propose, then we were there, and it..." He shrugged. "By the time you got back from the restroom, I decided to wait. Nothing about it was right, not the restaurant, not our moods..." He tilted my hand up. "Not this."

There was a heartbeat, maybe, where he expected me to protest, say everything was perfect. Or perhaps I imagined it and was projecting what my impulse was. Either way, I held my tongue.

"Then Julian blabbed about it, and..." Another shrug accompanied by a self-deprecating laugh. "Well, it wasn't like I could pretend that hadn't been the plan. It was clear you'd already figured it out anyway. It's not like you're an idiot."

"I didn't actually figure it out until I was in the bathroom." Already, with the two of us talking by the fire, just the speaking of truth on both of our sides, relief began to settle over me. "Although I think I was intentionally not figuring it out before then."

"I can't blame you." He continued to hold my hand but shifted where it wasn't so he could examine the ring, but simply keep contact. "I don't regret proposing. And I don't even regret when I proposed, only how, and where, and... with what." He gave a little eye roll. "That sounds crazy."

"No, I think I understand." With my free hand, I held up the stack of photos that had been used to torment my mother for nearly a decade, thought to the stores on Elkhorn, empty due to murder or arrest. "It's been a stressful few weeks."

"Yeah." We grew silent as he stared at the photos, a slight twitching throbbing in his jaw. I could tell there was more he wanted to say, so I stayed still, letting him pick his words. Finally, he met my gaze again and spoke with a soft clarity. "Branson taunting us at the Cozy Corgi that night. Saying the things he did about me not marrying you yet, things about our history, with him, with... everything." Leo released my hand and took the stack of pictures, giving them a shake. "The knowledge that everything could be taken away from us at any time, that no tomorrow is promised, as if I needed more proof." He put the photos back in my lap and held my gaze once more, looking deep. "There's not been any question in my mind that I want to spend my life with you,

you know that. I have loved you from the second I saw you, before it made any rhyme or reason to. Things are so good between us that I wasn't in a hurry. It's not like either of us felt we had to lock this thing down or one of us would walk away. But I also wanted to make it perfect, wait for the exact moment, do it in the right, most romantic way, and then... Branson. The Irons family. The..." He shook his head and finished with another laugh. "Well. With all that, I did it the exact wrong moment, and the exact wrong way, and in the exact wrong place for either of us."

There was comfort in his confession, as it was exactly what I figured had prompted the proposal in the way it had been done. But I didn't need to say that. "Leo, I understand. Like we've already said, it doesn't matter if the proposal was perfect. Whether it was done in the right place, interrupted, or not. The point is we're getting married, we *are* spending our lives together."

"True." His tone indicated he wasn't finished, and he tapped the diamond. "I knew this wasn't right, either. I thought maybe when it fit correctly, but..." He wrinkled his nose. "No, that's not true, either. I knew the minute you put it on that night." Another laugh. "No, *that's* not true, either. I knew the second I walked out of Aspen Gold it was the wrong ring. I didn't go in there planning on buying a big diamond, you're not a diamond type of woman, and I'm not a diamond-buying type of guy."

I didn't know it was possible to fall more in love with Leo Lopez, but yet, time after time after time he found a way to make me sink a little deeper in that seemingly endless well of love.

Before I could find the words to say that, he continued. "But then, I walked in there, barely got out that I was looking for an engagement ring when Julian showed me *that*"—he gestured toward the diamond—"that Fifth-Avenue tower-monstrosity type of thing, and I got... carried away. Maybe because of Branson and the Irons family, or maybe some deep Americanized male belief that we are told we have to buy the biggest and the best diamond to earn love or some such trash." One of his hands dropped and started stroking Watson. I didn't think he even realized. "And when I found out I could afford it, I said yes without thinking through the whole thing right then. I hadn't planned on proposing to you that night, before that very moment, hadn't planned on Prime Slice. I'd been hoping to... I don't know, something else, but then it just all... snowballed."

"I love you, Leo." For the first time in days, a fog seemed to lift. Even though I thought I'd figured out why the proposal and the ring had been what they were, it was such a relief to hear him confirm it. Further and further affirmation of the man he was, of the man I knew him to be, and of the relationship the two of us had. "I love us together. I love us apart too, but even more so together. And I love that you're both human enough to make this mistake and strong enough to not only realize it but talk about it."

"Thank you for not protesting, trying to convince me right now that you love that ring or that Prime Slice was your dream proposal." He grinned and cocked an eyebrow. "Do you mind if we get you a different engagement ring? I kind of hate that one."

I laughed so hard Watson flinched but stayed where he was. "Dear Lord. Yes please."

He beamed. "Unfortunately, one with hippos has already been called. So... no hippos, or cupcakes, for that matter."

"Believe me, Katie's ring is perfect, for *her*. No hippos for me." Another thought entered, and I tried to bite my tongue, trying to tell myself to be quiet, but didn't succeed. "And... no corgis for me either, not on my ring. Not about us."

"I know that." He lifted up off the footstool and

kissed me. "You're more than the woman who owns the Cozy Corgi, and we—as much as we love him, we are more than Watson's mom and dad." He hesitated a moment. "Do you mind if I pick out the new engagement ring? Or, after that paperweight on your finger, would you like to do it together?"

"Toge—" I stopped myself, a little surprised at the flash of disappointment that shot through me as I started that word, so I adjusted. "Actually... I'd like you to do it. Surprise me."

"You got it." When you love someone so much and see them day after day, sometimes you forget how beautiful they are, as you grow accustomed to their face. But Leo's smile radiated such that there was no denying how handsome my fiancé was, or how the light from his soul lit up everything around him.

"There's one more thing." I slid the ring off and held it up to him. "I don't know what you paid for this diamond, but it was way too much. It's fake. No solid proof yet, but I'm sure there's going to be. Julian had been switching out some gems and such from the residents' jewelry from Aspen Grove. He's a swindler. Unless you're a multimillionaire and haven't told me, there's no way you could've afforded the actual price of a diamond this size. So however much you paid for it believing it was real, I'm certain it was way more than the cubic zirconium is worth."

"You know, I was blown away by the price of it, but I didn't really consider it being fake. It's Aspen Gold, the reputation is solid. I guess... like I said, Julian was so excited for us, and we were both so caught up in the moment. I... well, I don't know what I thought. And then after—" He gave me an ironic grin. "—whether that diamond was real or not was the least of my concerns. I've been much more weighed down about that disastrous proposal, and that the ring was about the worst ring imaginable for Winifred Page—real, fake, or otherwise."

"Maybe they will give you your money back." I winced. "Although, I'm not exactly Vivian and Roger's favorite person right now, so... we might want to wait before we ask."

The second dirty chai of the morning was halfway gone, and the Cozy Corgi's doors had barely opened, allowing the breakfast rush to begin, when Susan called. Channeling her energy, I jumped right into the conversation after hitting Accept, skipping over any form of greeting. "What did you find out when you spoke to the Ericksons? You don't think Dawn has any more involvement than those animals, do you? And you think Julian gave them to her?"

"No, I don't think Dawn has any more involvement than those animals." Proving that skipping formalities was Susan's preferred method of communication, she jumped in seamlessly without an ounce of offense. "As far as Julian giving them to her... maybe."

"Maybe?"

"That's what I said." Susan growled but continued. "Dawn *claims* Julian saw her admiring them and actually nudged them toward her, that he started to tell her she could have them but then began arguing with his parents, who were in the back room. Stupid animals. I swear, the trash tourists waste their money on is beyond me."

"*Started* to tell her she could have them?" I didn't try to keep the skepticism from my tone. "I'm not sure how she would know what Julian started to say. But... I think it's a toss-up. Dawn's already proven she'd steal, but if Julian was midargument, from things we're learning about him, I think I can see him offering them to her out of spite."

"Yeah." Susan grunted. "I wouldn't trust that girl as far as I could throw her. She's a no good..." She sighed. "Actually, Dawn's real problem is that Becky needs to decide if she's the mother or not. It was painful to watch the two of them together. Reminds me of my own parents with Mark. Always had them wrapped around his little finger. He'd get away with murder and..."

When Susan trailed off, I glanced at the screen of the cell phone to make sure the call hadn't been disconnected, though I was fairly certain it hadn't been. I actually felt her annoyance grow through the phone line, though I hadn't the faintest idea what I'd done to prompt that abrupt switch. "You okay?"

"How do you do that?" Sure enough, when she spoke again, Susan's tone was full-on exasperated.

"Do what?"

"Well." Susan gave a frustrated chuckle. "I guess *that's* how you're able to wheedle so much out of people without them realizing it. *I* called *you*, and all of a sudden started talking about family drama." She pushed on before I could begin to think of a response to that. "And that's exactly why I'm calling you. I need you to put that skill to work on Dinah Zuckerman. *Quickly.*"

It was a good thing I hadn't taken a sip of the dirty chai or I might've choked. I didn't think I'd mentioned the taffy lady's name to Susan when we spoke the night before. Not intentionally, she'd merely slipped my mind after discovering the stolen crystal animals. "Really?"

"Yep. I just received an interesting call from her, saying the exact same thing the residents of Aspen Grove claim about their jewelry. I'd like to talk to her myself, but things have sort of exploded on our end, and I want her questioned before word gets out."

"Before word gets out on what?" My curiosity couldn't help itself.

To my surprise, prodding didn't seem to annoy Susan further. "I'll tell you as soon as you talk to Dinah. I don't want what we found out to influence your perception of her, either."

Stranger and stranger. "Okay. I'll go right now."

"Great. Take fleabag. Milton is a dog lover, so Watson might help."

Susan, of course, didn't bother with thanks, and sounded like she'd been about to hang up when she remembered something. "Oh, and Fred, go the back way or something. All of this quite literally just happened, but knowing Estes Park, Carl and Anna probably already know. And I really do want your take on Dinah uninfluenced."

She was gone before I could ask any follow-up questions. From my spot on the stool at the espresso bar, I looked down toward Cabin and Hearth. Though there was a morning glare on the windows, I thought I could see Carl moving about. Susan wasn't wrong, they did have the superpower of gossip.

Since Katie and Nick were elbow-deep in the breakfast rush, I darted behind the bakery counter, retrieved a to-go cup, and transferred in the remaining half of my dirty chai—waste not, want not, especially where caffeine was concerned. With the to-go cup in one hand and Watson's leash in the other, we exited through the back door. The river walk that ran parallel to Elkhorn Avenue was mostly free of tourists wandering over cobblestones that meandered through groves of pines and aspens.

As we continued after passing over Moraine Avenue, Watson offered a couple of compulsory barks at a small herd of elk grazing on the riverbank. Doubtlessly, within half an hour, they'd be wandering down the middle of Elkhorn Avenue, partaking in a sampling of the flowering planters for dessert. After a tug or two, Watson caught up with me.

At the base of a large hill—or what would've been a small mountain in most places—we reached the end of the row of shops on the south side and crossed back over Elkhorn Avenue, then darted past the waterwheel. Susan's advice had been spot-on, and not only because of the Hansons. With the detour, Watson and I had avoided walking past Aspen Gold. While I was certain I was the last person they ever wanted to see again, I might not have the willpower to refrain from darting inside and truly confronting them about the fake diamond their son sold to Leo. Likewise, I dashed past Alakazam, not wanting to run into Mark Green or his fairy assistant, as charming as I found Glinda. Without pausing to appreciate the cute window display, Watson and I slid in through the door of Taffy Lane.

Even in the rush of being on a covert mission, I couldn't help but appreciate the charm of the candy store, despite the fact I'd been in many times before. And though I hadn't glanced from outside, at the gentle mechanical whirling sound, I turned, momentarily mesmerized at the old mint-green saltwater-taffy-pulling machine, it's two sets of hooks whirling between each other, twisting a thick, pearlescent rope of baby blue taffy. Watson, too, stared up at the machine, watching the hypnotic weaving.

"Welcome to Taffy Lane." A female voice pulled our attention back into the shop, and Dinah halted when she recognized us. Though not unkind, both her expression and her tone shifted from the standard we all used with tourists to something a little less bubbly. "Oh, Winifred." I'd had enough interaction with Dinah, having bought candy at her and her husband's shop for my nieces and nephews, and mingling at city events, that I wasn't surprised when she was as quick as ever. "Let me guess, Detective Green didn't find my complaint valid enough to send an officer?" Her eyes narrowed, but she smiled. "No offense to you." Her gaze flicked to Watson, and then she ushered me in farther. "Although, if you don't mind moving away from the taffy machine, I'd rather not have to put dog hair in the ingredient list for our blue raspberry flavor."

"Oh, sorry!" We hurried away, and with all the smells catching his attention, Watson didn't fight against me at all as we weaved through the meandering trails of the shop. Unlike with Aspen Gold sharing one crooked wall with Alakazam, Taffy Lane somehow shared two, both of them jutting off at weird angles. It worked well with the décor, however. The Zuckermans incorporated the frequent 1960s styling of Estes Park, this time lifting directly from the game Candyland. The hardwood floors had been painted with paths of alternating blue, green, pink, orange, black, and yellow squares—scuffed with age—which made it feel like a person was walking along the game board. Old painted wooden signs hung above various sections in the shop, labeled Peppermint Stick Forest, Gumdrop Mountain, Lollipop Woods, Macaroon Meadow, Fudge Village, and of course, Taffy Lane, amongst others. It was a complete mashup of retro pinks, greens, and browns blended with the old-time candy shop finishes of glass counters, flashing colorful lights, and brass accents. While my bookshop and bakery might be the coziest place downtown, Taffy Lane competed for the happiest.

Unlike her shop, Dinah didn't feel all that happy. "I heard you were looking into Julian's getaway." She marched nearer, approaching the counter, which had small old-fashioned toys in little cardboard boxes for sale beside the cash register. "And I don't mind telling you the same as I told the police. I've held my tongue long enough. At this point, I'll tell anyone who asks."

Making sure to keep a tight grip on Watson's leash as if he might sneak away without my noticing —there was no doubt that he would overdose on sugar within three minutes—I leaned my hip against the counter, a comfortable distance away from Dinah. "I can't help but notice you said his getaway as opposed to his kidnapping."

The older woman snorted in disgust. "Please. That weasel had this planned since the day he arrived months ago." She smiled in a sarcastic way as I apparently pulled a face. "Oh don't be shocked at how I speak about him. If you knew Julian at all, you'd describe him in the exact same way. And like I said, I'm done holding my tongue. I tried to get Roger and Vivian to toss him out on his ear the minute I heard he was arriving. I knew exactly what was going to happen."

I was a little taken aback. "I guess I've heard some unfriendly things about him, but nothing quite as adamant as all of that." I considered for a heartbeat, and then instead of questioning why she called the police, decided on simply following Dinah's lead. "How did you know what would happen before he even arrived? Did you already know Julian?"

"Trust me on this. The LaRues have been Milton's and my close friends nearly since they moved here years and years ago. Actually, I'd say they're best friends—we both tend to be a little intentionally isolated, at least until Julian arrived." More disgust filled her features, but instead of anger, her voice took on a sympathetic quality as she leaned nearer and tapped on the countertop. "They've always been careful about what they said about their son. But it was easy enough to read between the lines. Julian was spoiled rotten, indulged, and treated with kid gloves." Dinah was on a roll and didn't require any prompting from me in the slightest. "I think Roger is a little more open to the realities of Julian, but to Vivian, he hung the moon, and she sees him as a victim. No matter what trouble he got into, it was *always* someone else's fault. Always." Dinah gave a little laugh. "I learned quickly to hold my tongue, as the first time I pointed out that possibly the common denominator in all of Julian's suffering was Julian himself, it nearly cost us our friendship. I didn't see the harm in keeping silent, *until* he moved back here and began working at his parents' shop."

Dawn's claim came back to me from the night before, that she'd been given—or stolen—the crystals while Julian and his parents argued about the taffy lady. "Did you confront Julian?"

"Not until recently. Just in the past week or so, in fact, and only a couple of times. Though they didn't end well. He basically called me trash and made some... well... derogatory remarks about us being Jewish." Dinah reached across the counter, pulling a yellow-and-orange-striped hard candy stick from a holder, unwrapping it absentmindedly as she spoke. "Before then, I was gently—" She gave a little laugh. "—sometimes not so gently, trying to get Vivian to see the light about how Julian was merely here to use them, to take advantage. Milton told me to hold my tongue, that we were going to lose our friends. But... what kind of friend would I be..." She let a shrug finish the statement for her.

I finally understood. The argument I'd overheard between Julian and his parents hadn't been over a girl they wanted him to date. It had been over Dinah Zuckerman. Calling his parents crazy that they would give anything she said a moment's credence. And them saying that he believed she wasn't good enough for him. Had the last part really been about Dinah's heritage? "Julian actually said horrible things about you being Jewish?"

"That's what I mean." Dinah had put the candy stick in her mouth and spoke around it. "He didn't learn that from his parents. Vivian and Roger are very accepting. They even participate in our Passover Seder with us on occasion. But... Julian... a complete bigot, and a self-serving manipulative one at that."

I halted. It wasn't that I didn't believe Dinah, it just clashed with what I'd heard from Delilah and Alessandra, what I'd witnessed from the LaRues themselves. As was so often the case, even after a momentary debate, I opted on the side of oversharing. Despite what Vivian and Roger wished, it didn't really seem like it was all that big of a secret anyway. "From what I've gathered, it sounds like Julian was actually the recipient of his parents' bigotry. They kept pressuring him to—"

"Yes." Dinah pulled the candy stick out of her mouth that time, giving it a little shake. "You're not wrong. And I've spoken to them about that, so has Milton. Why, our own Rebecca is a..." Her lips move soundlessly, and I could see her searching. "Well, she and Kelly were married three years ago. It wasn't easy for us to come to terms with, but you do what you must when you love your children. That was the only area I took up for Julian, but it doesn't excuse what he does to his parents." Dinah shook the candy stick again, then pointed at me as if I'd dared to argue with her. "Plus, that man is in his forties. It isn't like he is a closeted thirteen-year-old child anymore. *He* is responsible for his choices. *He* is the one who needs to stand up to his parents about who he is. Besides, he wasn't really worried about what they thought. He simply wanted to stay in their good graces for money and for new chances to swindle them."

While I'd always liked Dinah Zuckerman in an abstract-acquaintance kind of manner, I decided that in a lot of ways the two of us were kindred spirits. I suspected she wouldn't flinch twice at a bomb throwing, so I tossed one. "Why is Vivian ordained, and has she spoken to you about why Aspen Gold is registered as a church?"

"A *church*? And Vivian—a *minister*?" Diana laughed as if that was the most ridiculous thing she'd ever heard. The laughter cut off abruptly, and once more she proved she was razor-sharp. "Julian." She stuck the candy stick back in her mouth, that time biting off a hunk with a loud crunch. "Like I said, a weasel."

"You think he did that in his mother's name, behind her back?" The notion settled easily in my gut. "Why?"

She shrugged. "Money, what else? That's always what he wanted." After a few more crunches, her teeth clenched. "I really didn't want this to be a case of *I told you so* with them. This is going to break their hearts, but—" She accentuated the word by gesturing with what remained of the candy stick once more. "—it'll be worth it if it gets them to open their eyes and quit being taken advantage of. Hopefully, they won't believe whatever crazy story Julian concocts the next time he rolls into town—the thieving little weasel."

I experienced another realization then, though it was fairly obvious, given the accusations from Aspen Grove. "Did Julian steal from you? Is that why you called Su—Detective Green?"

"We can call her Susan. I've known that vinegar-filled girl since she was knee-high to a grasshopper." Dinah went icy cold. "And you tell me... taking a diamond worth thirty-five thousand dollars, does *that* qualify as stealing?"

Though I'd finished the dirty chai on the walk up and disposed of the to-go cup, I choked. "Thirty-five thou—" I glanced down to my ring finger, which was bare. After Leo's and my conversation the night before, he'd taken it with him. Though, surely not. That didn't make any sense. I forced my gaze back up to Dinah. "What do you mean?"

"What I mean is, poor little Julian LaRue switched my diamond when I took it in for cleaning and to make sure the prongs were secure—I do it every three months like clockwork, required by insurance—for a fake cubic zirconia rock, as if I wouldn't notice." Her eyes turned to fire. "I had my suspicion when I picked it up, mainly because he seemed a little too pleased with himself." She made a fluttering gesture with her hand. "Plus, something looked a little off about it, but I didn't quite let myself go there. Not until I heard he'd hightailed it out of town." She scowled. "Oh, *excuse me*, I mean was *kidnapped*." She finished with an eye roll and then continued. "I took it to Denver. I get ninety-nine percent of my jewelry from Vivian and Roger, but there's a jeweler I trust in the valley as well. I received confirmation this morning. It's a fake. I called the police, and"—another gesture toward me, going so far as to encompass Watson at my feet—"you two show up not twenty minutes later."

Though it didn't make any sense, I knew. Or maybe I was just catastrophizing and was wrong, but I didn't think so. "When did you take it into Aspen Gold?"

"Five days ago." Dinah didn't even have to think. "That little weasel had it for about three hours. Clearly, he planned it from when he'd cleaned it the first time as the replica was identical."

I pulled out my phone, opened the pictures, and scrolled to the one of the ring—I'd sent it to Percival and Gary upon request when they'd been at the convention—then angled it toward Dinah. "Did it look like this one?"

She leaned nearer, narrowing her brown eyes. "Yes. I can't swear that's the same one, of course—it's a standard cut. Nothing unusual about it except its size and quality. But... yes." Sharp again, that gaze flicked toward my bare hand, then rose to meet my eyes. "I heard you got a large engagement ring. When?"

My cheeks heated in embarrassment, though I'd

done nothing wrong. "Leo bought it five days ago from Aspen Gold, from Julian, but he didn't pay thirty-five thousand. He actually said it was shockingly cheap. We realized last night it was a fake, of course. And that I'm—" For once I managed to not stick my foot in my mouth about me proclaiming to not be the diamond type of gal and somehow insulting Dinah.

"He's worse than I imagined. So much more despicable than just doing it for the money. That little weasel thought he would really get it over on me. Pay me back for trying to turn his parents against him, no doubt." I didn't think I'd ever seen a smile so filled with hate before. "Probably thought I wouldn't realize mine was fake, all the while you're wearing *my* diamond around town."

"Really? You think Julian would do that?" I rushed ahead, realizing how that sounded. "I mean, be petty enough to waste making thirty-five thousand off you?"

That smile increased. "Oh yes. I completely do. And it's not like he didn't have countless other diamonds at his disposal that he could switch out and steal. Thirty-five grand is just a drop in the bucket if he'd been playing his cards right."

I was fortunate enough due to events that as long

as *I* played *my* cards right, the Cozy Corgi and myself would be okay, but couldn't fathom the idea of thirty-five thousand being a drop in the bucket of anything, but... though it didn't make sense to the way I saw the world, Dinah's theory felt right.

The door to Taffy Lane opened, making us whirl toward the sound.

Glinda was short enough, that for a moment we didn't see her past one of the large treelike displays making up Peppermint Stick Forest, but then she came into view, shimmery pink wings fluttering behind her with her speed. "Dinah, did you hear? The wizard just informed me that—" She halted with a blink, then smiled as Watson trotted happily toward her. "Oh, hello, sweet boy." She knelt, her earthy green-and-brown gown billowing around her. "I'm sorry, I don't have anything special for you. But come over to Alakazam when you leave. I'll get you one of the doggy treats we keep."

Watson whimpered at his favorite word.

Glinda simply cooed and patted his head.

"Glinda..." Dinah prompted, sounding a little amused, a response making it clear this wasn't an uncommon occurrence from the fairy who occupied the other side of the wall. "What tidbit did you discover from your wizard?"

"Oh!" Glinda flinched and stood abruptly. "Oh yes!" She sidestepped Watson, who followed quickly on her heels as she joined me by the counter, lowering her voice to a breathy whisper. "They just discovered Julian LaRue's body. Apparently, he drove his car right into Grand Lake."

Leaving Taffy Lane, I was so wrapped up in Glinda's news of the discovery of Julian's body, I completely forgot I was supposed to go the back way and walked directly down Elkhorn. At first, Watson struggled to return to the candy store after the undelivered promised treat, but once we were past the waterwheel, he changed directions, practically dragging me back toward the Cozy Corgi. Even with him yanking on my arm, I managed to hit Susan's name on the speed dial twice. Neither time did she answer. Not too surprising. Doubtlessly, she'd already known about Julian's fate when she called me and that had been the news she hadn't wanted to share yet.

In proof that miracles truly did happen, despite my lacking effort to remain covert, no storeowners rushed out as I passed their windows to try to wrangle gossip from me. As I approached Madame

Delilah's Old Tyme Photography, I realized what I was doing and halted as Cabin and Hearth came into view. There was no doubt that either Anna or Carl would see me, and if Glinda knew, the Hansons *definitely* did and there would be no avoiding them. Just as I was going to force Watson to jaywalk at a rushed angle to dart inside the bookshop, I recognized the figure approaching from the opposite direction.

Shelly Patel didn't notice us, but from her stride, she too looked to be on a mission. With a quick turn, she opened the door and stepped into the pet shop.

I debated for possibly the entire length of half of a heartbeat—Susan wasn't answering, perhaps the fire department had details around Julian being discovered in Grand Lake. For the first time, I abandoned any pretense of pride and bent so I could crouch walk in front of the windows of Cabin and Hearth, dragging a thoroughly offended Watson behind me. The miracle held out, as neither Carl nor Anna burst out the doors to not only demand answers but berate me for trying to avoid them.

Watson's glare as we entered Paws, and Flotsam and Jetsam letting out howls of delight and rushing toward him from where they'd been greeting Shelly, made up for any unpleasantness which we'd avoided from the Hansons. They crashed into Watson before he had a chance to even snarl—licking, nuzzling, and nipping my grumpy little man, in a practical tornado of corgi hair.

Paulie clapped in happiness and beamed at Shelly and me in turn. "Aren't they just the cutest? So full of life and joy!"

Shelly smiled at the tumble of corgis but took a few steps back, bumping her hip against the counter in her effort to avoid getting covered in hair.

Over it all, the sound of parakeet screeching, canaries chirping, chipmunk wheels spinning, and fish tank filtration motors humming added to the cacophony of barks and yips.

Watson burst free of the tangle, snarling and looking like a short-legged tiger emerging from a swarm of wildebeests. He barreled toward me, darting in one smooth motion beneath my skirt, bumping against my leg so hard I nearly fell.

Proving that it was neither of our first rodeos, I bent halfway, just in time to stretch out both hands to catch the two pursuing corgis before they used my skirt as a circus tent. "Breathe, boys, breathe."

Both the tricolor and the redhead with markings almost identical to Watson's shifted their attention onto me, lavishing my hands and arms nearly up to my elbows with licks and nose nudges.

Finally coming to the rescue, Paulie slid one hand through each of their collars, pulling Flotsam and Jetsam off me. Nonplussed, they merely swiveled, lavishing their affection on Paulie's arms instead of mine.

"Goodness. Just watching that made me tired." Shelly let out a breathless laugh. "And here I thought raising two teenagers was a challenge."

I flashed a quick smile but focused on Paulie. "Treats for all three of them, please. Quickly."

"Good idea." He sprang up, and though he released his boys, they stayed by his side as he grabbed three long beef-jerky-style sticks from the open container beside the cash register, giving one each to Flotsam and Jetsam, and then shoving the third underneath my skirt.

Shelly went a little bug-eyed at that and covered her mouth as she giggled.

Paulie didn't notice, and I could feel his hand brush my boot as he patted Watson's head when delivering the treat. After a second longer, he stood, looking thoroughly enamored of the whole situation. "All that was an unexpectedly fun way to start the morning. As good as coffee. Better, I'd say."

"I'd have to disagree with you there." Although it definitely worked just as well getting the heart rate going, I'd pick caffeine any day over Flotsam and Jetsam.

Still smiling, Paulie looked back and forth between the two of us. "Well, Shelly, you were here first, so I guess I should help you before Fred." He narrowed his eyes. "Although, I didn't remember your family having a pet." Those narrowed eyes were wide once more, and he gasped. "Oh no, are you here to arrest me because I set Prime Slice on fire?"

Shelly laughed again, louder that time. "Not hardly. And I'm the fire chief, remember, not Susan. I'm not here to arrest anybody. However... it is regarding Prime Slice." She spared me a glance. "Knowing you as I do, I'm certain you'll find out anyway, so you might as well hear from the source."

I was speechless for just a second, as I expected both of them to pounce on me with questions about Julian. Maybe gossip hadn't traveled quite as far and as fast as I'd suspected. I decided to go with it, as clearly I'd been wrong about Shelly having details, but was curious what she was going to say to Paulie. "When you're right, you're right, Shelly."

"Well..." She suddenly looked like she was reconsidering. "This really only concerns Paulie and

Campbell, but..." She reconsidered once more and shrugged it off. "Well, like I said, it's you. Winifred Page knows everything anyway."

Thank goodness for small towns. Instead of commenting, I simply smiled in encouragement.

Shelly refocused on Paulie. "I wanted you to know as soon as possible. I hate that you've been worried this was somehow going to get you in trouble." She reached out a hand to squeeze Paulie's shoulder, clearly experiencing that protective impulse that Paulie seemed to elicit in people. "None of the fire was your fault."

Paulie blinked, looking thoroughly unconvinced, and in the momentary silence, the gnawing of the three dogs chewing on their beef jerky sticks filled the void. "But... Campbell and I were playing swords and that flaming piece of meat—"

"It was only a matter of time," Shelly cut him off. "The place was a powder keg simply waiting for a spark. Honestly, it's nothing short of miraculous that it hadn't happened a million times over by now. The walls were practically drenched in lighter fluid."

"Lighter fluid?" I gaped at her. "It was intentional?"

"Tom Colter has been pouring a little bit more

on each and every day," Shelly confirmed. "It's a testament to good ventilation and the aroma of all the meat, seasonings, and spices that the place didn't reek to high heaven."

"That can't be right." Paulie scowled. "Why would the owner want to burn down his own restaurant?"

"Insurance." Why else? I couldn't help but recall Alessandra's impression of the man, and I shook my head at Shelly in disbelief. "So... Tom was just waiting for one of the customers to accidentally ignite it on fire. It was a setup."

"Exactly right." She nodded.

"Insurance?" Paulie still sounded full of disbelief. "He could've killed someone doing it like that."

"I don't think Tom even considered that. All he saw was dollar signs, and he's lived a rather charmed life. I doubt he thought for a moment he'd get caught or that his actions could harm anyone, burn down half the national park, or Lord knows what else."

That was brazen. "He actually admitted it?"

Shelly turned back to me, eyes twinkling with pride and humor. "Susan Green isn't the only one who can interrogate."

I couldn't help but laugh. "That is impressive."

She addressed Paulie once again. "Anyway, I wanted to tell you in person—you don't have anything to worry about."

"Thank God." The weight off Paulie's shoulders was obvious, and he slid to the floor, letting his back rest against the counter. Sitting between his two corgis, he began to stroke both of their backs as they took the final bites of their treats. "Still, I hate that Campbell and I were the ones who set the fire for him."

"You're... not..." Shelly paused, peering at both of us once more, clearly debating how much of an overshare to give into. When she finally shrugged, I could practically hear her thoughts of, *Well, they're going to know it all soon enough anyway.* "Julian lit the match."

"What?" *That* I hadn't been expecting. Even though the theory had been mentioned when I'd spoken to Delilah and Alessandra. "Julian?"

Shelly nodded. "We assume it was moments after Paulie and Campbell gave their impromptu sword fight. Unintentionally offering a distraction." She held out a hand to Paulie when he made a lamenting sound. "Still not your fault, so you just stop that!" When he nodded, Shelly continued, focusing more on me. "It was planned that night already. Maybe Tom is placing more blame on Julian than is warranted, since he's not here to defend himself, but... I don't think so. Julian was recently added as a partial owner of Prime Slice. So, he would benefit."

"Tom made Julian part owner of his restaurant?" I gaped at her. "I'd not heard of any connection between Julian and Tom."

"Well... it seems Tom and he were occasional..." She cleared her throat.

Paulie blinked in confusion.

I thought I understood. "They were having an affair?"

"Tom didn't specify, only Julian was holding some dirt over his head, and partial ownership was the price."

"Blackmail." I hadn't meant to speak but breathed out the word.

Shelly nodded. "An affair is only my guess... reading between the lines." Her eyes narrowed. "And you *didn't* hear that from me. I serve on the PTA with his wife, so..."

That time, Paulie and I exchanged glances.

Shelly continued with another clearing of her

throat. "*Anyway*... Tom says Julian came up with the scheme well over a month ago when Tom spoke about wanting to update and remodel but couldn't afford all he dreamed of doing. He claims Julian thought of the gradual soaking of the walls. Suggested that if Tom did it slowly enough, people wouldn't notice, that Tom would get away with it if he did it right in front of people's faces."

"In front of people's faces?" I glanced down at my bare ring finger.

Shelly didn't follow my train of thought and only nodded. "Yeah. I guess it's that frog in the hot pot scenario, or maybe the adage of the best hiding place is in plain sight... something like that. Either way, Tom claims it was Julian's plan. He admits he gradually soaked the wall, but swears Julian lit the match. As if those details matter when they were both in on it."

"It matters that it wasn't Campbell or me." Paulie sighed in relief again.

I felt bad that I hadn't realized how worried Paulie had been. For everything he'd been through, the man retained an innocence that was both endearing and admirable. I supposed that was what made so many of us feel protective of him.

Feeling my attention, Paulie looked up at me.

"And was there something I could help you with? I'm sorry to have kept you waiting, Fred."

Suddenly, I realized it was my turn to announce why I was there, and I didn't have a good reason anymore. I didn't want to be the one to spread word about Julian's death. It would only invoke Susan's ire. Instead, I used Watson as my go-to excuse. "There's no rush, but I thought I'd get some of the expensive buffalo jerky that Zelda and Verona used to have for Watson sometimes. He's been pretty patient through a lot of things the past few days, so I thought a special trea—something special is called for."

"Oh sure." Paulie motioned toward a display near Shelly. "Grab what you want. It's on the house."

"It most definitely isn't, but thank you." I smiled at him, then lifted the hem of my skirt to peer at Watson. "You're about to lose your hiding spot." Proving me wrong, he shuffled between my feet as I walked over to the display and picked out a couple of bags.

Shelly giggled again, shaking her head at Watson's antics, then paused to reach out and grab my hand. "Where's your ring? I swear that was the most gorgeous diamond I've ever seen."

"Oh! It's—" I wasn't sure what to say about that, either. Both in terms of how it might affect the case against Julian, or if it would impact Vivian and Roger, as I doubted they'd been aware of the switch, not to mention Dinah's privacy. I decided to skip over it entirely by offering the other aspect, as it was just as true. "Leo and I talked last night. It's funny, neither one of us feel like it's the right ring. Leo had the chance to buy it and was kind of overwhelmed but regretted it pretty quickly. We're not exactly big-diamond type of people."

Shelly bugged her eyes out. "You and I are *very* different women." She grinned, but the smile turned a little... something... sad, maybe? She lifted a hand, pulling out a chain around her neck so the silver pendant emerged from the collar of her blouse. "*I* was hoping for a diamond for our twenty-fifth, not the size of yours, of course, just a small thing in a gold locket I'd thought I'd dropped more than enough hints over, the kind I could put a picture of the kids on each side." She pulled the chain to its length so I could see. "But this is real silver and the initial of our last name."

I leaned in, inspecting the shiny capital *P* at the end of the silver chain. "It's beautiful. And looks good-quality, not that I know much about jewelry. I like how thick it is."

Paulie had stood and leaned in as well. "Oh!

That is nice. And the braiding of the chain is very delicate."

"I guess you're right." Though I doubted she could see it from her angle, Shelly peered down with a growing smile, as if seeing it in a new light. She gave an embarrassed laugh. "*Hopefully*, I didn't let my disappointment show. I don't want to be ungracious. And as Ajay pointed out when I opened the box, silver is the traditional gift for a twenty-fifth anniversary." Her tone softened. "Which is actually really romantic for him to have considered. Not to mention, with the toll of parenting lately, it's a miracle we made time to celebrate at all, let alone exchange gifts."

"It reminds me of my earrings, although the texture isn't pounded like these. I like silver, and the *P* is meaningful, just like the corgis." Trying to be helpful, I tucked my hair behind my ear and tilted my head toward Shelly. "These were a gift from Leo a long time ago. To me, they're a lot more romantic than diamonds. Like your necklace."

Shelly lifted a hand, taking the bottom of the three dangling corgis between her finger and thumb, rubbing it gently. "You are totally right." She let the earring loose and offered another laugh. "Still, twenty-five years or not, like I said, it was a miracle it happened at all. It barely had the chance to be romantic. Although *what is* with two teenagers, especially with everything going on with Ananya, Dawn, and Britney. If it's not the two of us fighting Ananya, then we're fighting each other over what we're supposed to do to help her." Shelly shrugged and I got the impression she was going to change the topic, but she paused, the debate clear.

After a few moments, I decided to prompt her, in case it was important. "What are you thinking? Is there something new going on with Ananya and the girls?"

"No..." Again she considered, cast a glance toward Paulie, then gave a little shrug. "I don't want to badmouth anyone, but I know Britney's been with you the past couple of afternoons at the shop. How often has Dawn come in?" She rushed ahead before I could answer, at this point clearly wanting to vent her feelings more than gather information. "It all started with her. She's a bad influence on my daughter, and Britney, too, as far as I'm concerned. Before Dawn came to school, Britney would come hang out with Ananya all the time, and things were just as happy as can be. Britney was one of the politest of all Ananya's friends. Then Dawn joined the mix, and both of them grew these horrible mean-girl attitudes.

And if you ask me, Dawn's mother only makes it all worse. But of course, Ajay says our focus should be on Ananya, not blame Becky or Zelda for them not parenting the way we think they should. Ananya has to make good choices regardless of what her friends do. And... I don't disagree with him there, but—"

"Ananya can come work here at Paws after school, if she needs something constructive to do," Paulie offered, clearly wanting to offer support but at a loss for what else to do. "Being around animals is good for the soul."

"Oh no." Shelly laughed. "You're too sweet of a man, Paulie Bezor. However, I like you too much to do that to you. *Trust me*, a teenage girl would eat you alive."

I joined in on her laughter, reaching out to squeeze Paulie's shoulder as Shelly had done moments before. "I've got to agree with Shelly on this one. Count your blessings, like me, that the only thing you have to put up with is corgi attitude."

On cue, Watson chuffed, glaring at the bags of buffalo jerky in my hand, clearly offended they traveled no closer to his belly.

Once more using him as an excuse, I forced payment on Paulie and left. I was tempted to fill Shelly in on what I discovered with Dawn the night before but didn't want to make things worse. And if Dawn's sticky fingers became public knowledge, which, it was a tiny mountain town, so of course they would, I didn't want to be the one to deliver the news of her being remotely connected to Aspen Gold.

"The fairy thinks he *drove* into Grand Lake?" Susan barked out a laugh. "Julian wasn't in any condition to drive *himself* anywhere."

"Maybe if he was a zombie." Officer Cabot spoke up helpfully from the other side of the table and wrinkled his nose in confusion. "Although, I don't think zombies have the mental capacity to operate heavy machinery."

"*Seriously?*" Susan looked on the verge of pulling her weapon.

"Well, yeah." Campbell nodded in earnest. "Driving a car requires executive brain functions that zombies wouldn't be able to—"

"Stop it. Plus, the autopsy hasn't been completed, obviously." Susan bared her teeth, then leaned sideways to peer downward through the one-way glass into Watson's apartment. "Make room,

Officer Fleabag. Officer Idiot is going to take a timeout."

Watson didn't so much as pause in his snoring.

With the lull after lunch, the bakery was empty. In what had become commonplace since the remodel, the tables beside the Cozy Corgi merchandise and Watson's apartment functioned as Scooby Gang headquarters, *not* that Susan would ever consider herself part of the Scooby Gang. She and Campbell sat on one side, Katie and I on the other, and as was also commonplace, a host of pastries piled in the middle. Nick had just delivered drinks as we sat down and was certainly listening in from the kitchen as he prepared more delicacies.

"I think you're spot-on about your zombie theory, Campbell." Katie reached across the table, patted his arm, and snagged an oaty ginger crunch bar as she pulled her hand back over, then refocused on Susan. "I take it that means murder?"

"What else?" She turned to look at me with an unusually pleasant grin. "In fact, the only reason I would think that it *isn't* murder is that *you* didn't stumble across him when you decided to go for a swim in Grand Lake or some such nonsense. It's kinda like that adage of the tree falling in the forest.

Does it really count as murder if Winifred Page doesn't find the body?"

I hadn't taken a drink of the dirty chai yet, holding the mug between my hands, warming them as I addressed Susan. "You're in an unusually chipper mood considering, well... you know, murder."

She waved that off. "It's not every day a killer makes it as easy as this one. If I'm correct, judging from the impact to the back of Julian's skull—which wouldn't have happened during an accidental wreck into the lake—the murder weapon was in the trunk, along with all the stolen jewelry from Aspen Gold. Though, technically, we don't have an official cause of death, and don't know if he was dead before or after his little swim." She made a face. "Either way, it hasn't been inventoried yet, but I'm assuming all of it."

"The amethyst geode?" I took an easy guess, considering it was the other stolen item that Julian hated that hadn't been in Dawn Erickson's bedroom. "It looked as if it was heavy enough to hurt someone."

"Exactly." Susan gave a dismissive nod as if that was obvious and continued explaining her good mood. "I mean really, with all of that in one location, even with a couple of days in fish-infested water—the windows were cracked, so they got in—unless we're talking about a contract killer, there's a mistake in there somewhere. We'll find fingerprints, hair, who knows, but there'll be something that'll serve as well as a signed confession."

"One of the theories we had early on was maybe some enemies from Vegas." Katie didn't sound convinced. "You might very well be dealing with a contract killer."

Susan had taken a bite of cream-cheese Danish and didn't bother swallowing before negating Katie's theory. "No, this was clearly desperate. It was only a matter of time before someone found Julian's car in Grand Lake. Granted, sooner than even I probably would've guessed, especially with it going to be frozen over in a matter of months. An avid boater just happened to be playing with one of his new toys, using sonar, as if he was going to fish for whales or something." She finally swallowed and gave an eye roll. "He's already asking for a reward since he discovered the car."

"How are Vivian and Roger?" At times, it was easy to get caught up in the mystery, putting puzzle pieces and clues together, and forget that there were actual humans involved. While, from all accounts, there weren't all that many who would miss Julian LaRue, I was certain his parents would be devastated, especially his mother.

Susan took a breath, and there was no humor or dismissiveness in her tone when she finally spoke. "Vivian is refusing to believe it, at this point, but Roger does. And we need to be thorough before they see the body. Including making him as presentable as possible." Surprising me, Susan's gaze turned sympathetic, and her voice took on a tone I didn't think I'd ever heard from her. "You spoke to Dinah?"

"Yeah, of course. You—" I started to say she already knew that but halted when her expression and tone suddenly made sense. I was so touched that it took me another second to be sure of my voice when I spoke. "You'd already figured out about my engagement ring, didn't you?"

"What about your engagement ring?" Katie twisted beside me. "Oh! I didn't even notice you weren't wearing it."

"I thought it might be better if you spoke to Dinah yourself, plus see if you came to the same conclusion I did." She didn't offer Katie an explanation and partially changed directions. "I also wanted to see what your reaction was to Dinah. Though I don't think she clobbered Julian and then drove him to Grand Lake only to shove his car into the water."

"We believe Julian switched out Dinah's diamond for a fake and sold the real one to Leo for cheap to rub it in Dinah's face." Unlike Susan, I took the time to catch Katie up to speed. "In a type of petty retribution, I suppose."

"Really? *That* was Dinah's theory?" Susan interrupted before Katie could respond. "She said that whopper was worth over thirty thousand. Julian despised her *that* much that he'd basically throw away thirty grand just to rub it in her face?"

"Well..." Campbell dared to speak up again. "If it's also true he's been trading out gemstones from the residents of Aspen Grove, who knows how many other times he's done that. It wouldn't take long to accumulate quite a hefty trove."

Susan shot him an impressed glance, then turned back to me. "Dinah thinks Julian thought that low of her, huh?"

"Yes. She claims she's had his number for years, even before she met Julian, just from the stories his parents told her. She's been trying to get Vivian and Roger to see their son for who he really is and to quit letting him take advantage."

Katie sucked in a long breath, a familiar sound

that let me know she'd added up some pieces. "*Julian* registered Aspen Gold as a church and somehow got ordained... er... got his mom ordained through identity theft." She halted then, looking disappointed. "Why?"

"I've been thinking about that since I talked to Dinah and finding out about my ring." Finally, I took a sip of my dirty chai, playing through my theory once more before speaking out loud. "There're a lot of variables, a lot of ifs that would have to be true for this to work. However, *if* Julian had been trading out valuable diamonds and gems and such, hoarding them away, and who knows what else, then he's been building up a little bit of a fortune. Dinah believes it was only a matter of time before he left town. And it's becoming clearer that Julian either thought it beneficial or enjoyable, or maybe both, to do his misdeeds out in the open. I'm getting the sense he enjoyed getting away with the obvious, or what he was making rather obvious, if a person knew to look." Thinking about Shelly's impression that Julian had been having an affair with a married man, I glanced toward Susan. "I'm sure you spoke to the fire chief about Prime Slice and Tom's connection to Julian?"

"Of course. Tom's a prime suspect at the moment, considering he had plenty of reasons to want Julian gone." Her pale blue eyes widened. "Huh. Beyond that thought, this does all flow with the new details we're learning about Julian. All right there in the open? Probably how he swindled the casinos in Vegas as well."

At Katie's scowl, I took a second to explain about Julian blackmailing Tom, what had been uncovered about the fire, compared it to what Julian probably did with Dinah's diamond, then tied it all back to his possible plans of tax fraud in his mother's name and Aspen Gold. Finally, I returned to Susan. "We'd have to see if the LaRues put Julian in charge of their finances or their books... or if he *took* charge, but it could be a matter of tax fraud, getting a larger rebate and pocketing the difference. Who knows how many schemes and plans he had going on that would all come due right before he left town. I'd say we've only scratched the surface, but it could add up to one massive sum. Again, that's only plausible if all these other things are true." Finally, the fog that had been billowing around Julian's disappearance was clearing. Each piece added up to a full, completely reprehensible image of the man. It seemed obvious it had always been just a matter of time before one of those pieces became Julian's undoing.

"Maybe his parents are the ones who drove

Julian into the lake. Imagine having *him* as a son." Officer Cabot had lifted a ginger oaty bar to his lips and paused midbite when all three of us turned to him. "What? I was kidding."

"I did wonder if they were in on it together at one point." Susan seemed to consider.

"There's no way Vivian had anything to do with Julian's death. Not in a million years. Roger..." I thought back to his dark expression as I confronted them about forcing Julian to date Alessandra. "I don't think so, but... maybe..."

"We've got a list a mile long of people who might want Julian LaRue dead." Susan cracked a grin. "Including a bunch of old folks at the retirement home. Maybe Mario gathered them all up, and they took a murderous little field trip of revenge." Her chuckle turned a little whimsical. "I can kinda see him doing that." Abruptly, as if she'd caught herself in the moment, she cleared her throat. "He's definitely got untrustworthy beady little eyes."

"No, he doesn't." Campbell sounded utterly lost, suggesting he hadn't noticed his partner's crush. "Mr. Toscano's got very good eyes. He's a handsome guy."

"He really is," Katie agreed and then sucked in another gasp, turning to me and clutching my hand.

"Oh, I forgot to tell you, I heard that Mario's been dating Delilah. When Anna came over to see what she could find out about Julian being found, she got sidetracked with that little detail. She's hoping Delilah will now quit fishing for Carl." She chuckled. "I know that's beside the point right now, but it just hit me."

Susan choked, went pale, and partially crushed what remained of the danish she'd been holding. "Delilah Johnson? Mario is... Mr. Toscano is dating *Delilah*?" I couldn't tell if she looked more disgusted or furious.

Atypically, Katie didn't seem to catch on, only looking confused. "Yeah, I mean really, it's not surprising. Like we've already said, Mario is drop-dead gorgeous, so is Delilah, and it's not like she doesn't get around."

I winced, mentally kicking myself for my lack of tendency to gossip. I'd not shared with Katie what I'd noticed brewing inside Susan for Mario, nor had I passed along that Delilah had been seeing him. I looked for a distraction, quickly, and found one. "Actually, after finding out about Tom, we may have another suspect, speaking of dates. Rion Sparks."

When Susan's pale blue gaze turned to me, the hard wall that shot up was a heartbeat too late, and I saw the hurt there, though it didn't seep out in her tone. "The wedding-dress guy, why?"

"Apparently he and Julian were... going on dates. If I'm reading between the lines correctly, Vivian accidentally pointed in Rion's direction yesterday by insisting *much* too strongly that he and her son were only meeting to go over a possible business collaboration... at her behest, no less. It was part of the drama between Julian and his parents. We should add Rion to the list. I didn't think much of it yesterday, not to mention getting sidetracked by Dawn stealing again. However, now that Julian is dead, not just making a getaway with a bunch of jewelry, that puts a new swing on things. If Rion found out about Tom and felt jilted, or was being blackmailed himself, or realized Julian wouldn't stand up to his parents for their relationship, then..."

Katie gasped for the third time and clutched my arm. "*I'm* going with you!"

"What?" I angled toward her, confused. "Going where?"

"To interview Rion Sparks, of course, at Day of Lace. In fact, let's go now." Katie spared an obligatory glance at the time and craned around to holler at Nick, "Fred and I are going to the wedding-dress shop, we may not be back in time for the afternoon rush, will you be okay?"

Nick leaned over the counter, a trail of flour across his forehead, proving that he had, of course, been listening. "You bet. Send pictures of whatever you try on."

Katie blushed, then gave a shrug as if caught as she turned back to us. "Well... maybe if there's time..."

With a scowl at Katie, Susan pulled us back on track. "A jilted lover *would* fit. Like I said, this wasn't professional. My guess is a solitary impulse bang on the back of the head with that geode—maybe not even a real attempt to kill, as there were no signs of struggle, no blood. Though again, maybe he was dead when he entered the lake, maybe not—followed by a sloppy attempt to make it look like a burglary gone wrong. However—"

"Actually..." I sat up straighter, Susan's words ushering in a thought and prompting me to cut her off. "A jilted lover *does* make sense."

She scowled. "Yes. I know. I just said that."

I laughed but stifled it quickly as Susan's glare turned deadly. "I mean with the fact the traffic camera caught Julian's car driving through town after dark. Maybe a late-night rendezvous gone bad."

Susan cocked her head, then gave an approving nod. "Agreed. We should check out this angle for sure, but..." Susan looked as if she was going to be sick. "The *last* place I ever want to go is Day of Lace. Being around all that... well... *lace* and tulle and junk would make me break out in hives. So please, by all means, *you* handle that one for me. Why anyone in their right mind would pay good money for a wedding when—" Her eyes went wide as she glanced between the newly engaged Katie and myself, before wheeling on Campbell as if it was all his fault. "Hurry up, Cabot. We can't spend all day here eating. Go find out if they finished cataloguing all that was in the trunk."

Katie practically vibrated in the passenger seat all the way across town. Moraine Avenue bisected the shops running up and down Elkhorn before it curved around a small mountain that sat behind the south side of the shops, curved again past Chipmunk Mountain and on down to another commercial area. Though tourists still frequented them, the stores and restaurants were much more spread out and not easily walkable between one another and were more targeted to locals. Day of Lace sat on its own, beside a large grove of blue spruce. While the relatively new construction building had traditional log siding on the front, it had a more modern take, with two solid walls of windows meeting at a forty-five-degree angle going up to a steep pitch as if it were a church—an aspect accentuated by the overall height and narrowness. Even from the large paved lot, where we parked, the two stories of wedding dresses shimmered white behind those towering windows.

Unsurprisingly, since there were only two other cars in the parking lot, Day of Lace was empty as we entered, save for a handsome man in a well-fitted gray suit. He smiled warmly as he headed directly toward us from where he was adjusting a long train around the wedding-dress display. "Welcome to Day of Lace, ladies. May I offer you a glass of champagne?" He missed a step when he noticed Watson. "Oh... uhm... we don't usually allow pets." There was a clatter from the balcony above, but he didn't seem to notice. "You know, the last thing most brides-to be want is a gown covered in dog hair."

"Simon!" someone called from above, causing Katie and me to look up. Though we'd only met a couple of times, I recognized Rion Sparks, whose suit was deep navy. "Don't you realize who this is? He's not merely a *pet*. He's the infamous Watson. And I believe, if rumor has it, the notorious Winifred Page and Katie Pizzolato are here to look for wedding gowns." Rion's tone was magnanimous but rang a little hollow, somehow.

"Oh, we're not—" I bit my tongue as Katie flashed me a glare.

"It's not the *main* reason we're here, but I

wouldn't mind looking around." Katie refocused on Simon. "And I'll take you up on that champagne offer."

"Of course." Simon's smile was back in place, but he didn't hurry off to pour champagne. Instead, he glanced toward the balcony, though from his angle, I doubted he could see Rion, then closed the distance between us, moving a little quicker than he had before. "What is the main reason you're here?"

Possibly I was reading into things, but I thought I picked up on a little trepidation in his tone. Before I could answer, Watson pattered forward a couple of steps, sniffing at Simon's patent-leather shoes.

Simon spared a glance down and patted Watson's head absentmindedly. "What did you say you needed?"

That time, I was sure, though he hadn't recognized us, now that we had been identified, our presence made him nervous, as if he knew why we were there. Strange. No one had mentioned Julian having any connection to anyone named Simon.

Katie seemed to pick up on his nerves as well and cast me a glance that stated clearly for me to take the lead.

So I did. "Julian LaRue's body was found today."

"We heard." Simon nodded, his eyes narrowing.

"Tragedy, to be sure. I can't say I ever met him. But I've seen him around town." That gaze flicked to Rion, who'd just made it to the base of the curving stairs. "He was a handsome guy."

Rion hurried over, even quicker than Simon. "Yes, it was a tragedy. We were sad to hear of his passing." He took Katie's arm without permission. "Now, I know *just* the dress for your body type. You'll look—"

"Vivian, Julian's mother, mentioned he had a connection to you." I wasn't about to relent. Rion wasn't even being subtle about trying to distract.

"Did she?" Simon's voice shot up as he crossed his arms and angled his stare toward the other man.

Rion halted, looked flummoxed for a second, then let out a heavy sigh before he dropped Katie's arm. "Yes. I'd hoped to keep it secret." He shot me a tight smile and shrugged toward Simon. "I went to Aspen Gold the other day. I... found a watch that I thought was perfect for you. Purchased it on the spot but needed to... uhm... have a couple of links taken out so it would fit your wrist." Rion refocused on me, staring into my eyes with a meaningful glare. "Simon is my *partner*."

Though it wasn't an act I engaged in frequently, nor one I could pull off with much conviction, I played dumb. "Oh? You two are in business together?"

"No." Rion shook his head and laughed. "Well, yes. Technically, I own Day of Lace, and Simon's the manager, but no, I meant... we're partners in life as well as business." Rion bent to pet Watson, as Simon had done, but Watson chuffed and waddled a couple of steps backward.

"A watch?" Simon sounded thoroughly unconvinced. "How nice. Is it a surprise? I haven't received it yet."

"No, you wouldn't have, unfortunately." Rion grimaced toward Simon. "The watch was one of the items stolen the other day. You heard about Aspen Gold being robbed, right?"

Simon just cocked an eyebrow at his partner, his arms folding tighter across his chest.

If it hadn't been so cringeworthy, Rion's performance would've been nearly laughable. Having no pity for lying, especially when done so pathetically and accompanied by flagrant cheating, I went with it. "Well, the good news is Detective Green said all the stolen merchandise was recovered, so maybe that watch will be repairable."

"Oh *great!*" Rion actually clapped his hands once and smiled through gritted teeth at me before clearing his throat that time, taking Katie's arm and offering it toward his partner. "I believe Katie was hoping for champagne, and maybe to try on some dresses. I was thinking one of the gowns from the Divina Malloy collection. She—"

"I'm perfectly capable of picking out a gown to fit Ms. Pizzolato." Simon's gritted-teeth smile resembled the one Rion had offered, but it softened somewhat as he accepted Katie's hand. "Come with me."

Despite the tension in the room, Katie uttered a little giggle of glee and paused, looking back at me. "Do you mind if I—"

"Are you kidding?" I shooed her forward. "Go on. Watson and I will be there in a few seconds."

I barely made it through the sentence before Katie whirled and practically dragged poor Simon away.

When I opened my mouth to speak, Rion lifted a hand and shook his head, waiting until the two of them were out of view, and then his gaze finally landed back on me. He was just as handsome as Simon, though maybe a decade older. His eyes were red-rimmed, strained. Clearly, he'd been crying or at least was on the verge.

"There was no watch, Rion." I went for the jugular. "*Vivian* claimed you and Julian met in hopes of forming a business alliance of some sort with wedding gowns and wedding rings, but that wasn't true, either. Though she was a touch more convincing."

"Am I a suspect?" He gave up all pretenses. "I promise you, I didn't even know Julian was dead until the rest of the town found out today. I figured he took the jewelry and ran, like they were saying."

"Rion, I'm afraid your word doesn't mean much. I've barely been here two seconds, and you've uttered several lies." I gestured downward. "Poorly enough, I might add, that even Watson, who is not so fluent in human, could tell."

At his name, Watson looked up hopefully, chocolate eyes bright as he glanced toward my hands, but when he found them empty of treats, lost interest with a forlorn sigh.

"*I* didn't kill him." Rion glanced over his shoulder, but nothing was there but racks and displays of wedding gowns. When he refocused on me, his voice was barely audible. "And yes, I was lying. So was Julian's horrid mother. But I *didn't* kill him, would never. Wasn't even a reason to. We... got together a couple of times. It was nothing more than that."

"Lovers' quarrels can explode. Especially of the secretive, illicit variety, I would imagine." I stole

Susan's term. "Everything indicates that Julian was killed in a crime of passion."

He snorted. "I was hardly the only one Julian saw from time to time."

So, he did know. "Did that make you jealous?"

The scowl he gave me was the first genuine emotion I'd seen from him, besides nervousness, and his tone dripped with everything the look implied— that I was some naïve innocent and unable to fathom how the real world worked. "Does it look to you like I have any reason to be jealous of Julian being with other people when *I'm* the one in a committed relationship?"

"In a—" I'd been about to throw the accusation of Julian blackmailing Rion over their relationship but barely caught myself from laughing at his use of that term. "The other member of that *committed* relationship of yours would have reason to be jealous, then."

He paled and shook his head. As he'd done with Katie, he grabbed my hand when he spoke. "Simon didn't hurt Julian. He would never. And he didn't know anything about it… us until you—"

I ripped my hand free of his. "You don't want to touch me without permission, Mr. Sparks."

Ever attune to his mama, Watson growled his support.

"Sorry." Rion stepped back and actually sounded genuine. "I didn't mean..." He shook his head again, his tone plaintive. "Listen, I don't blame you for looking into me, knowing what you know. Yes, I am not a good guy in this situation, but I'm *not* a killer. There's no reason to be. I'm sorry Julian is dead, but it wasn't like I loved him. He didn't love me, either. I love Simon. And I promise you..." Though he stayed where he was, he leaned nearer at that, holding my gaze. "I promise you, Simon didn't know. And even if he did, there's not one evil bone in his body. He would never hurt anyone."

Despite that Rion had already proved he was an inadequate liar on the spur of the moment, that didn't mean he couldn't pull it off if he'd been prepared, which he would've been if he was the one who'd killed Julian. However, he was clearly sincere in his belief that Simon was incapable of hurting someone else. But... given he also believed he loved Simon yet could do this to him, Rion Sparks' beliefs didn't hold any more weight than his moral character.

"Listen..." If anything, his tone switched yet again, growing simpering. "I heard you and Leo got engaged. Pick any wedding gown you like. I'll give it to you for fifty percent off."

An unflattering sound issued unbidden from the back of my throat.

Panic lit in Rion's eyes, and he clearly had misunderstood my reaction as he spoke hurriedly once more. "Okay, free. Any wedding dress at all. Any designer, any style, any price. It's yours, free. Just leave Simon and me alone."

As if he understood the implication, Watson growled again.

Unwilling to not have my own say, I leaned closer once more. "I know first-hand what it's like to have a man say he loves you while running around behind my back. I wouldn't wear a gown from here if you paid me. You are vile." When he sputtered, I pushed on. "And I promise you this, if you did have anything to do with Julian's death, half-price wedding gowns will be the least of your worries."

After a few more seconds of glaring, Rion looked to the floor in defeat, then stood aside.

Not giving a hoot about how much corgi hair we left in our wake, I stormed past him, keeping Watson by my side. I was going to find Katie and never look at Day of Lace again.

However, finding Katie was easier said than done. Though narrow, the building had quite the footprint, and I had to admit that even given its size, it dripped with an easy elegance. In a lot of ways, the styling of the interior, despite the log façade on the outside, echoed some of the Art Deco aspects of Katie's newly remodeled bakery.

I heard her before I found them, and I paused before entering through an arched doorway, caught by her happy, excited tone. "I'm so glad you like it. It's one-of-a-kind. Joe, my fiancé, had it designed for me."

"I never thought I'd like hippos on an engagement ring, but I do." Simon, though he'd been clearly upset, now sounded gentle and sincere.

"You're not the first person to say that." Katie giggled. "But hippos are magnificent. Did you know they can't jump, like at all, and their milk is pink? *Pink!* Well... that's proven to be an unlikely fact, but... I'm holding on to it anyway. In more factual news, a group of them is called a float. Isn't that perfect? A bunch of fat, happy little animals floating around, and they're actually called a *float*?"

Simon giggled too, and without Rion beside him, I realized something about his manner reminded me of Barry—though without the tie-dye tank tops. "I definitely can't say I knew that. But I'm rather glad that I do now."

"And..." Katie clearly wasn't done, and I could practically see her lean forward as she went on one of her trivia binges. "George Washington's false teeth were made out of hippo teeth." Her words burst forth, nearly tripping over each other. "Of course, I'm hoping the hippopotamuses who donated their teeth for our old president died of natural causes at a ripe old age *before* that particular sacrifice."

"I'm sure they did." Simon laughed again, then went serious. "Okay, got you all cinched up. See what you think."

I stepped through the doorway the very second Katie turned on the pedestal to look at her reflection in the three-paneled mirror.

We both gasped at the same time.

Katie's gaze lifted to mine in the mirror, and she beamed. "This is it, right? Surely not, it's the first one. But this is *it*."

The sight of my best friend in what without a doubt was going to be her wedding gown washed away every protest I might've made about her purchasing it from Day of Lace. "Oh yes." I nodded, casting a glance toward Simon, who smiled gently at the vision Katie made and then came to stand beside her, speaking to her reflection so I didn't have to look away from the entirety of her. "It's as perfect for you as the ring."

It really was. The gown was sleeveless but not too low-cut, with a formfitting bodice and a drop waist that flared into a near cloud of tulle. Unsurprisingly, the lace that covered the bodice and flowed to her hips before tapering off like a waterfall around the white tulle was a pale soft pink.

I could barely find my voice. "Katie Pizzolato, you're going to make the most beautiful bride in the whole world."

"I know!" She nodded, giggled, and a tear rolled down one of her full, happy cheeks.

Watson shoved his head between our legs, adding more hair to what already covered my broomstick skirt and weaving who knew how much through the tulle of the gown.

If he noticed, Simon didn't let on that he minded as he focused on me. "It's completely different than this one, but I have one that would be perfect for you as well. It's also from one of the Malloy collections. Would you like me to get it for you?"

I nearly said yes, so caught up in the moment with Katie, but then recalled what I'd said to Rion not even five minutes before. "No, thank you. This is Katie's time." When she started to protest, I jumped to the easiest excuse. "Unlike you, I don't have my real engagement ring yet. I think that should come first."

"Oh." Katie relented instantly and nodded her agreement. "That makes perfect sense."

A quarter of an hour later, Katie was back in her hoodie—which, surprisingly sported a chubby alligator decal and not a hippo—and the three of us headed back across the parking lot to my Mini Cooper, Katie talking a mile a minute. "I never dreamed a wedding dress would cost *that* much. Apparently, this Divina Malloy is quite the designer. I'm not sure how I'm going to swing that price tag, but—"

Footsteps hurried over the asphalt, cutting her off, and we both turned around to see Simon heading our way.

He was a little breathless when he reached us and spared a quick scratch on Watson's head, before launching in with a whisper, though there was no one else around to hear. "I told myself I wasn't going to ask, but I can't keep from it. Was Rion seeing Julian? He wasn't actually buying me a watch, was he?"

It wasn't really a question, but even so, Katie and I exchanged uncomfortable glances, trying to decide how best to respond.

"That's okay." Simon saved us. "That's all the answer I needed." He stood there in silence for a couple of seconds, and just when I thought he was going to turn around and walk away, his shoulders slumped as he let out a long breath. "This isn't the first time, you know."

Katie reached out a hand and took his.

Simon continued with his confession. "There was another who he saw behind my back for three years." He bugged his eyes out as if shocked by his own story. "*Three* years. I had no clue. Neither did the other guy. Poor fool thought they were going to get married. Then after reading some texts, I showed up on his doorstep." He snorted in derision. "I guess *I'm* the poor fool."

Katie made a sympathetic sound, but I couldn't help myself. "Why did you stay?" I glanced over his shoulder and saw Rion watching through the window. The distance didn't help, and I couldn't tell if his expression was angry or... worried and panicked. I hoped he could read my lips. "You don't have to stay. You could leave him this time."

"Yeah, I know." He shrugged one shoulder. "I

should. But... I love him. And at the end of the day, he loves me."

"But, Simon, if he really—"

"Fred." Katie cut me off, though not unkindly, and stayed focused on Simon, giving his hand another squeeze before she let it go. "I know we just met, but anytime you want to talk, there's countless cupcakes, cookies, brownies, you name it, waiting for you in the Cozy Corgi Bakery. And some ears willing to listen."

I marveled at her, both her kindness and her ability to let people be wherever they were without argument or needing to tell them what to do. If Simon did show up in the bakery, I'd probably let her have that conversation alone, as I didn't think I possessed that particular skill, nor would I be able to stay impartial where Simon's own version of Garrett was concerned. "Katie also makes a killer dirty chai. And they make a lot of things better."

"You okay?"

I flinched, so caught up in my own thoughts that Leo's voice startled me. Probably a good thing to bring me back to the moment, considering I was the one behind the wheel. After refocusing on the road, I spared him a quick glance. "Yes, just... thinking about things."

"I know you don't love being the center of attention, but remember, it's your family. And since they're celebrating our engagement, I'll steal some of the limelight from you." Though Leo attempted to keep his tone soft, I could hear the slight edge beneath it. "And of course, Watson will do his part as well."

"Oh no." I took another glance from the road to give him an encouraging smile. "It's not that. Honestly, that part will be wonderful. We've been so caught up in everything else we haven't had a real chance to celebrate our engagement yet."

He offered a smile as well, angled it to where Watson napped in the back seat, then let out a breath, speaking quickly as if ripping off the bandage. "So... you're still... excited about the engagement?"

I flinched again, whipping back to look at Leo. "What? *Of course* I am."

He cocked an eyebrow and pushed on tentatively. "Things at Day of Lace didn't throw you off?"

I *had* been thinking about what happened there, but it took me a moment to figure out what Leo meant. "Because of Rion and Simon? You think I even had the faintest worry that our relationship might mirror theirs?"

He shrugged. "I hope not, but..." Another shrug. "Of all times to see a couple like that, when you're in the middle of a bunch of wedding dresses, I would imagine it could mess with your mind a little bit, especially considering how the proposal and the ring—"

"Hey." I started to look at him once more, then decided he needed more than a passing glance. We were less than a few minutes from Mom and Barry's house, so after a check in the rearview, I pulled off to the side of the road, allowing whatever time we needed.

Watson roused in the back, peering through the window, clearly expecting to see Barry running toward him. When it was just the road on one side and trees on the other, he chuffed, cast me an annoyed glance, and lay back down.

I swiveled in my seat to face Leo as directly as I could and took his hand. "We've been through this. I'm not worried about the ring or how the proposal went, and as far as Rion Sparks and wedding dresses?" I gave an intentionally exaggerated eye roll. "He might be almost as handsome as you, but he is the anti-Leo Lopez if there ever was one." When Leo started to shake his head, I doubled down. "Trust me, I'm not worried about secrets, three-year-covert affairs, or any of that. I understand that life happens, and that relationships get messy, but Rion choosing to live that way reveals the core of who he is. There's a lot of unknowns in this world, but one of the few things of which I am completely certain is the core of what makes up you, and I trust it entirely."

"I know, but if I were in your shoes, I'd..." Clearly not done, Leo chose his next words carefully. "Actually, I don't have to put myself in your shoes.

I'm thinking about it while in my own shoes, which means you surely are."

"Thinking about shoes?" I forced a grin.

He snorted out a little laugh. "No. About... well, about Garrett." When I started to protest, Leo pushed on. "About Garrett and Branson... Lord knows I've been thinking about Branson. Here we are, newly engaged, and you're seeing the wedding-dress guy cheating, *with* the guy I bought your engagement ring from. *With* a stolen diamond in it. I know your history with Garrett—infidelity, and how he left your marriage. I know Charlotte betrayed you in your business partnership. And I *watched* Branson lie and manipulate you and all of us. This has got to be stirring that up in you. How couldn't it?"

Charlotte's face arose from nowhere in my mind. How funny, I'd not even considered Charlotte in all of this, and how she'd basically stolen our publishing house right from under my nose. When laid out in front of me, as Leo had done, even more than staring at the pictures taken in secret and going over Garrett's and my wedding album the other night, I had to admit, it was a long string of betrayal. It made me think of Dinah's words about Julian. *He'd* been the common denominator in all his problems. Maybe I should see it that way. That *I* had the issue. That *I* drew that sort of people to me. And if that was the case, then what did that say about Leo and my engagement, our relationship?

Leo shifted in the passenger seat, making me realize how long I'd been silent.

Even so, I thought a bit longer. Actually, *felt* a bit longer. While not infallible, I trusted my gut. And my gut *knew*, it just *knew* Leo was exactly who he said he was, who he'd shown himself to be, who I *knew* him to be. And... actually, that wasn't only a feeling. Wasn't only my gut. I'd had a mountain of evidence of the type of man who sat across from me accumulate over the years. And every entry gave witness to the exact same thing.

When I finally spoke, there was no hesitation, no flicker of doubt, nothing but complete surety. "Everything you just said is true. However, I know who you are, and who we are together. I trust you with every fiber of my soul."

Leo didn't hesitate. "I feel the exact same about you." He must have seen that I meant it completely, as Leo's relief was sudden and palpable. Even so, his eyes narrowed, but not in suspicion, more of curiosity. "Then what are you thinking? You've been off ever since you told me about what happened with you and Katie."

"You're right, and I've been thinking about it even before I told you. But again, trust me, it has absolutely nothing to do with us." That badgering sensation in the back of my mind again had been plaguing me ever since we left Day of Lace. "There was some connection at the bridal shop to what happened to Julian. I can feel it, and not merely that Rion was having an affair with him. Or Tom having an affair with Julian, for that matter."

Leo sat up a little straighter and seemed content to move on to others' relationship dramas. "But you said you didn't think Rion or Simon were responsible?"

"I don't. Maybe Tom. I've not looked into him yet. But..." Even as I spoke, I tried to play through differing scenarios and I just couldn't see it. "But there is some puzzle piece there that fits, revolving around betrayal. Julian seemed to peddle in it, to wallow in it. There's no way that didn't come back to bite him somehow. I can't quite see the shape of that betrayal-hued puzzle piece to know where it goes. But I can *feel* it, almost like it's stuck in the thumbnail of my mind."

"Thumbnail of your mind? That's a new one." Leo barked out a laugh. "Not to mention painful, having a puzzle piece stuck under your thumbnail, mind or otherwise."

"Yeah, I'm not sure where that analogy came from." I joined in on the laughter, clearly both of us ready to lighten the mood. "However, while not actually painful, it *is* distracting—that's all that's going on." I managed to shove it aside, distracting or not, and leaned in for a kiss. "You ready to celebrate?"

"Oh sure," Percival glowered at the literal feast spread over Mom and Barry's table. *"Fred and Leo* get meat, from an actual animal, not the kind where a whole bunch of vegetables decided to play dress-up."

Mom straightened from where she'd just delivered the giant platter of pork roast to the middle of the spread. "Don't worry, brother. Barry prepared a vegetarian pork roast as well. You can have some of his, if you miss it so much."

"Actually, it's full-on vegan this time." Barry entered from the kitchen, carrying a smaller platter, Watson nipping at the flowing hem of his white-and-yellow tie-dyed linen hippy pants. "And there's more than enough to share."

Percival's husband, Gary, bent closer, inspecting. "Seriously? But that's crispy skin on there?"

"Rice paper!" Barry practically crowed in triumph as he placed it by the larger pork version.

"Smoke and mirrors and a bunch of lies, that's what it is." Percival turned to Leo, lifting his voice dramatically. "You sure you want to marry into this family? I've told you before, it's not too late to run, but it's getting close!"

Zelda had just placed a bowl of mashed potatoes on the already crowded table and hooked a hand through the crook of Leo's right arm. "Oh, he's not going anywhere!"

"Nope!" Verona mimicked her twin by rushing forward and grabbing Leo's left arm. "He is ours, forever."

Completely unconcerned that their wives were hanging over a handsome park ranger, Noah and Jonah followed Gary's example and leaned down to inspect the vegan pork loin. "Rice paper..." Jonah poked the crust with his finger, then gave his brother the side-eye.

"If you're thinking what I'm thinking"—Noah's eyes lit up in excitement—"we can cover that new robot chipmunk body you finished last week and—"

Whatever horrible idea was about to be birthed into the world was cut off with a loud groan from Britney. "Stop. Just stop."

Zelda released Leo, turning to her daughter. "Watch your tone, young lady. We've talked about this."

"Seriously, Mom?" Britney dropped the pendant she'd been fingering around her neck to gesture toward Barry's faux-pork loin. "That's Grandpa's dinner. The last thing here any of us want to envision is it covering some stupid chipmunk invention that—"

"I think it would be cute," Christina piped up from across the room, nudging Leaf with her elbow.

He rose to the occasion. "Yeah, me too."

"*You* would." Britney rolled her eyes at her younger sister and their cousin.

"See, Leo?" Ocean, Verona and Jonah's oldest son, apparently saw things from Britney's point of view. "You may want to take Uncle Percival's advice, run while the getting's good."

Leo shot me a wink. "Nah, I'm not going anywhere." He turned a concerned glance to my brothers-in-law. "However, if any rice-paper-covered rodents show up on Chipmunk Mountain, I'll know whose doors to come knocking on."

Britney made a gagging sound, and Barry threw back his head with laughter.

. . .

Rice-paper-skinned robots and teenage angst aside, as the fourteen of us crowded around the long table—with Watson and a baked chicken breast below—we got to the business of making sure not an ounce of the engagement feast went to waste. Everything else got pushed to the side. There were no distracting thoughts of Rion and Simon in the back of my mind, no concerns about fake diamonds that had turned out to be ridiculously real, and I managed not even to ponder about the mystery surrounding Julian's newly discovered body. On the way over, I'd planned on asking pointed questions to Gary and Percival about the LaRues, what they might have noticed during the convention before Vivian and Roger had to leave—if they had significant connections to Dinah Zuckerman or were privy to any gossip about other clandestine romances Julian might have been involved in, as they seemed to be abundant. Instead, without much effort at all, I gave myself over to the warmth and laughter of my family surrounding me, to the presence of my fiancé by my side, and was present, fully, in the moment.

A long time later, after the table had been cleared and we'd all gathered in their living room to let dinner settle, Mom stood to announce it was time for dessert. Instead of picking something up from

Katie's bakery, as was typical, she'd made a Mexican spiced chocolate cake.

"Here." Leo popped up. "Let me help." Before he followed, he leaned over, kissing the top of my head. "You stay here, relax."

Watson, who of course had been napping by Barry's feet, sprang to life and scurried after Leo.

As the two of them disappeared into the kitchen, Percival leaned forward, finally bringing up the inevitable. "So, darling niece, rumor has it you and our beloved baker made a trip to Day of Lace this afternoon. I was glad to hear it. To my knowledge, they don't possess any broomstick wedding dresses. Were you able to find some you like?"

"Now there's a thought I could get behind." I shot him a wink as I smoothed out the sage-green broomstick skirt I'd chosen for the night. "I didn't think to ask. But I bet they could special order one."

"I will murder you myself." He sniffed, and Barry dared to laugh, earning himself a glare, before Percival turned back to me. "Seriously, please tell me you found at least one you like. I think a mermaid style would look divine on you. Maybe an empire waist... What was the style you wore in your wedding to Garrett?"

"Percival!" Gary gasped and swatted Percival's bony shoulder. "Really."

"Oh." Percival actually sounded abashed. "Sorry. I... wasn't thinking."

"No big deal." Despite the wedding album throwing me off somewhat the other night, hearing Garrett's name and being reminded that this wouldn't be my first wedding dress barely caused a glitch at all. It seemed like such different events. Garrett and Leo couldn't be more different. And the Winifred who'd said yes to her first marriage was vastly different from the Fred who said yes to Leo. Even so, I skipped over the question. "I didn't try any dresses on today. Katie did. Found the perfect one. It's—" I barely caught myself. "Well, I suppose that should be a surprise for when she walks down the aisle. But I will say, it is the most perfect wedding dress for Katie that I can imagine."

"So... covered in hippos?" It was Verona, and there wasn't a bit of judgment in her tone.

"Shockingly, no." As happy as I was, my heart warmed at the memory of Katie in her gown. "But it's something."

"The *something* I was desperate to see was your ring." Percival let out an exaggerated sigh. "And I missed it."

I laughed. "No, you didn't. As soon as everything gets sorted, go over to Taffy Lane, you'll be able to see it on Dinah's finger, since it's hers."

"What?" That time, Percival gasped and exchanged a scandalous glance with his husband. "Well, *that's* news." He refocused on me, leaning forward and twinkling his fingers together. "Please tell me I can pass the news on to Anna and Carl. I love it when I can beat them to the juicy stuff."

I couldn't believe that tidbit hadn't traveled around town yet. Although, I supposed that it had only been that morning, but it felt like ages ago. And in the scheme of things, there'd been a murder to gossip about, which was much bigger than my engagement ring.

"So much stealing around town these days." Percival hadn't waited to get my permission to tell the Hansons. "I heard about that girl." He snapped his fingers as if it would help him remember, then looked toward Britney. "That friend of yours, what's her name? The girl who steals everything?"

Britney stiffened, and the whole room went silent.

Though he didn't speak, Gary nudged his husband in reprimand once more.

I couldn't blame him. I wanted to nudge Percival

myself. My uncle was always outspoken but typically showed a little more tact than that.

However, unlike with his wedding-dress misstep, Percival didn't regret that comment and doubled down with Britney. "I remember some of my own friends back in the day. There was a period I ran around with quite a rough crowd. But please, dear, don't get sucked into the stealing. It's most unattractive. And you're better than that."

All blood drained from Britney's face at becoming the center of attention. Beside her, Ocean shifted uncomfortably as if in sympathy pains.

"That's what I tell her." Zelda latched on, clearly desperate to reach Britney through whatever means necessary. "Britney is better than that. And so is Ananya. And while my heart goes out to Dawn, having been homeschooled by a stressed-out single mother—and to Becky for that matter, I can't even imagine a teenager on my own—I'm not okay with her bad influence on you. It should be the other way around. You and Ananya have huge stable and supportive families. *You* should be influencing *her*."

"Oh yeah." Britney shot up, finding her voice. "*Totally* stable. Ananya's parents fight like crazy, and Ajay's nothing more than a deadbeat." She began to tremble. Over her shoulder I saw Leo and

Mom appear in the doorway from the kitchen, clearly alerted by her volume. "Have you looked around this room? How many crystals are you wearing, Mom? Are you absolutely certain that their *powers* don't conflict with each other?" She turned to Percival. "And you're sitting there wearing a purple fur coat in the middle of the living room all desperate to play gossip with your old fat friends? Fred only wears one type of skirt and acts like her chubby dog is just as important as the rest of us." Britney transferred from ghost white to beet red as she picked up speed. "And Grandpa cooks vegetables every day to pretend like they're meat so he can —" Her gaze slid to Barry's, and she gasped, her hand covering her mouth, tears springing forth instantly. "Grandpa, I'm... I'm sorry. I—" With a cry, she darted across the room, seemed to debate which doorway to try to escape through, then surprised us all by throwing open the front door and running out into the night.

Barry stood instantly, holding a hand out toward Zelda and Noah, who looked like they were going to chase after their daughter. "I'll go. She and I—"

"No." I stood too. That puzzle piece that had been lodged in the thumbnail of my mind came into focus in the middle of Britney's diatribe. "Let me talk to her. I think I know, at least partly, what's going on."

For a second, it looked like Barry was going to argue. He and Britney had a special relationship, and he, more than anyone else, would have the most pull with her.

"Give me five minutes, okay?" I gave him a meaningful look. And when he nodded, I hurried after Britney, but paused in closing the door behind me when I realized Watson was rushing along beside me.

The night was cool and cloudless. The full moon and the star-laden sky provided all the illumination needed. Britney had come to a stop at a little log table and chair set several yards away from the house. Her elbows were on her knees, her face in her hands as she wept.

Watson trotted a few paces ahead of me, reaching Britney first. When she didn't notice, he nudged against her knee with his nose.

After a second, one of her hands lowered, and she stroked his face. She didn't look at me as I took the chair opposite her. "I didn't mean to say those things. And Grandpa, I don't care if he... It doesn't matter what he eats or cooks. I just..."

"He knows that." I reached out and stroked the

top of her shoulder gently. "Britney, Barry knows that. He loves you more than life itself."

That only made her choke out another sob. "And I love him."

"He knows that too." I kept my hand where it was, trying to figure out what to say next. Maybe I should've had Barry come with me. Finally, I leaned nearer with a whisper. "Are you okay?"

She choked out a sob laugh. "Do I look okay?"

Despite myself, a laugh escaped, a half-crazed thing. "No. I guess not."

Britney giggled then, but it was mixed with more tears.

I studied her for a couple of minutes as she continued to pet Watson, other puzzle pieces I'd not even realized had been in front of my face the whole time suddenly coming into focus. Britney's defense of her friends, Dawn specifically. Saying that she had a rough time. Britney's disrespect, which, granted, spread out to everyone lately, but seemed especially toxic when directed at Ajay Patel. That's when it clicked, when she'd yelled that he was a deadbeat a few moments before. Shelly had been right—Dawn had shown up, and not too long after, Britney began acting very unlike herself. On one hand, all those months could be summed up to typical teenage angst and attitude. We'd all assumed. But I was suddenly certain we'd all been very wrong.

"Britney?" I squeezed her shoulder and paused until her tear-filled gaze lifted to meet mine. "Have you been keeping a secret?"

She shook her head, but her wide eyes said differently. One hand stayed on Watson and the other worried over the pendant at her neck once more.

Noticing, I realized my thumb was doing the same thing where my engagement ring was supposed to be. Not bothering to stop, I thought through things again, not wanting to push too hard, especially in the wrong direction. Dawn's mom had complained that Ajay compared her daughter to Ananya. And I recalled how Ajay had acted in the Cozy Corgi when the three girls and all the parents had gathered for an intervention. "Britney, is Ajay having an affair with Dawn's mother?"

To my surprise, Britney, instead of looking horrified, snorted out in disgust. "I hate him."

Another memory came back to me, one of Britney spewing her rudeness at Ajay Patel and questioning why he could tell Dawn what to do if he wasn't her dad, and me taking on the parental role and reprimanding her. I'd taken a slightly wrong turn and only scratched the surface of what Britney knew. "Ajay is Dawn's father, isn't he?"

That time, when Britney's eyes went wide, her jaw went slack as well. For a heartbeat it looked like she was going to shake her head and deny it, but then she slumped, letting out a breath that sounded like she'd been holding it forever. "Yeah."

Though I'd already figured it out, I blinked and stared at my niece, dumbfounded. "He's her dad."

I said it more as a statement to myself, trying to come to terms with it, attempting to take in all the ripples of implication, but Britney interpreted it as a question. And now she didn't have to hold it any longer, all the details gushed forth. "Dawn hit it off with Ananya and me the second she showed up at school. It was a couple of months before she told me that she and Ananya have the same dad. She made me promise I wouldn't tell anybody, that I wouldn't tell Ananya."

"*Ananya* doesn't know?" I hadn't had time to think that far, but I guessed I would've assumed all three girls would've shared the secret if Britney knew. But at the realization, my hurt for her compounded. It had been bad enough to think of Britney holding such a secret from the adults in her life, but even from her life-long friend? Knowing that her best friends were actually sisters and she couldn't say anything?

"She isn't keeping it from her to be cruel." Britney apparently interpreted my reaction as judgment on Dawn. "She has had to keep it secret her *whole* life. Dawn sobbed and sobbed when she told me." Britney lifted her hand from Watson's head and grabbed mine. "She's not bad. She's hurting. And her mom and her stupid, horrid dad made her keep it a secret. That's why she was homeschooled for so long. She swore she wouldn't tell. It took her years of begging and pleading and promising. And now that scumbag comes over to their house, and she has to pretend she doesn't know when Ananya talks about her dad being out of town for business again."

"He's still—" Once more the pieces were coming so thick and fast I barely had a chance to grasp them, let alone perceive them coming. I swallowed. "Ajay is *still* in a relationship with Becky?"

"Yeah." Britney bugged out her eyes, sounding teenager all over again. "What did you think we were talking about?"

And that's why the situation revealed at Day of Lace that afternoon had stuck. My subconscious had figured it out before me. It all came down to betrayal. Although bad, Simon discovering about three years of his partner's double life was a walk in the park to Shelly Patel finding out her husband had a secret family for at least the last sixteen years, judging from Dawn's age. Maybe longer?

"Fred, please don't tell. Please." Britney pulled my attention back to her, squeezing my hands tightly. "Dawn will be so mad I told. And Ananya will be hurt I didn't tell her I knew this whole time. And I just want—" She broke off, astutely reading my expression. "You're going to tell."

Chances were if what Britney knew was the entire story, I still would've told. Although I would've had to think about it. The implications of what that revelation would do to a marriage, to the children involved... I wasn't sure where I would fall on what choice would cause the least damage. But at the revelation of Ajay's secret life, and recalling Shelly's disappointment of her anniversary gift, I thought I'd figured out one of Ajay's secrets Britney didn't know.

I knew who killed Julian LaRue. And *that*, I definitely couldn't keep secret.

Aware it would hurt Britney, I nodded. "Yes. I'm going to tell. But... I need you to keep it a secret from Dawn and Ananya for a little while longer. Just one more night." I held her gaze. "Okay?"

Tears fell again, and at last she nodded.

"I'm so sorry." Though we didn't even come close to having as deep of a relationship as hers and Barry's, I pulled Britney into my arms, holding her tight. "I'm so sorry you had to hold the secret for so long."

Britney stiffened.

I held her tighter. "I'm so sorry you were hurting and none of us knew."

She folded in upon me then, her tears finally feeling like a release.

After a while, we headed back to Mom and Barry's house, Watson flanking the other side of Britney.

I squeezed her hand as we neared the door. "I need you to keep it from your friends for one more night, but let's fill in the rest of the family. You've had to hold this on your own for far too long."

"I figured it out, you're paying me back because I didn't tell you about Julian's body being discovered when I called you." Susan entered the holding room of the police station. As her arms were occupied carrying a large cardboard box, she used the heel of her shoe to slam the door closed behind her. "What I can't figure out is why I'm allowing this nonsense." She dropped the box onto the metal table as if to prove a point.

The clanging of the impact reverberated around the hardscaped room, causing Watson to whimper, then chuff toward Susan.

She pulled her head back, staring down her nose. "Listen here, Officer Fleabag, anyone talks to me that way has a death wish."

Though Leo chuckled at their exchange by my side, I couldn't wait and began pulling out plastic bags, laying them over the table.

"Hold on." Susan slapped a large hand on the table, intentionally making it reverberate again. "Were you born this morning?"

I glanced up at her, thinking she was addressing Watson once more and found her pale blue eyes boring into me. "Um... no?"

"Apparently you were." She reached behind and pulled a bunch of white gloves from her back pocket, tossing a pair to Leo and myself before shoving her hands into her own. "Not that protocol is the name of the game this evening—especially when you drag me out of my pajamas and my house right when I was getting ready to settle down and restart watching the entire series of the *Golden—*" She cleared her throat. "But still, fingerprints, please."

I felt an adequate amount of shame at my lapse in judgment, especially being a detective's daughter.

Leo, on the other hand, made a humming noise as if lost to consideration. "Now that's a question I've never pondered before. What kind of pajamas *does* Detective Susan Green wear?"

Susan went white.

"Do you think the fuzzy kind with little booties attached?" Leo peered down at Watson, as if expecting him have something to offer in the debate.

Watson cocked his head back and forth, ears twitching.

"You're right. I'm betting a yellow rubber-duck pattern."

Susan banged on the table for a second time. "Just because I didn't come with my own weapon doesn't mean I can't step right out into the hallway and snag one off the first officer walking by." She brought her other hand down equally as loud, so all her weight was supported and leaned forward. "Keep talking about my pajamas, Lopez."

After Britney and I had filled the rest of the family in on what had been weighing on her shoulders for the past many months, I'd called Susan, suspecting there'd be some tangible evidence if I could get to what was recovered from Julian's drowned car. However, I stayed vague, knowing I'd rouse Susan's curiosity and guarantee her allowing me to take part, even if it did heighten her grumpy mood.

Apparently satisfied Leo and Watson were done pondering her sleepwear, Susan turned her glower toward me. "The murderous geode isn't here, it's still in lockup. You didn't need it for whatever scheme it is that you're not sharing?"

"No. Not the geode." Now that I had on gloves, I

returned to the bags, unfastening them and spreading the jewelry out on the table.

"What exactly are you looking for?" Susan remained leaning over the table but turned her attention toward the jewelry. "I'm tired of you playing games."

"I'm not exactly sure. But I'll know it when I see it. A locket, I think." Nothing was triggered in the first couple of bags—some loose diamonds, a couple of rings, a tangle of necklace chains. There was a small bag within the larger second bag, and I held it up. "Loose pearls. I bet Charlene will be glad to have these back."

"Thank heavens," Susan practically growled. "Glinda has called me each and every day asking me if they've been recovered, even with my threatening to tear off her stupid fairy wings."

"Wait, her wings are real?"

She glared at Leo long enough that his chuckle died away, and Watson plodded to the far corner of the room, sniffed, then curled up. Finally, she refocused on me once more. "What prompted all this, exactly? Don't think for a moment that from now on I'm going to allow you to start pulling me all over the place on your harebrained schemes."

I moved on to another bag "I'll tell you. But I

think it'll speak for itself if I can only find the right —" I sucked in a breath as I spread out the contents and a gold locket was revealed under another tangle of necklaces. "This is it." The spark of excitement evaporated the second I picked it up. "No. There's no diamond."

As Susan began to pepper questions, I did a quick search of the rest of the recovered jewelry and sank back against the chair in defeat. I'd been so sure.

"I'm sorry." I forced myself to meet Susan's gaze. "I was wrong. I thought there'd be a certain locket here that would prove Julian knew Ajay was having an—" My gaze returned to the diamond-less locket.

"I know that look." Susan grunted and focused on Leo. "Don't you?"

He chuckled softly but addressed me instead of Susan. "You figured it out."

"Yes. This time for real. The locket isn't here." It had been in front of me for days. In front of everyone. Just like all of Julian's other misdeeds. Laid out for the whole world to see, if they only realized what they were looking for.

"Fred." Zelda's eyes narrowed as she opened the door, though not unkindly. "Leo, Watson." She stood aside as Noah approached from behind. "Come on in. What in the world?"

"Sorry to drop by unannounced so late." I entered, Watson and Leo right behind me. "I should've called. I was just too... excited." That was true enough, but I also didn't want to give Britney any forewarning. I thought she'd be honest; catching her off guard would make that more likely. "May I speak with Britney?"

"Why?" Zelda's tone went cold and hard, though clearly not because of me. "What did she do now?"

"Nothing." I reached up and squeezed Zelda's forearm reassuringly. "She's not in trouble. But I think she may have something we need to figure out who killed Julian." When both Zelda and Noah's eyes went wide in fear, I realized my mistake.

Leo did as well and beat me to the explanation. "Britney didn't have anything to do with it. If she does have what we're thinking, she doesn't realize what it means."

"Her new locket." Noah turned and glanced toward the darkened hallway that I knew led to Britney's bedroom. "She said it was a gift from Dawn."

"Her locket?" Zelda swatted at her husband. "Don't be silly. How could that..." Her gaze turned back to Leo and me. "Oh. It's stolen from Aspen Gold too, isn't it?"

They surprised me, especially Noah. Stumbling upon it so quickly. They so often seemed lost in the clouds. "Maybe. Yes. But again, like Leo said, Britney probably doesn't realize it."

Fury cutting over her face, Zelda whirled. "I'm going to—"

"No, wait." I reached out again, grasping her arm once more. "Wait, please?" Though she hesitated, Zelda looked ready to argue. "Let me, one more time."

Noah slipped his hand into Zelda's.

She nodded.

Leo stayed behind with them to explain. Watson and I walked down the hallway, and I knocked on Britney's door. When there was still no answer the second time, I twisted the knob and pushed it open slowly, peering in, thinking she was probably sleeping.

"Mom!" Britney hollered, loudly enough that it could have been because she was a moody teenager, or simply that the white earbuds that matched the ones Dawn had been using impaired her volume control. "You need to *knock*! How many times do I —" She turned, flinching when she saw me, then ripped the earbuds out, her volume dropping instantly. "Fred."

"Hi!" I gave a little wave. "May I come in?"

"Sure." Britney shuffled the papers she'd been going through to the side, covering them with a pillow, then patted beside her on the comforter and offered a quick smile as Watson joined me crossing her room. "What's going on?"

Instead of answering, I sat and glanced at her neck. With her sleepwear tank top, it was more easily identifiable, and I knew instantly it was the right one. Though small, I could see why it appealed to Shelly. The gold was a soft, warm finish, and a diamond was set in the center of the oval, delicate petals engraved around it in a sunburst pattern. "Did Dawn give you that locket?"

Like I'd noticed a few times the past days, Britney's hand rose and encircled what I'd thought had been a pendant. I could see panic, quickly followed by lies beginning to form behind her eyes, but then she sighed and dropped her hand. "Yes. She did." Britney's volume increased then, as did her speed. "But she didn't steal it. I swear. She wouldn't lie to me. I asked. I wasn't going to wear something that was stolen."

Hidden in plain sight. Flaunt it for everyone to

see, but not really see. Yeah, by now that was completely a Julian LaRue trademark. "Did Julian give it to her the same way he gave her the gold-and-crystal animals?"

Britney blanched that I'd figured it out and seemed to relax. "Yes. At the exact same time. Dawn said he pulled it out from underneath a cabinet, laid it beside the animals, and then walked back to some other room where he was arguing with his parents. She gave it to me as a thank-you. She *swore* he gave it to her, that it wasn't stolen."

Dawn left out that little detail when I caught her with the animals. Though, not surprising. "As a thank... Oh, for claiming you stole the corgi from the bakery?"

Britney nodded.

"I don't think Dawn lied to you. I don't think she stole the locket." I held out my hand. "May I have it?"

She hesitated, looking from me to Watson, then back. "Will it get her in trouble?"

"No. It won't." Part of me felt like I was lying. It wouldn't get Dawn in trouble, but it would hurt her family, cause her pain.

"If she didn't steal it, why do you need it?" She

hesitated still, and this time when she looked toward Watson, her gaze stayed on him as I answered.

"I can't tell you that, Britney. I'm sorry." Maybe I could have, but I didn't trust she wouldn't tell Dawn. Didn't know if Dawn realized what the locket might prove or not. "I can only promise you it's the right thing to do."

Britney continued to stare at Watson, who stared right back, a pleasant expression on his sweet face. "You don't want me to tell Dawn about this either, do you?"

"No, I don't." I might not tell Britney everything, but I wasn't going to lie to her. "Like I said at Mom and Barry's, I need you to keep the secret one more night. If I'm right, there won't be any more secrets tomorrow."

"You're always right." She looked to me then, and proved once more that her intelligence was just as quick as her temper. "This is going to ruin Dawn's family, isn't it?"

No, I wouldn't lie to her. "I'd say it already is, wouldn't you?"

With a sigh, she lifted both her hands, dipped behind her long hair to unfasten the necklace at the back, and handed it to me. "Here you go."

. . .

As we'd agreed, we stopped a quarter mile from Glen Haven, where Susan waited in her cruiser. She'd insisted on a compromise. She wouldn't go storming into Zelda and Noah's home, as long as we didn't expect her to sit around at the Estes Park Police Station.

Leo and Watson climbed into the back seat, while I hopped into the front.

Susan barely spared a glaring glance at Watson being in her car before snatching the locket from my hand. "So you think this is what cost Julian his life, huh?"

"I think so. We didn't have any tools in the Mini Cooper, and I wasn't about to ask Noah or Zelda for any and risk upsetting Britney. But... see this?" Not taking it away from her, I twisted the locket so Susan could view the back. "This little golden plate looks like it was attached later, with these little bitty screws." It was well done, proving that Julian truly did have talent in the jewelry business. The thin backplate looked decorative, though the industrial-style screws didn't exactly match the romantic etching and petal pattern of the front. "If it's proof of what I think it is, and if Julian continued to operate in that flaunting way of his, then he'd made it where this could be taken off, instead of soldering it on."

She held it closer to the overhead light, then wordlessly reached across me into the glove compartment and pulled out a little kit. "I think I have that screwdriver I use on sunglasses in here. It might work." It only took a couple of seconds to locate, and sure enough, it did. In less than a minute, the four screws were gone, and Susan slid the backplate off. She peered at it, then grunted. "It's too dark. And the letters are too small." She held it back up to the light.

I leaned closer so I could see the words for myself, etched in gold.

Becky
25 into forever
Ajay

"Becky... Not Shelly." While it didn't make a lick of sense, the locket was clearly the missing piece to it all.

"How are they late? They're literally on either side of the store." Ajay paced, his arms folded, back and forth behind the antique sofa in the mystery room.

Shelly swiveled, reaching a comforting hand toward her husband from where she sat in the corner of the antique sofa, closest to the fireplace. "They're not even two minutes late. Give them a moment. *We* just got here ourselves. If Zelda is like me, she's probably debating if she wants to face this or simply change her name and run away to a different town."

From her spot on the opposite side of the sofa, Becky laughed darkly. "If I had a nickel for every time I've considered that."

"Well, teenagers will do that to you, I'm learning." Shelly cast a quick glance toward Becky, but it was dismissive at best.

Becky flashed a barely discernible glare the other woman's way.

The tension was like static in the room and felt like an ember popping from the fire might ignite the very air. That had been there between the three the other time we were together, but I had chalked it up to stress around troubled children and each of the mothers blaming the other's daughter for being the bad influence. Perhaps I was picking up on more as I had a fuller picture this time.

"Oh, one second." I pretended my phone buzzed, and I pulled it out of the pocket of my skirt and stepped out of the mystery room toward the wood-panel elevator set behind the slope of the staircase leading up to the bakery. Lifting it to my ear, I mimicked Ajay and paced, nodding and mumbling in case they were watching.

The night before, the three of us had debated the perfect location for this confrontation. The police station seemed too obvious and would get all tensions running high before they even arrived. The real toss-up had been between Aspen Gold and the Cozy Corgi. Susan had leaned toward the jewelry shop, thinking that bringing Ajay back to the scene of the crime might make cracking him easier. I figured she was right. However, Leo pointed out it was more believable at the Cozy Corgi, as we'd already done that before, where they'd discussed multiple infractions from the three girls together, and was logical, considering Britney worked there in the afternoons. My only concern on that was customers going back and forth from the bakery or possibly wandering into the mystery room for a book, but even as I started to offer that as a drawback, I decided it might actually work in our favor, if one or all of them wanted to avoid a scene.

While Watson didn't offer any direct input, he did have a small interruption of flatulence as he napped in the corner, which both drew a moment of disgust from Susan and seemed to tip the scales in the Cozy Corgi's favor, as she suggested it drove home the theory that the more comfortable they were, the more likely they were to let something slip. And someone would need to slip to answer questions the jewelry didn't provide. Were we dealing with a solitary murderer or a pair? Susan and Leo were voting that Becky played a part, though whether large or small they weren't sure. I... wasn't so sure.

Dropping my phone back into my pocket, I reentered the mystery room. "Zelda says they're running about ten minutes behind, to go ahead and get started."

"Probably trying to read whether *her* daughter is innocent in a crystal ball." Becky started to roll her eyes, then caught herself and offered the word toward me, "Sorry."

"It's okay." I waved it off. "I don't think the twins use crystal balls. And while I don't have teenagers, I've learned that my stepsisters can make a liar out of you, so maybe they've started."

My joke fell flat, even earning myself a glare from Susan, which I suppose wasn't all that unusual. From his napping spot in the sunbeam near the front windows, Watson let out a long snore in his sleep. It might've been a judgment on my poor joke, but I chose to believe it to be a rousing utterance of support.

Ajay grunted in annoyance and continued pacing. I couldn't get a good read on him—whether his unease was more trouble with his daughters, being in the room with both of his women at the same time again, or if he was more on edge since Julian's car had been recovered the day before. Probably all three.

"Well... let's get on with it." Susan gestured toward Watson's ottoman. "Fred, if you'll do the honors."

We'd already determined that I would lay out the stolen goods on the ottoman so Susan could stay standing at the ready, just in case. We didn't expect any trouble from Ajay, but you could never know. In that vein, Officer Cabot and Leo—who'd called in late to work—waited above us in the bakery, in case.

I knelt by the ottoman, opening a small leather satchel, which Susan had provided. "Like I said when I called you all this morning, Katie found a stash of stolen items hidden behind some of the large bags of flour in the bakery." As I spoke, I began to lay out a variety of things, some Cozy Corgi merchandise, some crystals from Chakras, an antique cameo from my uncles' shop, and a few other things we'd collected from downtown earlier that morning to represent our faux treasure chest of stolen teenage goods.

"*I'm* here because things are a bit different this time," Susan spoke up, and whether intentional or just on reflex, her hand came to rest on her holstered weapon. "You need to realize that I'm doing this as a *favor*. We're talking about three local teenagers. I'm hoping an intervention will work, but we'll all need to be on the same page. I don't want anything to end up on their permanent records."

"Permanent records?" Shelly sat up straighter, and for the first time held a bit of aggression in her tone. "All three girls are minors. And as bad as stealing is, it's hardly a felony at this level, nothing coming close to ending up on a permanent record."

"Well..." Susan drew out the word and pointed to a diamond ring I'd just laid out beside a Cozy Corgi magnet. "The rub is that *some* of the items in this bag match some of the jewelry stolen from Aspen Gold the other day."

Both of the mothers gasped, each looking horrified and disbelieving. Ajay finally froze in his pacing. He moved a couple of steps closer, then stopped at the center of the couch to lean over the back of it to get a better view while gripping the edges with white knuckles. "That's not possible. There's no way anything the girls did is connected to that."

"Well, *of course* not." Shelly was all mama bear.

I dared to peer at Becky when she didn't speak. She'd gone slightly pale and glanced up at Ajay, who didn't notice. It looked like Susan and Leo had been right after all.

"I'm afraid it *is* possible." Susan gestured as I pulled out a diamond bangle and added it to the collection. "That... bracelet thingy was part of a set, which—"

Watson appeared from nowhere, giving a massive but clumsy leap onto the ottoman, catching his right back paw on the edge. He glared at me as if

I'd tripped him, before doing his normal and spinning a couple of circles before crawling up to nap, covering the bangle, diamond ring, and half of the other fake stolen merchandise.

"Are you kidding me right now?" Susan leaned down partially to glare at Watson. "Move it, fleabag."

Watson didn't budge, didn't even open an eye, which considering it had been a second, two tops, there was no way he'd already fallen asleep that quickly, so it was pure stubbornness.

"Quit worrying about the dog." Ajay's tone was hard, and I thought I caught just a tremor of fear behind the anger. "Think about what you're saying. You're accusing our daughters of—"

"I'm not accusing them of anything." Susan straightened, forgetting all about Watson. "At least not yet. We're merely laying out the evidence of what we found in the bakery. And like I was saying, that bracelet was part of a set." She motioned toward me. As she continued to speak, I pulled out a small bag with two teardrop-diamond earrings and laid them next to Watson. "Those were recovered from the trunk of Julian's car, which, as you may have heard, went for a swim, with unconscious or murdered Julian in the front seat."

"Stop this right now." Shelly stood, anger

matching her husband's. "I'm not hearing another word. You're getting closer and closer to accusing Ananya of murder, which is the most ridiculous thing I've ever heard in my life."

Another glance toward Becky. She'd gone even whiter and was openly staring at Ajay.

"And these." I pulled out a small baggie with Charlene's pearls. Ajay didn't react to them, which suggested he hadn't really paid attention to the items he'd taken from Aspen Gold.

"I said *stop!*" Shelly looked on the verge of leaping across the ottoman to grab Susan's pistol.

Watson lifted his head when she yelled, answering with a quiet, threatening growl.

Time to go for the kill—I pulled it out. "And this locket." I spared a covert glance toward Ajay. He'd gone from looking worried and shocked to completely and horrifyingly baffled. A little guilt bit at me as I knew this would hurt, but I pushed ahead. "Shelly, isn't this the one you told me you wanted? Do you think Ananya might have known and taken it for you?"

"What locket?" Shelly glanced down with a sneer, barely giving it a glance before refocusing on Susan. "I don't know what your game is, why you're trying to pin this on my daughter, but I will—" She froze, glancing down at the locket and began shaking her head. "No, she wouldn't do that. She wouldn't. Of course not. This is just coincidence." She sat and reached for the locket.

"Of course she didn't. This is ridiculous." Ajay leaped forward, having to teeter totter over the back of the sofa as he reached to snatch the locket before his wife could take it. He missed.

"She wouldn't. Ananya wouldn't hurt anyone." Shelly held the locket with trembling fingers and looked toward Becky. "Neither would Dawn. None of them would."

"Shelly..." I made my voice a whisper, trying to make it gentle. "Turn the locket over."

Ajay cast a hate-filled glare my way.

"What?" She looked at me like I was crazy.

"No! Don't listen to them. This is nothing but—" Ajay lunged again, trying to snag the locket from Shelly.

He would've managed it if Becky hadn't reached out as well, grabbing Ajay's arm and yanking it back, then addressing Shelly through gritted teeth. "Turn it over."

Shaking, Shelly turned the locket over. Confusion grew as she read the inscription, then more emotions than had names crossed her face. "Ajay...

I..." Twisting once more, she looked at her husband, then Becky, then back again. There was an expression of confusion, then repulsion, but only the briefest of each. As her body went slack, Shelly seemed to accept it, and I knew the look that entered her eyes then—puzzle pieces, maybe some she'd been pondering over for years, and others appearing in that moment, all snapping together in a heartbeat. "You two."

With her own trembling fingers, Becky stretched out her hand and took the locket from Shelly. As she read the inscription, I could see another set of puzzle pieces clicking into place, and I realized that I'd been right about her. At least partly.

As if a million miles away, I heard more customers come into the Cozy Corgi but didn't bother looking over. Ben would do his best to make sure they didn't come into the mystery room.

"You..." As Shelly had before, Becky stood to glare at Ajay, anger and hate bubbling from out of nowhere. "You made me a part of this. I felt like something was off, but I trusted you. I believed you." She whipped toward Susan. "I swear to you, Detective, I did not know. I did *not* know."

"Stop this." Ajay made a motion like he was going to grab at Shelly but looked like another part of him wanted to dash for the front door, and in the internal conflict became frozen. "That... that thing wasn't even there. Julian didn't have—"

"What do you mean you didn't know? Didn't know what? You've clearly been having an affair with my hus—" Shelly, still focused on Becky, gestured toward the locket in Becky's hand and then sucked in a gasp, only then catching Ajay's words and seemed to realize the other implication. She looked toward her husband. "You... you killed that man?"

"Dad?" At the voice in the doorway, all of us, even Watson, turned to see Dawn, her red hair seemingly on fire, lit from behind with the sunlight streaming into the windows. She was flanked on either side by Ananya and Britney. "You killed someone?"

"*Dad!*" Shelly's voice went up nearly three octaves as the third and final shock hit her, and she looked between Dawn, Becky, and Ajay.

Once more, Ajay seemed like he was internally being torn apart, part of him ready to run, another to fight, and another to protest. Instead, all strength left his body and he collapsed to his knees and began to cry.

Ananya was the only one who started to go

toward him but stopped and remained in place when Dawn grabbed her hand.

"Ajay Patel." Susan removed her cuffs as she walked around the ottoman and the matching sofa, casting a remorseful glance toward the girls, who hadn't been part of the plan—no one had wanted any of this to happen in front of them. "You're under arrest for the murder of Julian LaRue." Officer Cabot, Leo, and Katie came down from the bakery as Susan read Ajay his rights. Before leading him away, Susan looked toward Becky. "Do you need to be handcuffed, or are you going to come willingly?"

"Mom!" Dawn rushed in, throwing her arms around her mom. "You didn't. You didn't!"

"No. I *didn't*." Becky held her daughter close, sent another hate-filled glare toward Ajay, and then addressed Susan. "I picked Ajay up in Granby the day of the robbery... the murder, I suppose. He said he was driving back from work and his car broke down. I didn't suspect anything until the car was found yesterday, but I wouldn't quite let myself go there." She refocused on her daughter. "I'm going to go with the police, but I didn't hurt anyone. I'll be back tonight."

Still crying, Dawn nodded into her mom's shoulder.

Becky looked around frantically, toward Shelly, then toward me. "Can Dawn stay with you? Please."

"She'll stay with us." Ananya was in tears too, but lifted her chin defiantly, and sent a pleading stare toward her mother. "She's... she's my sister."

I'd seen many acts of love throughout my years—selflessness, graciousness, and strength. But watching emotions whirl over Shelly Patel's face in that moment, only to solidify into strength as she met Becky Erickson's gaze, might've been the purest act of love I'd ever seen. "Dawn will be with *us*. She will be safe and cared for until she can be with you."

With that, Cabot read Becky her rights and led her away.

We put up the Closed sign and locked the doors to the Cozy Corgi, giving Shelly, Ananya, and Dawn all the time they needed in the mystery room.

Britney sat on the floor of the bakery, her back against the shelves, and Watson, though he was right next to his little apartment, nestled between her legs.

Leo and Katie had gone to fetch hot chocolates to give us some space, and I joined her on the floor. Zelda did the same on the other side, while

Noah sat on a chair beside Zelda, ready to spring into action.

"I'm sorry I told." Though her eyes were bright with tears, her cheeks were dry, and her voice was genuine, but suddenly sounding so grown-up.

"Oh, baby." Zelda leaned against Britney's shoulder supportively. "I understand. I do... but... why couldn't you wait just a couple more hours?"

Britney sniffed. "Sam was home sick today and heard that Ajay and Shelly were coming down here. He texted Ananya, warning her that she might want to skip school before their parents came to get her." With one hand she continued to stroke Watson, and with the other she reached for mine, holding it tightly as if pleading for forgiveness. "When she showed the text to Dawn and me, I just... well, there's already been so many secrets. I couldn't lie to Ananya anymore about knowing she had a sister, and I couldn't add to it by lying to Dawn that I didn't know what was happening. And she was asking why I wasn't wearing the locket. So... we skipped and came here." Finally, the tears started. "What are they going to do? This will ruin both of their lives, and I... I'm the one who—"

"*You're* the one who will be their friend, the one who won't judge them for what their parents did." I released her hand and put my arm over her shoulders, pulling her close.

Zelda hummed her agreement and put her arm on top of mine so Britney was fully surrounded.

I spared a quick smile to her, then spoke to Britney again. "*You* are the one who was brave and strong enough to try to hold on to this secret so you wouldn't ruin anyone's family. And you are also the one strong enough to speak out when the time was right. I'm proud of you, and I love you."

As Dawn had done with her mom, Britney pressed her head into my shoulder and let the tears fall.

It seemed all the shuffling about had not sat well with Watson's breakfast that morning, as he let out a large belch, which made Britney giggle. By the time the first round of hot chocolate was ready, we were lost in a mix of tears and laughter.

"Ajay had poor Julian tied up in the back room of the jewelry store all afternoon." Anna Hanson made certain she had the full attention of everyone gathered for the breakfast rush the next morning in the Cozy Corgi Bakery. "Then forced him to drive to Granby at gunpoint, where he beat him in the back of the head with a rock and put him in the lake." She lifted a finger, scanning the crowd until it narrowed in on Lavender Kelly, an aspiring filmmaker and Nick's girlfriend, who was back in town from visiting her family in LA. "You're writing this down, right? This could be your next documentary."

"That's..." Lavender scrunched her eyes. "That's not exactly how I heard it."

From the other side of the bakery counter, Nick chuckled, but at Anna's glare, he cleared his throat and returned to taking cinnamon rolls out of a pan.

"That's because that isn't exactly how it

happened." Myrtle Bantam clucked from a nearby table.

"Well, I never." Anna swiveled, searching for her husband. "Carl! Isn't that what you told me when you got home after talking to Jed?"

"Well... yeah." Carl shrugged, and his round cheeks pinked, matching his shiny bald head. "But Jed was a little sauced."

"When *isn't* that donut maker sauced? Really, if you two are going to peddle in gossip, at least make sure your sources are sober." Myrtle was thoroughly unimpressed and turned to me where I was trying to simultaneously drink my dirty chai and keep from choking from laughter. "Why are you so quiet over there, Fred? We all know *you* know what happened. Fill us in."

There was a time I would've thought twice about simply telling all the details to the mostly full bakery, but really, we'd all been through so much together, and it wasn't like they weren't all going to know anyway. At least they should get the details right.

"Anna got quite a few things correct." I offered her an apologetic smile and started in. "Julian was hit with a rock, an amethyst geode, to be exact, that Vivian and Roger kept near the cash register. In order to keep his secret, Mr. Patel hit Julian in the back of the head. He then tied and gagged Julian in the back room, took his keys, locked up the shop, and came back that night with Julian's car when everyone was asleep. Then... drove to Granby, untied Julian, and sank the car in Grand Lake. From the way it sounds, Julian never regained consciousness and drowned."

Anna sniffed and looked at the little scroungy white dog in her arms. "That's almost word for word what I said."

Myrtle opened her mouth, clearly getting ready to educate Anna on alternative facts, when Athena placed her hand on top of Myrtle's and shook her head.

There were other details in the middle. That Ajay had attempted to make it look like a robbery—stolen the security VHS tapes and put all the evidence in the car, but there was no need to get into minutia. It still made my skin tingle to know that when I'd gone to pick up the engagement ring that evening and no one answered, Julian was tied up and unconscious in the office, with Ajay just waiting for the cover of night to return.

"What I don't understand is why that Erickson woman is free and walking about." Apparently needing the last word, Anna changed topics. "She's an accomplice, helped her *married* boyfriend prepare for the drop-off."

"Not exactly." I raised my voice, making sure everyone could hear me clearly that time. "In preparation, Ajay drove his car to Granby earlier in the day, so he'd have a way home in the middle of the night. When he was up there, he called Becky, telling her he'd been driving to his job when his car broke down, and that the soonest a tow truck could come help him was several hours away. She went up to get him, not thinking anything of it. At that point, no one even knew Julian was missing. Later that night, Ajay drove *Julian's* car, with Julian and the stolen jewelry in it, into Grand Lake, then hiked to where he'd left his own car and drove back home. There was no reason for Becky, or anyone, to be suspicious."

"No reason to be suspicious?" Anna's voice shot up again, making Winston yip.

From his apartment where he'd sheltered from the crowd, Watson answered with a bark of his own.

That, of course, sent Winston into ecstatic hysterics. After several seconds of thrashing, he got his way. Anna placed the diapered dog on the floor, and he scurried like a rabid energizer bunny across the bakery and disappeared with a loud smacking of the dog-door flap.

Anna smiled indulgently to where he'd run and then refocused on her point. "That jezebel had been carrying on with a married man for nearly two decades! What do you mean she had no reason to be suspicious?"

Myrtle groaned. "As horrible as it is, Anna, an affair and murder aren't exactly the same thing."

"Aren't they?" Anna pointed again, that time at Carl. "Why, if *my* husband was unfaithful, I can promise you there would be murder."

I barely heard Katie's giggle before she used the espresso machine to loudly steam milk to cover the noise. Which made it harder for me to keep a straight face as well.

"I am curious." Lavender dared to speak up, raising her hand as if she was in school. "How did the mistake happen with the names on the locket?"

It was the best question yet, and I wasn't surprised that the sharp documentary maker was the one to ask it. That time, I did debate how much to share, as it really wasn't my story. However, once more I settled on it being better for the truth to spread around town rather than a bunch of made-up theories, which often was more harmful to the innocent—in this case, Shelly and all three of Ajay's children. "From what I understand, when Ajay called in to order the anniversary present for Shelly, he'd been fighting with Becky on the phone right before, so she was on his mind. At least that's what he thinks happened as he's not sure why he would make that mistake either. He didn't realize until he went to pick it up and Julian pointed it out, asking why he was getting jewelry for someone who had a different name than his wife. Ajay tried to play it off, but over the last month, Julian started blackmailing him. Ajay finally had enough and..." I edited then, not wanting to bring in Dawn's name and how Julian had given the locket to Ajay's daughter the very day Ajay decided to be done with it—to kill Julian, get the locket, and make it look like Julian left town. Ajay's one flaw, or at least his first one, was he hadn't made sure Julian still had the locket before hitting him in the back of the head with the geode.

"See?" Once more Anna piped up, saving me from figuring out how to explain without involving Dawn, still using her finger gesturing heavenward. "And *that's* the cost of sin, right there. It will always find you out. And besides that, that's what he gets. One relationship is complicated enough." She looked toward her husband. "Isn't that what I always tell you, Carl? I say, Carl, you can barely manage to keep *one* woman happy, don't bother with two." She nodded emphatically. "Isn't that what I say, Carl?"

"Yep." He nodded as well, acquiescing as ever. "That's exactly what you always say. I can barely manage to keep one woman happy, so stay away from Delilah Johns—" His eyes went wide behind his spectacles, and Anna let out a little scream, and the entire bakery went utterly silent. Except... for one loud snort behind the espresso machine. Then the entire bakery was lost to what seemed like an unending cacophony of laughter. Even Anna chuckled a time or two, though she swatted at Carl, but even that seemed lovingly, for her.

Later that afternoon, Anna and Winston returned, and as it was between busy times in the bakery, we had the space mostly to ourselves. After an entire day of napping, Watson surprised all of us by initiating a nip toward Winston's wiry tail, and then the two of them took off in a race, scurrying over the hardwood floor and weaving in and out of table pedestals and chair legs.

I gaped at my chubby little corgi as he slid across the floor and bumped into the wall, only to roll and then take off like a bullet, barely evading Winston's crooked, snapping fangs, before barreling down the steps into the bookshop, Winston yipping and happy in excitement at his heels.

"Well, that's something you don't see every day." I was tempted to rush down into the bookshop to watch what would happen next, but as I didn't hear any crash of book displays, I figured by the time he reached the bottom floor that Watson became winded, and they'd probably be curled up together by the fire by the time I got down there.

"Winston brings out the best in people." Anna had also been focused on where the dogs had disappeared and turned to smile to Katie. "Now, due to Carl's faux pas this afternoon, I want two ginger oaty bars for me, one for him, two lemon bars for me, one for him, and three almond croissants for me and two for him. We'll save a couple of those last ones for breakfast." She started to refocus on me, then turned to Katie again. "Oh, I might as well try your quiche of the month, whatever it is, while I'm here."

"It's fig, bacon, and smoked maple bourbon." Katie was already reaching in to retrieve one.

"Oh, that sounds heavenly. Make it two." Anna waited until Katie slid the plate of two quiches, with a fork and napkin, to her before launching in. "Now,

I wanted to talk to you two alone, which is why I waited until now—you know me, the queen of discretion. I was—"

"I thought you were the queen of gossip?" Katie just couldn't help herself.

"I am." Anna paused with a scowl. "Although Percival likes to claim *he's* the queen of gossip." Her busy finger from that morning returned and pointed at me. "Speaking of, I don't appreciate you sharing the details around that massive stolen diamond Leo gave you with Percival, when I'm right across the street." She shook it closer to my face, not giving me a chance to respond. "Such behavior should negate the generosity I'm about to offer, but I love you both too much. So I'll overlook it. *This time.*"

I started to laugh, and then her meaning caught up with me, and I straightened as a sinking sensation plummeted in my gut. "What do you mean? What generosity?"

"Well, really, Winifred. Must you look so insulting?" Not giving me a chance to respond, she took a bite of the quiche, not bothering with the fork, returned it to the plate, and then in a smooth motion grabbed both Katie's and my hand with hers. "I wanted to tell you that I'm going to—" She spoke with her mouth full. No crumbs went flying, but she halted abruptly and chewed a couple of times in silence before giving all her attention to Katie. "Well, that's marvelous. How do you come up with your flavor profiles?"

"Oh, Pastor—"

She didn't get a chance to finish before Anna continued. "Like I was saying. I wanted to tell you that I'm going to throw you both a joint engagement party. Invite the whole town. We can't have two of our most beloved old maids get engaged and not have a proper celebration."

"Old maids?" Katie guffawed at the exact moment I squeaked, "Party!" No wonder my gut plummeted.

"Yes, *party*." Anna released us as one, took another bite of quiche, groaning before capturing my hand once more and inspecting the bare finger. "Are you still engaged? There's no ring?"

"Yes, I'm still engaged." And I tried to hurry onward. "But there's no reason for a—"

"Wonderful!" Anna nodded, and it was decided. "Now, I don't know when, but relatively soon. I also don't know where, *but*—" She growled suddenly. "It will *not* be at Habaneros. Marcus Gonzalez is entirely too loosey-goosey with that stupid cheese fountain of his. Not classy at all." She'd finished one quiche and held up the other. "These on the other hand... Katie Pizzolato, I may have to hire you to cater this party."

"You..." Katie had to clear her throat to keep from laughing, though the corners of her lips didn't succeed in hiding her reaction. "You want me to cater my own engagement party?"

"Well, it's for Fred too, of course." With a sigh, Anna looked through the windows down across Elkhorn Avenue. "I know you're friends with those nasty Pink Panthers, but really, do I have to invite Delilah Johnson. She is just—" Anna stiffened, leaning forward, bumping her head on the glass like I had done many times before. "Look at that. Absolutely scandalous. Why, if I was Shelly Patel, I would forbid it."

Katie and I both looked down at Elkhorn to where Britney, Ananya, and Dawn walked over the sidewalk and disappeared into Madame Delilah's Old Tyme Photography.

Anna tsked. "Not only that, but skipping school to go spend time with the likes of *that* woman."

"It's past three, Anna." Katie managed to keep the chide mostly out of her tone. "School is done for the day. And you know I'm not one to defend Delilah very much, but those three girls have been through a lot, especially Dawn. I bet they're getting their picture taken together. Maybe a moment to help capture when two of them found out they were sisters."

"I bet you're right." I didn't even try to wipe away the tear that rolled down my cheek. "And I bet you anything it was Shelly's idea."

TWENTY-SEVEN

The second time I received a proposal from Leo Lopez, I knew it was coming. I couldn't remember the last time I'd gotten a call from him in the middle of the day to come meet for lunch in the national park. Nor, since he'd taken over the restructuring of Chipmunk Mountain, could I recall the last time he actually worked as a normal ranger in the park itself. There was only one explanation—we'd go on a hike with a picnic lunch, maybe to one of the more secluded lakes, and he'd propose.

The timing was perfect. Over the past couple of weeks, now that September was in full bloom, so was the gold of the aspen leaves—such a pure joy-filled color more than anything Aspen Gold had to offer. Maybe he'd pull out his ukulele. I'd heard him practicing a few times; he was getting pretty good. Not proposal good, but even that would be rather charming.

Unlike the first time, when I'd felt trapped in the bathroom at Prime Slice, there were no nerves, no panic. Just the pleasant and surprisingly giddy dance of butterfly wings in my stomach.

From the tongue-lolling grin Watson was giving from the passenger seat, he felt the butterflies too.

As much as I loved Estes Park and the mountains, as much as I never got used to its splendor, it'd been a while since I'd driven to the national park. Between the Cozy Corgi and snooping into mysteries, most of my time was spent on Elkhorn, darting around town, walking through my own dense woods around my cabin. I hadn't continued the drive past the shops on Elkhorn to the entrance to Rocky Mountain National Park in a while, and as always, it took my breath away. The sweeping meadows were revealed as we turned the last bend and glistened in their panorama frame of rugged purple mountains. With peaks white with an early snow, the golden streams of Aspen gleaming in the sunlight resting between groves of pine and spruce seemed all the more spectacular.

Yes, a perfect day for a picnic proposal.

A sense of déjà vu washed over me as I approached the entrance, the little tollbooths designed to look like tiny log cabins spread out at intervals across the road. They were where I'd met Leo nearly three years ago, bringing an owl feather from the Cozy Corgi—which I'd been converting from a taxidermy shop—to the park rangers to see if it held a clue about a murder. Reaching over, I stroked Watson as we approached, while part of me stayed caught in the past, reliving the moment I'd knocked on the tollbooth window and startled Leo. He'd completely taken my breath away as I had been convinced a young Oscar De La Hoya had dressed up in a park ranger uniform.

I had no clue what life had in store, all the twists and turns, all the joy.

The silhouette of one of the rangers shifted in the middle tollbooth, and I pulled the season pass out of my visor—it didn't matter if you didn't get up to the national park that often, if you lived in Estes Park, you bought a season pass; it's just what you did.

As I hit the button to roll down the window and started to hand over the season pass, Watson took a flying leap, his hind legs landing on my lap, nearly knocking the wind out of me and practically threw himself to the window. It didn't take a crackerjack supersleuth to put those puzzle pieces together. Unless Barry or Ben had found a new career, Leo was waiting on the other side of the glass.

"Well, hey there, cuteness. What brings you up here today?" Leo's warm voice made those butterfly wings flap quicker.

"I got a call from a certain park—" I turned toward him, stopping when I realized he'd been addressing Watson, not me.

"Hold on, buddy, you're going to need this." Leo disappeared inside the tollbooth but only for a heartbeat, before leaning out and snapping a collar around Watson's neck. "There. Now you're ready."

Watson licked Leo's hands as he pulled them away and then seemed to realize he'd been betrayed. He scooted backward across me, landing once more on the passenger seat, tilting his head down, trying to bite at the new collar. While he adamantly refused to dress up, he was used to wearing a collar, but I saw the problem quickly enough. This particular collar was indeed, at least as far as Watson would be concerned, a costume, as it sported a red-and-black plaid bow tie. He looked utterly adorable; annoyed, but adorable.

I ruffled the fur of his face, which he jerked away from. I turned to Leo. "Are we having a fancy picnic?" Might as well pretend like I didn't know what was going on, even if Leo was more than your average supersleuth as well and certainly knew I wasn't fooled.

His thick brows knitted. "No, no picnic."

"Really?" Might as well play along. "What, then? Discovered a new poaching ring that Watson needs to be dressed up for?"

"Something like that." Leo leaned his elbows on the little edge outside the booth's window, his eyes slightly dreamy as he peered down into the Mini Cooper. "I think I fell in love with you the minute I saw you, right here." He chuckled softly. "You were so beautiful, so flustered—asking me how old I was, bumping me in the nose with that feather." He gestured with his chin to where Watson sat scowling. "And with the cutest dog I'd ever seen in my life at your side."

What I thought had been butterflies before had apparently merely been ladybugs, because at that moment, I realized there indeed was no picnic, and they really took off, making me feel just as flustered as I had the very first time—more so, actually.

"I know we're already engaged, and I know we've been clear about being together forever for a while now, but... I want to get this right." Leo had been leaning out in such a way that his hands were folded over each other, and he had moved them so a small black box was now revealed in his palm. "Winifred Wendy Page, there is no human on the face of this earth that I respect or admire as much as you. There's no one that makes me laugh, no one who soothes my soul, no one who's able to clear away the shadows and the dark the way you do. I might have fallen head over heels in love with you the second I saw you right at this very spot, but I only fall more and more and more each and every passing day."

His hands moved, opening the black box, but I couldn't tear my gaze away from his beautiful eyes.

"We both know there will be bumps, twist and turns, struggles, and more shadows." Those honeyed eyes glistened as he spoke. "But I want to go through all of them with you. Stand beside you whatever comes. Walk through life's journey holding your hand." His voice, thick with emotion, cracked. He cleared his throat and gave a little laugh, then cleared it again. "Will you marry me?"

"Yes!" I shot up so quickly that I managed to both hit my head on the window frame while simultaneously getting yanked back to my seat with the seat belt.

Watson grunted his annoyance at such a display.

And Leo laughed. "God, I love you."

With my head smarting, I unbuckled my seat

belt, and actually opened the door to slide out—like a normal person—then closed it behind me so Watson didn't get any smart ideas. I threw my arms around Leo's neck and pulled him halfway out of the tollbooth in a kiss.

I don't know how much time passed, several seconds, at least, before I heard the applause. I kept my arms wrapped around his neck and broke the kiss to look around.

Somewhere in there, though I'd been too captivated with Leo to notice, the park rangers had set up a line of cones behind me, blocking the paths to the tollbooths. There was only one car waiting, but apparently, they didn't mind as they weren't honking. A glance the other way revealed Nadiya and several of the other park rangers gathered near the far tollbooth, right beside the ranger station, clapping wildly, throwing in a few catcalls and cheers as well. They rushed our way.

"I lied." Leo pulled my attention back to him. "Since you said yes, there *is* a picnic."

Less than twenty minutes later, we indeed had a picnic spread out beside a lake; however, it wasn't one of the smaller, secluded ones. It seemed the park rangers had taken some liberties and blocked off all the trails surrounding Bear Lake, so we sat on a black-and-red plaid blanket, which matched our still-disgruntled Watson's bow tie, and the massive body of water acted as a mirror, flipping the mountain streaming with gold upside down, making the entire world look like a fairy tale.

"You didn't put this on. Did you even look?" We hadn't even opened the basket when Leo pulled the black box out of his pocket, clearly unable to wait. "Care to see it? I promise no large diamond, fake, stolen, or otherwise."

There, by the onslaught of his ranger friends, and true to myself, I hadn't even thought about the engagement ring as I'd been captured by pure giddiness and floating on pink clouds—very *untrue* to myself, but immensely pleasant. Yet now that the black box was in front of me, I found myself a bit breathless. "Yes, please." I didn't quite know what to expect. If I had to guess, it would be a solid band, gold or silver, I wasn't sure.

He opened it, and my breath caught.

It wasn't what I would've pictured or come up with myself, but it was...

I lifted it out of the box, marveling at the delicate thing.

"Here, may I, please?" Leo took the ring from me and slid it on my finger.

A tingle of joy traveled down my spine.

"This was a group effort." Leo spoke as I stretched out my hand, holding it out in front of me, completely captured. "It was Charlene's pearls that got me thinking. I almost asked if I could buy one of hers, but didn't want anything associated with murder or theft, at least not a second time." He gave a quick chuckle before continuing. "So, I talked to Percival. One of his antique friends in Denver deals in old jewelry and sent up a few selections to Victorian Antlers for me to see. Apparently that pearl is over a hundred years old. I like the aged sheen on it." He laughed again. "Percival about killed me when he found out I was going to have it cut in half."

I finally looked up at him. "I bet." I couldn't keep my gaze away from the ring too long and shifted back, twisting my hand slightly. "You had it cut so it would lie flat?"

"Exactly, so it would lie flat," he repeated in agreement. "Besides the diamond being completely wrong, that was one of the things I realized when I saw it on you. You're not the kind of woman who wants some big thing protruding from her finger, no matter how pretty."

"You are so right." The two pearls—or, the one pearl cut in half, I supposed—sat side by side, at an angle so the lower one sat near the medial side of my finger, while the top one sat closer to the knuckle of my little finger. Each was bookended by a simple, small rose gold ball, making four in total, before giving way to two thin rose gold bands set parallel on either side, a small space between. I twisted again, letting the light catch the gold. "It's perfect. I think I probably would've chosen silver, as I always find gold so gaudy, but this... is so warm and soft."

"I went to Joe's jeweler friend in Lyons. Turns out he can do things *not* involving hippos." Leo smirked. "There's not as much copper mixed in as typical in rose gold, so it doesn't turn pink, just warms it up like you said. And I thought that matte finish suited you and your skin tone."

Again, it was a direction I never would have considered, or even known enough about jewelry to consider. But he was right. The soft rose gold had a gentle gleam, was better than anything I could've imagined.

"There's one more part." Leo patted the blanket beside us. "Come here, grumpy."

Watson grumbled but did as he was asked, always willing to give Leo anything he wanted.

"Good boy." Leo ruffled Watson's fur on top of his head and glanced at me. "Check his bow tie."

Though strange, I did as he asked, leaning down somewhat to get it level with my view. There, between the folds on the right side of the bowtie, was another ring, secured tightly with the thin black ribbon, that had just managed to blend in. "Yours?" It looked too thin for Leo.

His answer was to simply wait for me to untie it.

Watson snorted and nudged my hand away.

"You're always *you*, aren't you, buddy?" Laughing, Leo reached behind Watson's neck and unclipped the collar he'd put on at the tollbooth.

Watson gave a mighty shake, letting loose hairs fly, and then stretched in an exaggerated manner as if he'd been tied down for the past hour.

Sparing Watson an eye roll, Leo untied the string and handed me the small gold ring. "Do you recognize it?"

"Recognize it? You know me, I don't pay any attention to people jewelry. I might've seen this a million times and not—" Etching glinted on the inside as I twisted the ring. My breath caught, and I pulled it closer. My hand began to tremble, and my eyes filled with tears, obliterating what I'd read, but I didn't need to see it again. I'd know it anywhere.

PO&CP 1975

Phyllis Oswald and Charles Page, who'd been married in 1975.

Through the tears, I looked at Leo. "I... I don't understand."

"It's your mom's wedding ring."

A laugh burst from me. "Yeah, I realize. But I don't understand. The diamond is gone, and why does Watson have it?"

He took the band from me. "May I have your engagement ring back?" He held out his other hand, palm open.

Fingers still trembling I slid it off and handed it to him.

He held my engagement ring in one hand, my mother's wedding band in his other as he spoke. "A couple of weeks ago, the night we had the engagement dinner with your family—before Britney confessed everything she knew—I was talking to your mom in the kitchen. I asked if I could use her wedding band for yours."

"I... I still don't..."

With a smile, he pushed on. "The jeweler in Lyons took off the diamond, he's making it into a pendant Phyllis can wear. And this..." He held up his hands and then slipped the golden band between the two rose gold bands, sliding it in place under the pearls. "You will have your dad and your mom, whose marriage I know you hold as a model for all others, with you always—a part of what made you, *you*. Combined with our ring—a part of what will make us, *us*." Another smile. "I guess we're not supposed to actually use this part until the ceremony, but..."

He held it out, and I slid my finger through.

It was hard to see through the tears, but the old soft gold was perfect with the matte rose gold—an easy, elegant, timeless blend between the two. The setting of pearls lay flush on my finger, just a gentle slope. I never knew I could feel such a thing for jewelry, for a ring. Barely able to tear my gaze away from it, I beamed at my fiancé. "Leo, it's... I'm..." I sniffed, completely unable to get out the words.

As he so often did, Leo reached out his large hand to cup my face, stroking his thumb over my cheek, and smiled gently. His eyes were the deepest pools I'd ever seen. He didn't need me to say anything else. He'd known it was perfect, and beyond. After a few moments, he leaned in and kissed me.

After a few *more* moments, either feeling left out

or simply overcome with joy... or maybe just wanting to get this show on the road so he could get treats, Watson bounded over, propped a foreleg on each of our knees, and began licking our faces.

Help Fred and Watson solve their next murder hot on the trail of...

<u>Yowling Yetis</u>

Book Twenty-Two of the Cozy Corgi Series

Read the complete Twister Sisters Mysteries series now!

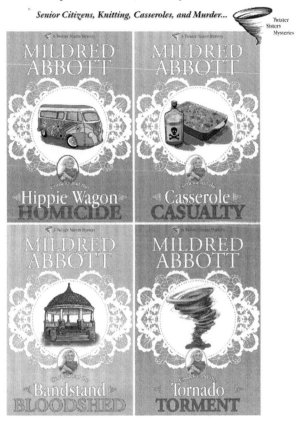

Link to Twister Sisters Mysteries

Katie's Oaty Ginger Crunch Bars
recipe provided by:

CLOUDY KITCHEN

Never miss a scrumptious recipe:
CloudyKitchen.com

Follow Cloudy Kitchen's creations
on social media:

Cloudy Kitchen Facebook
Cloudy Kitchen Instagram

KATIE'S OATY GINGER CRUNCH BARS RECIPE

INGREDIENTS

Base

- 300g all-purpose flour
- 1 1/2 tsp baking powder
- 1 tsp salt
- 2 1/2 tsp ground ginger
- 300g brown sugar
- 135g rolled oats (old-fashioned oats)
- 225g unsalted butter, cold from the fridge is fine
- 90g golden syrup

- 1 tsp vanilla bean paste or vanilla extract.

Ginger Topping

- 135g unsalted butter, cold from the fridge is fine
- 125g golden syrup
- 2 Tbsp ground ginger (dial back to 1 1/2 Tbsp if you don't want a super intense ginger flavor)
- 325g icing sugar / powdered sugar
- 1 tsp vanilla bean paste or vanilla extract

INSTRUCTIONS

1. Preheat the oven to 350°f / 180°c. Grease a 9" x 9" (23cm square) tin and line with two pieces of parchment paper, so that there is paper sticking out of the tin on all sides, forming a 'sling.'
2. In a large bowl, sift together the flour, baking powder, salt and ground ginger. Add the brown sugar and rolled oats, and mix well to combine.

3. In a small pot, melt together the butter, golden syrup, and vanilla. Add to the dry ingredients, and mix well. Press the mixture into the tin. Bake for 25-30 minutes, until lightly golden on the edges. Five minutes before the base is done, prepare the topping.
4. For the topping, add all of the ingredients to a medium pot in the order listed. Heat over low heat, stirring constantly, until smooth. Pour over the hot base, and leave to set at room temperature. Slice into pieces with a hot knife.
5. Store in an airtight container. Can be kept in the fridge, but bring to room temperature before eating.

A FEW WEE TIPS FOR MAKING OATY GINGER CRUNCH:

- I use Golden Syrup in this recipe. It lends a certain flavour to the slice, and I haven't tried substituting it. It's in the base and the topping, so I would

recommend getting some if you can! I get mine on Amazon.
- This is super sweet. It's meant to be that way. Just a word of warning. I like cutting it into tiny wee slices to snack on throughout the day.
- I use a fair amount of ginger in the topping, so if you don't want it to be super 'spicy,' you can dial back on this a little.
- Make sure to add the ingredients for the topping in the order specified, so that the sugar doesn't get all stuck to the bottom of the pot. It makes for lumpy icing. If you do end up with lumps, the immersion blender fixes everything. Trust me on that one.
- I have put the measurements for butter, golden syrup etc. in grams. It's considerably easier to measure the golden syrup in grams - if you use a measuring spoon, lots of it gets left behind because it's so stuck. Get yourself a scale if you don't already have one! Best $10 you will spend.

- This makes loads. It makes great gifts, but the recipe can most definitely be halved and made in a smaller tin (a loaf tin would likely work well), but ensure you adjust cooking times.

Merchandise

visit MildredAbbott.com

PATREON

Mildred Abbott's Patreon Page

Mildred Abbott is now on Patreon! By becoming a member, you gain access to exclusive Cozy Corgi merchandise, get a look behind the scenes of book creation, and receive real-life writing updates, plans, and puppy photos (becuase, of course there will be puppy photos!). You can also gain access to ebooks and recipes before publication, read future works *literally* as they are being written chapter by chapter, and can even choose to become a character in one of the novels!

Wether you choose to be a villager, busybody, police officer, super sleuth, or the fuzzy four-legged star of the show himself, please come check the

Mildred Abbott Patreon community and discover what fun awaits.

Personal Note: Being an indie writer means that some months bills are paid without much stress, while other months threaten the ability to continue the dream of writing. Becoming a member ensures that there will continue to be new Mildred Abbott books. Your support is unbelievably appreciated and invaluable.

*While there are many perks to becoming a patron, if you are a reader who can't afford to support (or simply don't feel led), rest assured you will *not* miss out on any writing. All books will continue to be published just as they always have been. None of the Mildred Abbott books will become exclusive to a select few. In fact, patrons help ensure that writing will continue to be published for everyone.

Mildred Abbott's Patreon Page

AUTHOR NOTE

Dear Reader:

Thank you so much for reading *Jaded Jewels*. If you enjoyed Watson finally getting Leo to propose to Fred, I would greatly appreciate a review on Amazon and Goodreads—reviews make a huge difference in helping the Cozy Corgi series continue. Feel free to drop me a note on Facebook or on my website (MildredAbbott.com) whenever you'd like. I'd love to hear from you. If you're interested in receiving advanced reader copies of upcoming installments, please join Mildred Abbott's Cozy Mystery Club on Facebook.

I also wanted to mention the elephant in the room... or the over-sugared corgi, as it were. Watson's personality is based around one of my own corgis, Alastair. He's the sweetest little guy in the world, and like Watson, is a bit of a grump. Also, like Watson (and every other corgi to grace the world with their presence), he lives for food. In the Cozy Corgi series, I'm giving Alastair the life of his dreams through Watson. Just like I don't spend my weekends solving murders, neither does he spend his days snacking on scones and unending dog treats. But in the books? Well, we both get to live out our fantasies. If you are a corgi parent, you already know your little angel shouldn't truly have free rein of the pastry case, but you can read them snippets of Watson's life for a pleasant bedtime fantasy.

LOTS of exciting things are in the works and will start arriving in the second half of 2021! Book Twenty-Two, Yowling Yetis, will sneak up on you by Halloween. A brand new series (featuring a friend or three of Fred's) is also getting ready to launch this year. And you'll meet a sweet little mutt named Gumbo in a short story coming in July. Don't worry, the Cozy Corgi isn't ending—not even close! In the meantime, again, please continue to share your love of the series with friends and write reviews for each installment. Spreading the word about the series will help it continue. Thank you!!!

Much love, Mildred

PS: I'd also love it if you signed up for my newsletter. That way you'll never miss a new release. You won't hear from me more than once a month, nobody needs that many newsletters!

Newsletter link: Mildred Abbott Newsletter Signup

ACKNOWLEDGMENTS

A special thanks to Agatha Frost, who gave her blessing and her wisdom. If you haven't already, you simply MUST read Agatha's Peridale Cafe Cozy Mystery series. They are absolute perfection.

The biggest and most heartfelt gratitude to Katie Pizzolato, for her belief in my writing career and being the inspiration for the character of the same name in this series. Thanks to you, Katie, our beloved baker, has completely stolen both mine and Fred's heart!

Desi, I couldn't imagine an adventure without you by my side.

A.J. Corza, you have given me the corgi covers of my dreams.

To the members of Mildred Abbott's Cozy Mystery Club on Facebook, thank you for all your help and feedback. I have so much fun with you!

Donna Keevers Driver, thank you for helping name Taffy Lane! Soooo perfect!

Jackie Hoffman, Levernier Kathy, Melodie

Nathan, and Polina Posner, thank you all for helping ensure Dinah is a fully developed character. I'm excited to see where she and her candy store will go!

A huge, huge thank you to all of the lovely souls who proofread the ARC versions and help me look somewhat literate (in completely random order): Melissa Brus, Cinnamon, Ron Perry, Bernadette Ould, Victoria Smiser, Lucy Campbell, and Sue Paulsen. Thank you all, so very, very much!

A further and special thanks to some of my dear readers and friends who support my passion on Patreon: Mike Martinez, Karin S. Kramer, Adrienne Singleton, Linda Brizendine, Melissa Brus, Jan Gillespie, Victoria Smiser, Heather Martin, Alisha Framel, and Mary Liberty. You are helping to make sure there will continue to be new Cozy Corgi installments and new, exciting Mildred Abbott cozy mysteries. I'm humbled and grateful beyond belief! So much love to you all! Thank you!!!

ALSO BY MILDRED ABBOTT

-the Cozy Corgi Cozy Mystery Series-

Cruel Candy

Traitorous Toys

Bickering Birds

Savage Sourdough

Scornful Scones

Chaotic Corgis

Quarrelsome Quartz

Wicked Wildlife

Malevolent Magic

Killer Keys

Perilous Pottery

Ghastly Gadgets

Meddlesome Money

Precarious Pasta

Evil Elves

Phony Photos

Despicable Desserts

Chattering Chipmunks

Vengeful Vellum

Wretched Wool

Jaded Jewels

Yowling Yetis

Lethal Lace

Pesky Puppies

Deceptive Designs

Antagonizing Antiques

Malicious Malts

Salacious Socialites

Dastardly Ducks

Stormy Stars

Baffling Bachelorettes

Bamboozled Brides-Coming Soon

(Books 1-13 are also available in audiobook format, read to perfection by Angie Hickman.)

-the Twister Sisters Mystery Series-

(*4-Book Series*)

Hippie Wagon Homicide

Casserole Casualty

Bandstand Bloodshed

Tornado Torment